Between Takes

By the Author

The Edge of Yesterday

Just One Taste

An Intimate Deception

Between Takes

New Horizons Series:

Unknown Horizons

Savage Horizons

False Horizons

BETWEEN TAKES

by

CJ Birch

2022

BETWEEN TAKES

ISBN 13: 978-1-63679-309-2

This Trade Paperback Original Is Published By
Bold Strokes Books, Inc.
P.O. Box 249
Valley Falls, NY 12185

First Edition: December 2022

Credits
Editor: Shelley Thrasher
Production Design: Susan Ramundo
Cover Design By CJ Birch

Acknowledgments

A great big thanks to Bold Strokes for all their amazing support, especially Shelley Thrasher, my editor, for always steering me in the right direction.

The idea for writing a story about an intimacy coordinator popped into my head a couple of years ago after reading an article about the emerging field and how needed it is. If anything, the last few years have shown we have a long way to go in the industry. I want to thank everyone who spoke with me on the subject (too many to name). Any errors are my own.

I want to thank my wife, Maire, for being my test audience and always giving me honest feedback.

Again, writing about a city I've lived in for almost twenty years made things a lot easier. Sadly, there is no loft building with a rooftop hot tub overlooking High Park, but there should be.

Everything else in the story regarding buildings and landmarks exist. There really are beach bluffs in the east end of Toronto. There really is a restaurant at the top of one of the tallest buildings in Toronto with a swaying elevator. And there really is an amazing old observatory north of the city.

And as always, I want to thank my readers for sharing my make-believe worlds with me.

Dedication

For Maire

Chapter One

The crushing heat enveloped the currently minimal world of Evelyn Harper. Oppressive, feet-scorching, ice-cream-melting sultriness was exactly what she craved. She wanted to hold on to these last minutes of freedom.

It reminded her of those days as a child when she had to put a towel on the seat before getting into the car. The windows would roll down, and touching any metal surface came with a risk of getting burned. The grass had turned brown, the annoying bugs had—mostly—disappeared, and obligations loomed. Evie's least favourite time of the year.

The end of summer.

Evie turned over on her back and adjusted the straps of her bikini top, so it didn't fall off and flash her breasts at half the condos in her neighbourhood. Why couldn't she be happy about starting work again? Maybe because she'd spent her entire summer doing exactly that. In Estonia, of all places. While lovely and charming, the temperature hadn't gotten much above the twenty-degree mark. As a native of southern Ontario, she'd acclimatized to the scorching heat and humidity that accompanied summer. And Evie fucking loved every second of it.

She was desperate to milk the last of these hot summer days before the weather turned cold and blistery and dull. Tomorrow would also bring the beginning of a new season—the second on one of the hottest shows, currently sitting number one on several streaming sites. As the lead, she could expect eighty-plus-hour work weeks for the next several months. The schedule sounded gruelling, but over the last year she'd bonded with most of the crew and cast of the show. It felt more like a family. Gossiping with friends didn't feel like work most of the time. Most of the time.

Evie's sun disappeared as a shadow stretched overhead. She squinted up at the silhouette. "You're in my sun."

Shane presented a highball glass containing a light-green liquid. "I'm perfecting the mojito. Try this."

Evie propped herself up on an elbow, careful to keep her top up with her other hand, a maneuver she'd perfected as a former heliophile, and reached out for the much-needed refreshment. "Aren't they perfect already?"

"This one uses like two percent of the sugar. I know you'll be heading into calorie hibernation for the next few months, so I thought I'd come up with a weekend unwinder for you."

Evie grinned and took a sip. "How thoughtful. You know the easiest way to cut out calories is to stop drinking altogether." She let the flavours run over her tongue before nodding her approval. "It's good." She took another sip. "Really good. How'd you make it sweet without so much sugar?"

Shane plopped down on the lounge chair next to her, pushing her to the side to make room. "You don't want to know." His tall, robust frame took up most of the lounger as he leaned back.

They sat in comfortable silence as they surveyed their domain. Shane and Evie had roomed together since they met second-year university. Since then, they'd both safely concluded that the best thing about being in their thirties and having good jobs for once in their lives was that the accommodations had improved.

Their dream apartment had replaced their former horror walk-ups featuring mice, skeevy landlords, and water shortages. The only thing missing in their current two-story loft with a rooftop patio in one of their favourite neighbourhoods on the west end was a pool. Did that sound a bit greedy? Sure. Evie could live without one if it meant they had twelve hundred square feet and manageable rent. At this point she could afford to live alone, although she couldn't imagine not living with Shane. At some level she knew the time would come when they both met someone else and moved on. Until then, though, they had an unspoken agreement that they would live with each other.

Like a two-page spread out of a magazine, the whole top floor was theirs. And unlike a lot of lofts in the city, it wasn't one large box with high ceilings. Designed with two rooms, one of which was on the second floor and overlooked High Park, both were private. It had doors that shut and locked, not always the case with some of the apartments they'd lived in. And the best part was Shane's dream kitchen. A giant island ran the length and could seat up to four. A giant gas stove that rivalled anything Shane cooked on at work sat in the middle like a king on its throne. And it had enough cupboards to stash all his gadgets.

The spacious living room nestled against one whole wall of windows with a view of downtown. Converted from an old factory, long forgotten in this neighbourhood, it stood in the best location—huddled between trendy shops and restaurants, across from the park and a block from the subway. No Torontonian could ask for better.

An obscenely loud chime came from Evie's phone tucked under the chaise. "Crap. That'll be the hair and makeup people."

Shane popped up. "Oh, good. More guinea pigs." He stopped at the door to the stairs leading down into their loft and turned back. "Maybe don't greet them in your floss."

Evie adjusted her white, polka-dotted bikini top, or as Shane called it, her floss, shoved her sunglasses back into her hair, and scowled. "Please. Give me some credit." She grabbed her thin cover-up made of turquoise linen and threaded her arms through it. "I'm not an exhibitionist." She walked past him down the stairs, the fabric ending at her upper thighs and swishing as she strutted down the stairs, her bikini peeking out every other step.

"If you weren't a lesbian..."

"And you weren't male..."

"We'd have made a great couple." Shane finished the much-said refrain.

Evie stopped at the bottom and patted his cheek. "We do make a great couple. It's just not a romantic one."

Shane smiled at her with the affection of an older brother. "You go get decent. I'll grab the door."

Two hours later Evie emerged from hair and makeup a flaming goddess. She watched as Bianca fussed with a few stray hairs, amazed at the transformation. She was still Evelyn Harper, but a hyper-unrealistic, unattainable version of Evelyn Harper. Later, after the photoshoot, she would receive touch-ups that would make her even less realistic.

When Entertainment Weekly, the reason behind this photoshoot, had approached her to shoot in her house, she'd thought they wanted a low-key, relaxed, "this is me" kind of style. However, EW was an entertainment magazine, which meant it was in the business of selling fantasy. They assumed people wanted escapism, to bask in the beauty that movies and television created. They didn't want to know that until two years ago Evie used to steal toilet paper from work, or that for weeks she lived on only rice and oatmeal because she'd blown her food budget on a Metropass so she could get to work on one side of the city and auditions on the other. Being a server had barely paid the rent, and her most notable credit to date before starting this show was Kelpien #1 on Star Trek: Discovery.

Shane, always her champion, had said, "Imagine how Kelpien #2 felt. They didn't even get a credit. And you almost got that gig on American Gods. How cool would that have been?" She'd smiled and laughed because any role was better than serving the pretentious fucks who frequented the restaurant she worked in.

She thought it strange how fast you forgot the fear and anxiety. The struggle to make rent, pay bills, buy food, and simply live had been sometimes overwhelming. Some nights she would get home from work, grab a beer from the fridge, and sit in her closet in total darkness. Her makeshift cocoon provided comfort: the smell of fresh laundry hanging above, four walls of safety, the hum of the city far distant, as if she could push life and all its scariness into the background as well.

And then she'd gotten a callback, and in almost an instant her life changed. She went from choosing between food and transportation to having her face on a billboard in Dundas Square. She hadn't seen it; a friend had texted the find. She was too afraid to take a look. Why? Not because it might all disappear. What if seeing herself three metres high as Abby Bruce the Social Queen made it all too real, and she started believing the illusion? No one starts out famous. They aren't divas from the beginning—maybe some are. Since that first day on set she'd been asking herself what the turning point was. When did the talent start believing the hype?

She stared at the sexed-up version of herself in the mirror. Gone were her freckles, any skin imperfections, and limp hair from lounging in the sun all day. All gone. Her green eyes were perfectly sculpted so that they appeared mysterious and sensual. Her lips were inviting, and her skin resembled that of porcelain dolls on creepy infomercials. The more she gazed at herself like this, the more she thought of herself as Abby, the mother of two, whom she played on a television show.

By the time she entered her living room, the photographer had shown up with two assistants and several duffel bags of equipment. Shane was entertaining Emma, the makeup artist, with what Evie lovingly called his stories from the trenches.

Shane was a sous chef at one of the more upscale restaurants on King St. West, which touring performers from the nearby shows frequented, some of whom were famous, and many of them demanding assholes. Evie preferred his stories about the actors who showed up and bought a round of drinks for the restaurant or the ones who left thousand-dollar tips. They weren't his favourite because he usually pulled them out only for women he was trying to impress, and the nice stories weren't funny.

Shane liked to be funny, especially when he had an audience. Emma—young, blond, pretty—was leaning on the island counter toward Shane, ready to buy anything he was selling.

When the photographer, Petra, approached her, she jumped off the couch. "Good. Excellent. If you're ready, let's get started." After that Petra didn't say much of anything. She let her assistants do most of the work. She moved around spots with her camera, taking shots and nodding to herself. Every now and then an assistant would run over and exchange cameras with her. Evie couldn't tell how she was communicating with them to let them know she wanted a different one.

Her first photoshoot had been a disaster. She had no idea what she was doing or why they kept changing cameras so often or why one of his assistants kept running up to her with a tiny black box with what looked like a Ping Pong ball chopped in half. He kept holding it up to her head and calling out a number. Then he would run back out of the shot.

Evie's favourite photographer had been an older gentleman who'd treated her like a friend he'd met for coffee. The entire time they talked about old movies. Evie had a soft spot for the classics. On her night off, she loved to make some popcorn and curl up and watch an old movie. Anything from the 30s, 40s, or 50s would do, but she preferred the B-movies, the ones that most actors tried to forget about when they became famous. She detected something desperate and unleashed about their performance. For every Rear Window was a Green Fire.

While talking, the older man had been snapping pictures, and the result was incredible. Evie came off as relaxed and approachable, whereas most of her photoshoots made her appear haughty and bored.

Occasionally one of Petra's assistants would slide up to Evie and politely ask her to turn one way or the other. She worried Petra would fall into the latter category of photographers. She was still in a bikini, this one so tight she was afraid the girls would spill over the fabric of the bra. It probably cost more than she used to make in a month. A flimsy cover draped over her arms did a poor job of covering anything.

Petra handed the camera to one of her assistants and paused, contemplating Evie with her hands on her hips. "Okay. Now that we have the sexy stuff, let's do something more fun."

Evie raised her eyebrows. She could take that statement a lot of different ways.

"Let's get you into something casual, something you could relax in."

By the time the crew finally left, Evie was emotionally exhausted. She'd once spent a summer earning money posing for art classes, which was harder than it looked. Maintaining the same pose for twenty or thirty minutes was a skill. After a class she'd feel electrified, yet not because ten strangers had scrutinized her naked body for an hour and a half, but because she found something magical about watching people create and find inspiration from her form. The experience was the opposite of sexual. A photoshoot put her on the spot in a completely different way because the intent, whether the photographer intended it or not, was sexual. It was their purpose.

Shane handed her a drink. "You know what we need?"

Evie took a sip and laid her head back on the couch. "A bath and a good book?"

"The opposite of that. It's the last night of summer vacation. And you know what that means."

"Can't we skip that this year? I just want to wash all this off and be done with it."

Shane nodded. "Okay." He propped his head on his bent arm and stared, eyes wide and round. "That's no problem. If you want to bail on a decades' old tradition, I will understand completely."

"You're such an asshole. You know that?"

He stood from the couch. "I'll even go run your bath for you." He checked his watch. "It's only like seven, but we should totally order a pizza and maybe some wings."

She banged her head on the soft cushion of the couch. "Ugh." She knew exactly what he was doing, and she hated him for it.

Ever since university they'd had a tradition that had started during second-year exams. The night before Evie's first exam, they went out to a club and got drunk and danced until the club kicked everyone out in the early hours. Evie had shown up the next morning—in all honesty—still a little drunk and aced her exam. They continued the tradition all through university and well after. Anytime something important was about to happen—the start of a new school year, or new job—they would go out and live it up the night before. The wildness had gone out of the event by the time they hit their thirties, but the tradition remained.

A few years ago, when Shane had started working his cushy corporate cheffing job, he'd had to take a bunch of health certifications and had begged off going because he'd gotten dumped and didn't feel like it. Evie had guilt-tripped him so hard he'd finally relented.

Well, this was his revenge. Shane was the type who would sit on the other side of the bathroom door telling her how totally fine it was that she wasn't going, and how great he was that he wasn't pushing her into doing anything she didn't want. All the while, her bath cooled, and her guilt grew.

She sat forward and looked down at her reflection in the glass coffee table. "He'll keep calling me and calling me until I come over…he'll make me feel guilty."

Shane launched over the back of the couch. "This is ridiculous."

In unison. "Okay, I'll go, I'll go, I'll go, I'll go."

And loud enough the neighbours could hear. "Goddamn it."

Shane squeezed Evie into a giant bear hug. "Life moves pretty fast. If you don't stop and look around once in a while, you could miss it."

"Let me go wash this crap off my face and get into something more appropriate." Evie was still in a robe after changing out of her last outfit for the photoshoot.

"You might want to spruce up a bit." He lifted the sleeve of a very old, very worn robe that appeared to have survived moths, the Great Depression, and the sinking of the Titanic. "But I say keep the makeup as is. It's perfect for the club we're going to."

She raised a brow and sipped the mojito he'd handed her earlier. "Sexy time in Slutsville?"

"Not even close."

Chapter Two

They want sixteen fifty for a one-room that doesn't even have a bathroom." Simone Lavoie stared out the giant floor-to-ceiling window overlooking Queen Street West. Even the view appeared ugly: a busy intersection in the west end with a Starbucks, a homeless shelter, a furniture store, and a Pizza Pizza making up the four corners.

"It'll have a bathroom."

At the sound of a gruff voice, Simone pulled her cell phone from her ear and turned to see two men, one of whom had let her in the apartment, carrying a plastic shower shell into the kitchen.

"Hold on a sec," she told her brother as she followed them down the narrow hallway. She peeked her head into the kitchen, no bigger than some people's walk-in closets, and saw the men shoving the shell into a corner between the fridge and what looked like an uninstalled garbage disposal.

"I'm going to glue this in so you have a shower. You can multitask." He shrugged as if this were a perk that should've been included in the Kijiji ad.

Simone stood for a second, lost for words—something rare for her—then rolled her eyes and turned to leave. As she stormed out of the apartment—a second-floor "studio" above a sushi restaurant—she heard the man grumble, "Then don't live at Bathurst and Queen."

It was Simone's second day apartment hunting, and it was quickly shaping up to be the worst experience of her life. Out on the street engulfed in the cacophony of traffic and people, she remembered her brother and lifted the phone back to her ear. "Gabriel? Ugh. Why did I think this was a good idea?"

"Because you were sick of Montreal, and this is a great opportunity for you."

"And the rent alone is going to suck up everything I make. Anything decent is almost double what I'd pay in Montreal." This was the fifth apartment she'd seen that day and wasn't even the worst by far. She leaned against the hot brick of the building and watched the chaos around her. A never-ending line of cars passed through the intersection, hobbled by yet more cars and pedestrians, some who waited for the lights and others who crossed when they saw an opportunity. She wasn't used to this chaos. Perhaps it was the light, or the lack of green space, or the architecture? Something felt off.

"Answer me this. Can you afford a higher rent? If so, pay it. You'll appreciate the apartment more, and in the end, you won't hate the city as much."

Gabriel was right. She'd been looking at places the same price she'd paid in Montreal, and obviously the city didn't meet her expectations. Too late to keep searching, it was best to admit defeat for today and head back to the Airbnb she'd rented for the week.

"Sometimes you're smarter than you look."

He chuckled. A sad sound, not his usual jovial roar. "What's wrong?" she asked.

A pause, then, "It's Maman." Simone rolled her eyes but stayed silent. "I brought Marissa home for dinner—"

"How'd that go?" Simone snorted.

"It was as if I'd brought home a biker chick named Bertha with tattoos all over her face."

"And what's wrong with biker chicks?" Simone dodged a cyclist as she crossed the street to catch a streetcar.

"You know what I mean. Maman treated her like she wasn't worth her time. She didn't ask any personal questions or engage her in conversation. When Marissa asked about her, she gave one-word answers. She had no interest at all in getting to know her."

Gabriel had to be serious about her. He rarely brought women home to meet their mom, and if he did, he certainly didn't care about her reaction. This was someone special. She didn't know the first thing to say to her brother to make him feel better. Genevieve Lavoie was pigheaded and could hold grudges for several lifetimes. The last thing you wanted to do was get on her bad side, a place where Simone currently sat because of her sudden move to Toronto. Genevieve had grown up in a small town in Quebec, spoke English only when absolutely necessary, and didn't feel anywhere outside of Quebec was worth her time. Even Montreal, where Simone had settled after university, was far too anglicized for her liking.

"Was Marissa speaking English?"

"She tried French, but you know how Maman is. It wasn't good enough for her. Why the fuck they insist on teaching Parisian French when the country speaks Quebecois makes no sense."

"Give her time. She hates change." That was the only advice she could offer. Nothing could forcibly change their mother's mind.

The only person who ever spoke English in their house and got away with it was her father. Simone had learned, at a very early age, never to argue with her father, for any reason. It was an unspoken rule in their house. She'd spent most of her childhood afraid of him. As the middle child of three, it had somehow fallen on her to protect her younger brother and older sister from the strange conversations that seemed to happen whenever anyone agitated her dad.

Not that it had been terribly difficult to do that. They'd grown up in a small town surrounded by farms and forests, easy places to escape. By the time she was eleven, things had settled into a routine. She and Mani, her older sister, would pick up Gabriel, who was the youngest, and head into the woods at the end of their street. Out there in the world of make-believe and fairies, they could say whatever they wanted—in whatever language they chose—play games, read each other stories, and forget everything happening at home.

Sometimes she could pretend her life had been this idyllic romp spent exploring caves and climbing trees. It was easier when talking with Gabriel. He didn't remember much because he was four years younger, too young to remember the really bad years, before her dad got help. But Mani remembered. Two years older, she had nightmares and misunderstandings mixed with her memories. She'd been too young to really understand, but old enough to remember the chaos that could descend on their home.

"Have you spoken with Mani lately?" Simone changed the topic before Gabriel could get too agitated about their mom. She'd always been close with Gabriel because—as the most similar—they had banded together against their mom and bonded over their concern for Mani.

"She left me a voice mail a few weeks ago saying she'd started a new job in Halifax. You know how she gets when she starts something new. All excited until it actually starts to feel like work. She hasn't responded to any of my texts though."

Simone suspected Mani had already moved on from that new job. She hadn't spoken to her sister in years. All her information was filtered through Gabriel, who got bits and pieces—usually voice mails left in the middle of the night so he couldn't question Mani's decisions or voice his concern—two things Mani hated. It was one reason she never called Simone. According to her there was too much judgment.

By the time she'd gotten off the call with Gabriel, the streetcar was descending into the underground, where she'd catch a subway to the east end.

She had a meeting with the line producer, Jess Cirillo, at the studio, even though her new job didn't officially start until tomorrow. Jess was in charge of the day-to-day production of the show and wanted to fill her in before she met everyone. Already Simone could tell she would like working with this woman, whose directness cut through all the bullshit.

Gabriel had been right. This was a huge opportunity for her, and standing at reception in the gigantic sprawl of buildings that housed the soundstage for the show she would start working on tomorrow, she was still surprised at how easily this gig had fallen into her lap. And at the perfect time in her life too.

"Simone, hello." Simone watched the mop of dark, curly hair bounce in through a side door. "Thanks for coming in today. I wanted a chance to talk to you before things get crazy." Jess, no bigger than five-two max, bounded up to Simone and pumped her hand a few times before pulling her toward the door she'd just come through.

As soon as they were inside, an even more hectic environment than Simone could imagine stampeded past. Crowds of people rushed by, not walking, but physically running as if their speed helped them save lives. It looked like a scene out of a disaster movie rather than a soundstage. Some carried clothing, while others clutched tablets or boxes or piles of scripts, everyone shouting and talking and calling out to people as they streamed by.

"First table-read tomorrow, so everyone's freaking out." Jess led Simone into a small office stuffed with boxes and a small desk. "Have a seat. It's not fancy, no window, but as my mom used to point out about my room, it has a door that closes and locks. So basically this is paradise for me." Jess slid a large tablet onto her desk and plopped down. "I'm so glad you're here."

Simone wasn't sure if she meant her office or the job in general. Jess's desk was covered with neat stacks of papers, a pile of multicoloured scripts, thick file folders arranged like Tetris blocks on her desk. "I want to thank you for joining the team—and it is a team. After a year of filming, we all work well together." She rearranged her coffee mug so she could lean forward and put her elbows on her desk. "I wanted to have this opportunity to go over some things about the schedule and give you a chance to ask any questions you might have." She took a breath and continued as if she were giving an Oscar speech and had only a few more seconds before the music began. "You were a dancer, right? Ballet?"

Simone nodded. "I can tell. You have that form, and you walk like a dancer, with your toes pointed out a little."

"I was never a professional dancer. I didn't love it enough to give my whole world to it. I studied movement and went into choreography."

"Is it a strange transition?"

"From dance?"

"To switch from choreography to becoming an intimacy coordinator?"

"Not really. A large part of my job is still choreography and movement. I deal with added elements and subtlety for sure."

"Of course. That makes sense." Jess riffled through one of her towers and produced a light-blue page. "This is the call sheet for tomorrow. We're usually pretty good at sticking to the times on there. Although the first week is usually a bit of a misfire." Before Simone had a chance to look at the sheet, Jess continued. "You'll have a chance to meet everyone tomorrow and sit down with them and get a feel for the different personalities you'll be dealing with. Did you get the first script?"

"I did. I had a few questions about some of the language in one of the scenes."

"Okay." Jess nodded, her curls bouncing enthusiastically. "You should talk to Cameron and Rob." She picked up her tablet and typed a few lines. "Anything creative-related goes through them as the show runner and head writer. Anything to do with scheduling or logistics you can come to me about." Jess leaned forward, her lips tightening into a straight line. "I really want you to feel welcome and supported here." She punctuated that sentence with a quick smile and sat back in her chair. "Now. Do you have any questions for me?"

Simone settled in the hard chair and intertwined her hands on her knees, unsure where to begin. She now had so many. Someone knocked at the door, and a woman in her early twenties, maybe even late teens, popped her head in. "Sorry to interrupt, Jess. Cynthia is in a panic because two of the actors didn't get the schedule for the table read, and they're still on vacation." The chaos and noise from the hallway filtered in.

Jess swiped her finger across her tablet's screen. "Who were the two?"

The woman consulted a slip of paper. "Emily Moyer and Hani Badaki."

Jess checked her tablet. "Hani has only two lines in the next episode. They'll be fine without her." Her finger quickly scanned down a page. "Emily has three full scenes." She drummed her fingers on her lips. "Have Jill come in and read her part. She can do a good Emily being Sonya. The table read's mostly for the writers anyway."

The woman smiled and ducked out, leaving the room in silence once again.

"Sorry. Where were we?"

"When we spoke earlier you had mentioned the need for an intimacy coordinator. Why wasn't one hired during the first season?"

Jess opened her top drawer and pulled out a hair elastic and spent several seconds taming her curls into a bun atop her head. "All shows should be required to have an intimacy coordinator. The day-to-day filming moves so fast that a lot of the hidden emotions, things people don't show, get steamrolled over. Another truth is that we have a lot more intimate scenes this season. At least one per episode as opposed to last season, where there were maybe three or four in the whole season. And one more truth is that…" Jess turned to look at a poster on her wall—an old print advertising Shakespeare's King Lear with a giant red king chess piece breaking apart and becoming a flock of crows. "I think one of our male leads is propositioning day players and trading sex for better parts." She fidgeted with the mug on her desk, spinning it around several times. "I overheard two women talking about it in a club bathroom. They didn't name who it was, so I can't be sure. But all these reasons add up to the fact that we need you here to make sure everyone's concerns are being met. And of course Cameron jumped at the chance because of the whole Me Too movement. He wants everyone to feel safe and comfortable on set. We all do."

"I'm certainly glad for the opportunity. I agree that this position needs to be more mainstream. As for the matter of the actor trading sex for…better parts? I'm not sure exactly what—"

"Nothing. It was something I wanted you to be aware of. I'm sorry to say it's the main reason I thought of hiring for your position in the first place. Sexual misconduct shouldn't be the wake-up call, but it doesn't change the fact that I'm glad you're here now."

"Have you ever worked with an intimacy coordinator?" Not all sets welcomed her. Some appeared standoffish, which made her job difficult.

"I have, but not to this extent before. An indie film called Your Choice. You might have heard of it?" Simone shook her head. "No? Oh, well. It was—anyway, they could afford to hire one for only two days. So not to the extent where you'll be on set most days."

"What I do takes time. And not everyone is happy that this time should be what one director I worked with stated was 'wasted on worrying about what the actors are feeling.' And that's bringing it down to a G-rated level." As she spoke, she used her hands and body to emphasize and imitate as needed. "I want you to know I'm excited to be here. I'd just like to know if I'm going to…" Simone crossed her legs and leaned forward. She wanted to be straight with Jess. It was always best to be up-front about expectations. "Basically I want to know what sort of egos I'll be dealing with. The more I know now, the easier it will be for me to navigate them. Does that make sense?"

Jess smiled widely. What lipstick she'd been wearing had long since worn off, much of it a red trace on her coffee mug. Still, her smile was her best feature, brightening her eyes. She had a mischievous sparkle then. "This is going to be a fun season. I can't wait to shake things up a bit." She stood and grabbed her tablet. "Let's go meet this episode's director." Her smile, if possible, grew brighter.

CHAPTER THREE

The club was called Everything For Sale, tucked down an alley, hastily cleaned for the night guests, in the Discovery District. The front housed a gothic bank on Bay Street, which accounted for the cavernous basement where the club was located.

"I'm going to get recognized looking like this." Several people had pointed at Evie, whispering into someone's ear, as they passed the long line sweeping down the alley and around the corner onto the main sidewalk. She'd changed into the tightest pair of black jeans she owned and paired it with a camisole that covered the important parts and left her back exposed. Regardless of who she was, eyes would turn. Evie killed in that outfit.

Last spring she could go to the grocery store and walk down the street without anyone giving her a second thought. A normal, safe life. Things had changed since she returned from Estonia. Unsettling. She couldn't go into a coffee shop without someone turning around to stare. This was Toronto, where no one gave a shit who you were, so they rarely approached her. Occasionally someone would come over and ask for her autograph or, more often, a picture of the two of them. Evie was always polite and in fact preferred that directness to the stares and pointing. But there was no helping it. If she went out without a hat and glasses, she would be recognized. And here she was looking almost identical to her TV counterpart, practically begging for it.

Shane squeezed her hand, keeping a steady pace as they passed the line to the front. "We're skirting the line, so of course people are going to point and whisper at us. Don't worry. When we get in, you'll see why I chose this place."

They stopped in front of a grey metallic door at the back of the alley. Two large men and a long line of hopeful people dressed in club wear were the only clues they'd found the entrance to an exclusive night club.

Shane leaned in and whispered something to one of the men dressed in a black, long-sleeve shirt clinging to the muscles underneath. He nodded and checked a tablet on a small table next to him. Halfway down the list his eyes stopped, and he turned to the equally forbidding bouncer with his hand on the door. The door opened, filling the alley with a heart-pounding beat. They stepped inside, enveloped in darkness.

The entrance stood on a platform overlooking the club below, or would have if it wasn't almost completely dark. Evie grabbed the railing in front of her to get her bearings. The blackness jarred her senses. After a minute, when her eyes began to adjust, she noticed the tiny glow of lights. Not completely dark. The stairs leading down had tinted LEDs along the edge, and the bar at the far end, which wrapped around an entire corner, had the same tinted LEDs along its surface. Every few seconds, as a certain beat hammered through the throng, coloured spotlights danced throughout the room, illuminating the mass of bodies on the dance floor.

"See," Shane yelled into Evie's ear. "If someone recognizes you in this, they either know you personally or you told them who you are."

"What did you say to get us in?"

"I know the manager. He was the assistant manager of Titans when I worked there."

Evie nodded. She was done talking. Evie loved clubs because no one expected a conversation. All she had to do was move.

"Let's grab a drink," Shane screamed in her ear. Evie smiled, grabbed his hand, and carefully guided them down the stairs, following the path of LEDs.

After threading their way through the throng of people, Evie pulled herself toward the bar, squeezing in between two women in stilettos. Amazingly, as soon as she stepped up, the shapes of people and the bar bloomed. Those on the dance floor became one large horde of black. The bartenders and the people standing along the broad counter popped in the light.

Evie turned her gaze to the back of the bar, the drinks' menu, written in neon paint, easily readable under the black lights. Blind as a newborn kitten without her glasses, Evie squinted up at the small font. A giant understatement. Evie was so blind she once ordered a tuna ceviche instead of a four-cheese dip. She was too embarrassed at the time to say anything and had been forced to eat fish, something she hadn't done since she was a teenager.

"Order for me. I can't read the menu."

Shane raised an eyebrow. "What are you going to do without me?"

Evie shook her head at him. She had no plans to do without him. She wasn't worried about herself finding someone else and leaving their platonic twosome. She was worried about Shane. He was, without a doubt, the sweetest person she knew.

They'd met when she was still questioning her sexuality and had decided to give it one more shot, thinking maybe high school had been the problem. Perhaps it had something to do with the maturity level of the boys she'd been dating. She and Shane had hit it off immediately. They liked the same movies, the same music; they even shared the same favourite book, In Cold Blood, by Truman Capote. Evie loved true crime and always had a book or podcast on the go. It helped her get through the sometimes-interminable wait times on set.

For their date, Shane took her to a homeless shelter where he volunteered. He worked in the kitchen, helping make meals for the residents. He'd shared his love of cooking, explaining how his grandma had taught him from the time he could reach the stove. For him it meant home, family, and safety, yet working at that kitchen had made up his mind for him. He wanted to cook for people, to see the joy on their faces when they bit into something and experienced the unexpected. He still volunteered on his off time at a few different shelters in the city.

Afterward, he'd taken her to his favourite chip truck, where they served authentic poutine. At the end of the evening he'd walked her back to her res and they'd exchanged numbers, both knowing what they had was much better than a quickie relationship.

Evie stopped dating men after that night. The few relationships she'd had over the years were brief, superficial, and mostly about sex. She occupied her mind with other more important things, like getting her career going. For now, that satisfied her.

Shane raised both arms, each holding a drink, and slid out from the bar. He handed Evie something tinged red. "Enjoy it. That's the last drink I'm buying here. They charged me over forty bucks for these." He twirled the tiny straw and took a conservative sip. "Forty goddamn bucks. That's more than they charge at a Leafs' game."

"Since when have you been to a Leafs' game?"

"Remember the hostess from Elephant and Castle? Her brother had a connection. I went once, and once was enough."

They found a corner with fewer people and a little protection from the noise. Evie used to love dance clubs. It was a way to feel without having to be on all the time. The industry she worked in was full of too many energy suckers—people who demanded your attention all the time. She was also done with sitting on the sidelines. Evie downed her cocktail and motioned for Shane to do the same. When he refused, she pulled him onto the dance floor anyway.

The DJ switched gears from a frenzied techno beat and mixed in some deep house. Evie soon lost Shane to the crowd, enveloped into the darkened mass. Every few minutes the dance floor would flare up, the strobing effect adding to the confusion of undulating bodies.

She caught sight of Shane as a flash of light illuminated the dance floor for a few seconds, his hand held high, protecting his twenty-dollar drink.

The deep bass created a hypnotic pulse that surged through her. Abandoning all thought, Evie closed her eyes and ignored everything except what it felt like to be here in this moment moving with hundreds of bodies.

Warm, strong hands gripped her hips and pulled her back against an undeniably feminine body. Evie flicked her gaze back to see, in the dim light, an eyebrow lift and the quirk of soft, red lips. Was this a question of permission?

At this instant, being in this club was as close to anonymity as she could possibly get. And why not enjoy herself? It's what she'd come to do—let off some steam before she had to settle back into fourteen-, sixteen-hour days, forced onto a gruelling diet—or else Des would give her that disappointed look when she had to alter a costume—with basically no social life. And she had no obligation. She could melt into the darkness of the crowd when she'd had enough or her partner grew too curious or insistent.

Evie turned, fully mesmerized by those crimson lips somehow still visible in the darkness. They twisted into a wicked seductive smile while the hands coaxed Evie closer and the two of them began to move in unison to the beat. They were already feeding off each other's movements, fuelled by one another's energy. Evie wrapped her arms around the woman's slender neck, fitting against her like a lens snapping onto the body of a camera.

The pulsing drive of the music invaded her, thumping and throbbing along her skin, skimming her like a caress. Their two bodies became coiled, surging with the crowd as the music grew louder and faster. It vibrated through Evie—trawling, pulling, arousing. The woman slid her fingertips along Evie's bare back, creating a devastating sensation that travelled from her back all the way to her toes.

Evie closed her eyes to the experience and slipped closer, pressing firmly against the woman, near enough to feel her breath on her ear, catch the scent of her perfume—something floral, definitely exotic—recognize the heat pulsing against her.

An erotic tangle, deeply provoking, and Evie was lost to it, sucked in by the crowd, the noise, the unexpected delight of it. For a mindless second she'd given up control, something she held precious, and dove deep into simply feeling. As the music crested, ready to spill over in climax, Evie could feel herself building.

The frenzy of the beat hit, coloured lights flashed, the crowd surged, and the woman was gone, swallowed by the billowing mass. Evie was left in the cold, unable to find her again.

Chapter Four

The moka pot gurgled, alerting Simone to its readiness. She removed it from the burner and turned off the heat. A forlorn Keurig sat in a corner, unused and unwanted. Years ago, Simone had learned, if you want good coffee when you travel, you must bring your own. After a disastrous trip to the Bahamas in the late aughts, she'd begun to bring her own grinds and a moka pot anytime she travelled. Even if it meant sacrificing something else for space. Coffee was important, which was why she couldn't understand how the Keurig became the go-to coffee machine of the hospitality industry. Perhaps because it looked clean and efficient. It apparently didn't matter that it tasted like something had shat in dirty water. It came in a variety of colours and could blend into any decor as if it truly belonged. As if it said, "Hi. I will be your morning perk." That's of course what owners thought it said. What it really said was, "Hi. It's more important I meet a certain aesthetic than fulfill your caffeine dreams."

She poured herself a cup, tucked her iPad under her arm, and headed for the fire escape that doubled as a balcony.

Today she'd be meeting the cast, sitting down to voice expectations, run through concerns. It was important to set the foundations of trust early at the beginning. And she was excited. Jess had introduced her to Michael Scott, the director for the first episode of the season and, according to Jess, the main director for the series. She almost seemed giddy at the prospect of something new. A new challenge, a new beginning. Simone had worked as an intimacy coordinator for the past three years—not long enough to become stale; it was the province that had become stale. Or, rather more, the inhabitants of said province. Until now she'd worked on small projects, plays, indie films. This was mainstream, a project that would finally legitimize her career.

The sun rose over the roofs on the other side of the street, breaking through the blue tint that engulfed the old row houses. Already muggy, the air would only get worse throughout the day.

"Best to get started early." She pulled her tablet out to begin a new search, with new parameters. If she was going to get an apartment she wanted, she would have to be willing to spend at least twenty-five hundred a month. "Fucking highway robbery."

First Simone opened her email. She'd made a few enquiries last night and wanted to check to see if she'd gotten any responses. Two out of the three had gotten back, but only one was available to see today. She responded and added that date to her calendar.

By the time she finished her coffee, the city had awoken. It was garbage day. The slow, steady pace of the recycling truck as it came up the street drowned out all other traffic. As it passed, it left a trail of liquid in its path so foul it could be used as smelling salts for the dead.

Simone lifted her mug off the tiny wooden table and climbed back into the window.

Out of the shower, she checked the weather—another scorcher—and pulled out a summer dress that looked both professional and feminine. Perfect for her mix of apartment viewings and meetings that morning. It made her appear capable of taking care of an apartment as well as doing her job.

Clothes were everything…

As was the aesthetic she strived to create. She wanted people to notice her, because growing up the second youngest in a giant Francophone family, she'd been overlooked most of her life. All her cousins were loud, with big personalities, who would hold court at family gatherings spouting opinions about this or that. Simone was subtle. She didn't like raising her voice or having to shout to be heard. Clothing allowed her to simply exist as she was.

Before leaving the apartment, she checked every appliance, taking pictures of each on her phone. She obsessed about leaving things on or unlocked. Without those pictures, her day dissolved into worry and anxiety. They represented verifiable proof her apartment wouldn't burn down.

Her phone dinged, alerting her that her Lyft driver was two minutes away. She locked the door, taking a video of herself doing so, and headed down the stairs. On the way, she passed a woman with dreadlocks taping a note to the bulletin board on one of the floors. Simone didn't stop to read it. Her Lyft driver Raul in the red Acura parked in front of the house.

Evie pulled her glasses case out of her bag and set them next to her script at the table. Always the first to arrive. No surprise. The eager beaver. Lucas, her younger brother, still teased her about that trait, although he no longer pretended to be a beaver.

When they were younger, he'd jut his front teeth out and dance in circles, driving her crazy. She couldn't fathom why now. The taunting ended his first day of high school, when Kristen Mason, one of Evie's friends, watched with disdain, the level of which only a haughty sixteen-year-old could muster, and said, "What a moron."

Those words, out of the mouth of his crush, wounded him deep. He didn't talk for a whole week.

The upside, Evie never endured his stupid beaver dance again. The downside? He spent the next two years trying to exact his revenge. The closest he ever came was soaking part of her arm with a water balloon aimed at her chest. Kristen stopped coming over after that.

Charlotte Newson, the next to arrive in the cast, played Evie's best friend on the show. Over the course of shooting last year, they'd become good friends off the show as well. It was strange how that happened. After spending countless hours together, you became family, which was accurate. You didn't choose your family. It chose you, much like the people you worked with on set.

The two of them couldn't have been more different. Short and bubbly to the point of almost being obnoxious, Charlotte had no filter between her head and her mouth and talked nonstop. Their shared love of the macabre had finally won Evie over. Charlotte was a true crime nerd as well, listening to podcasts about serial killers and brutal murders, which directly contrasted with Charlotte's apparent nature. When you pictured her, at least when Evie did, she imagined a 1950s housewife in a housecoat gossiping over coffee with the housewives along the street. And her part on Social Queen wasn't that different, maybe updated to the twenty-first century.

Early in her career she'd been known for darker roles. Charlotte got her start playing gritty characters on crime shows, which eventually landed her a supporting role as an FBI psychologist in a spinoff that ran for over a decade. That's when she became fascinated with the minds of serial killers. She'd done a ton of research for the role and found the more gruesome the details, the more she liked it.

Charlotte grabbed a cup of coffee, skipped the fancy pastries, as had Evie, and took a seat next to her. "Wow, honey. You look positively… What did you do during the summer? Camp underground?" In contrast, Charlotte's skin glowed a warm caramel, offset perfectly by her white blazer in which she'd pushed her sleeves up to her elbows like on the original Miami Vice.

Evie flipped her hair over her shoulder and gave an impish smile. "It's the new pasty look. All the redheads are wearing it."

"I had a cousin like that. She'd burn the second she went out in the sun." Will Stagg took a seat opposite them, his plate topped with several dripping pastries. "One year her family went to Italy, where they have all those topless beaches—" a wistful look brightened his eyes—"and she got second-degree burns on her boobs, couldn't wear a bra for weeks." He took a mouthful of danish. "Ruined her summer."

"That's what happens when you bring the girls out untrained." Charlotte pushed her breasts together. "You can't just expose them all at once. A little at a time until they're used to the sun." She laughed at Will's expression. His eyes had fallen to watch her hands lift her breasts until the tops were exposed over the flimsy camisole she was wearing under her blazer. Evie's gaze had also wandered over to the display. Charlotte let them drop, and they all watched them bounce back into place.

Will cleared his throat and took another bite of his danish. He swept brown hair off his face and glued his eyes to the script for the next ten minutes.

No matter how much time she spent with Will, Evie never felt like she was getting to know him. He was agreeable in such an extreme way, as if when not acting, he aimed to get you to like him. She'd first met him during auditions. She couldn't say she liked him then, and that hadn't changed.

Will played Ben, her husband on the show—a down-on-his-luck writer jealous of his wife's supposed fame. In the first season he'd sat back and watched as his wife wielded "truth" like a forged weapon that could be repaired and rebuilt at will. Last season had set the stage for some epic showdowns that they all knew would equal big ratings this season. The season finale had ended during a scene at a big fund-raiser with Abby Bruce, Evie's character, getting hot and heavy with her daughter's soccer couch, played by Ian Davies.

Evie flipped through her script while they waited for everyone to trickle in. The studio sent scripts out a week before shooting began, which meant hers had sat waiting on the kitchen island for when she returned from Estonia. She'd blushed as she read the first scene. Rumour had it they'd hired an intimacy coordinator, and if anything, that made her even more trepidatious. If she heard someone say "it was only acting" one more time, she'd stab them with one of those metal straws they'd given out last year. Right in the jugular.

Of course it wasn't real. Of course she wasn't actually going to get naked on a backyard balcony and let Ian Davies plow her from behind while she watched the lights dance on the water of his pool. It was a TV show. She would, however, have to simulate that act and make it look convincing. And before she had to do that, she would have to talk about it, and choreograph it with a stranger. She worried they might have a sit-around and talk about their "feelings."

"Did you guys get to the part where Abby tells off Sophia's teacher?" Ian Davies set his coffee down on the table, choosing a seat next to Charlotte. "I cannot wait to see Evie act the shit out of that scene." Ian held his fist out to Evie for a fist bump. Ian was big on fist bumps.

Evie punched hers to his and pulled back, imitating his explosion. Ian made the sound effect for both of them. He grinned at the group, flipping open his script. Ian reminded Evie of a golden retriever like the one she'd grown up with, which wasn't an insult to Ian or Angus. It didn't matter if it was five a.m. and they were in makeup, or three a.m. outside freezing their asses off waiting for a shot to be lit, Ian always had a smile. And it wasn't an act. It was like his optimism was ever-flowing and internal. She considered him the glue of the show. He kept everyone laughing during long days and gave the best pep talks.

Last year she'd had a difficult scene with her onscreen daughter, Sophia. She'd had to yell at the poor girl, who was only eight at the time. Mia, the actress, of course, took it like a pro—she'd been acting since she was three. Evie, however, was a basket case. Ian pulled her aside and shared a story with her. Early on in his career he'd played Dean Corll, the Candy Man, a serial killer from the 70s in a made-for-TV bio-pic. Corll killed young boys, at least twenty-eight, and getting inside the mind of that sick piece of shit was the hardest thing Ian had ever had to do. If he'd had a choice now, he'd never take such a role. It was too dark for him to handle.

It was one thing to take on a role that was all darkness and have to slog through. Abby Bruce might be a self-absorbed questionable wife and all-round sucky human being, but her heart was mostly in the right place. The scene was important for Abby's character arc. She was angry because she was scared for Sophia's safety. She was yelling out of fear and love. Having that talk with Ian had put the whole thing in perspective.

Now, whenever Abby had a hard scene to film, she would look at the importance of it compared to the storyline and how it built her character. It was the only reason she'd be able to get through all these intimate scenes this season. Abby and Ben's marriage was all about the kids. Ben spent more time worrying about money and his career than he did about being a good, loving husband to Abby. This was her way of finding a little bit of happiness. And if she was going to have to pretend to have illicit sex with someone, at least it was Ian.

Michael Scott, the episode's director, entered the room and shut the door. By now the room was full. Four writers were occupying chairs along the far wall; Jess Cirillo, the line producer, stood in the corner with her ever-present tablet; and around the table sat six of the episode's main cast.

"Hello. Let's get started," said Michael—never Mike—with an air of impatience, as if they were already behind schedule before they'd started. When he stopped at the head of the table, he wasn't much taller than Ian, who was sitting to his right. What hair he'd had was long lost, and any strays that dared remain were shaved to the scalp. Evie swore he wore the same outfit every day. That, or he had a closet full of replicas. Dark jeans and a light blue polo from Lacoste. Ian joked he'd seen him wear a Fred Perry once, though he had to admit, it was light blue.

Michael flipped open his script. "Julian, can you please read the action parts."

Julian, one of the writers sitting on the edge of the room, opened his script. "Exterior, dusk. Abby is bent over a balcony, half naked, her body jerks forward. The camera pans up to reveal Justin thrusting behind her."

Before Julian could continue, the door opened, and Cameron Buck, the executive producer, poked his head in. "Sorry to interrupt, everyone. I wanted to introduce you to the newest member of our team." He pulled the door wide and ushered in a woman wearing an expensive-looking dress with straps and a subtle black-and-turquoise pattern. As she surveyed the room with intense eyes, they stopped on Evie for several seconds, then continued. She smiled, and when she did, the cool facade fell away to reveal warmth. Like the sun coming out on a cold winter day to melt the ice.

"This is Simone Lavoie, our intimacy coordinator. I want all of you to welcome her into the family. We've all worked really hard to get the show to where it is—number one in Canada, the US, and the UK and trending in France and Australia." The writers' section of the room uttered a light cheer. "This season is going to be even better. We'll be pushing our comfort zone, and Simone is here to help us do that. We want everyone to enjoy the process. We're a team. No, even more than that. We're a family, and I know if we support each other, we'll do amazing things."

Simone raised her hand, with long slender fingers, and waved it in greeting. When she spoke, she had a slight accent. "Thank you for welcoming me. If possible," she looked back at Cameron for confirmation, "I would like to meet some of you today, get familiar with each other." Her gaze fell back on Evie and stopped. Evie was not going to be able to get out of this scene.

Chapter Five

Simone stood at the door looking in. Evelyn Harper's dressing room was on the second floor of the large studio building. Originally someone's office, the building had once been a warehouse for a department store at the turn of the twentieth century.

According to Jess, the production company had originally taken over the building to film a series that hadn't made it through the first season. Social Queen took over afterward, fitting the entire production into the enormous space. All the interiors were shot in the studio, even some of the exteriors with the help of green screens, creative lighting, and good editing.

Evelyn sat at a dressing table flipping through her script making notes. An uneaten salad sat next to her, an open thermos with something steaming.

She was unquestionably the woman from the club last night. Nothing eased Simone's stress more than dancing, a throwback to when she was younger. For the first two decades of her life, she had been passionate about becoming a dancer. Two shot knees and a broken ankle had curtailed that ambition early on, and she'd transitioned into choreography.

Dance was in her heart, her comfort space. Whenever she felt out of control or anxious, all she had to do was hit a club and lose herself in the crowd. It didn't even matter what kind of music or club. It soothed her to feel without having to think. She didn't share this preference with many people. The trauma of losing her dream felt too personal.

Last night she'd danced—flirted—with a woman who looked familiar. She couldn't place the face until she'd entered the room during the table read. And even then she wasn't a hundred-percent certain. Now she was.

Without removing her gaze from the script, Evelyn scooped up her hair and pulled it into a messy bun on top of her head, revealing a tiny bird tattoo on her neck. Simone remembered that tattoo from the night before. Dark as it had been in the club, she found the long, slender neck with the outline of a phoenix hard to forget.

She rapped her knuckle on the door frame. "I'm sorry to intrude on your lunch, your quiet time, Ms. Harper. Do you have a moment?"

Evie replaced her fork and stood. "Simone, was it?" Evie reached forward and shook Simone's hand in a firm grasp. "You can call me Evie. Evelyn was my grandmother and sounds like an old person's name. The name worked great for her, I guess. She had five kids and lived to be a hundred and two."

Simone suppressed a smile. Right away she found Evie charming. "It is Simone." She'd been named after Simone Signoret, a French actress no one except lovers of French cinema had ever heard of. Her mother adored old movies and would sit for hours and watch them with her father. It was one of the few things she'd seen them share. Simone looked around for somewhere to sit. The dressing room wasn't small. It had ample room for a couch, which currently held a suitcase's worth of clothes, a dressing table with a mirror, a full-length mirror, and an overstuffed chair that looked more ornamental than functional. A large window with lush blackout curtains looked out over a side street with train tracks running between buildings.

A more industrial area of the east end, this part of the city contained mostly commercial warehouses and historical buildings, a throwback to when most things were shipped by train in the country. It made it difficult to reach on transit, something Simone hadn't considered when she took the job.

Evie grimaced at the mess on the couch. "I'm a slob." She shrugged. "I usually like to have extra clothes here in case we run late. It's nice to have a choice of what to change into." Evie scooped up the pile of clothes in her arms and dumped them on the chair to her left. "Please. Have a seat." She indicated the now-vacant spot.

Simone observed Evie as she sat at the dressing table. She picked up a pen, clicked it a few times, seemed to notice her fidgeting, and replaced it.

"Are you nervous?"

"No—I'm…I'm…I think it's important that you're here. Everyone does. I'm just…" She scratched her elbow, folded her arms, unfolded them, placed them on her lap, and picked up the pen again.

Evie was nothing like Abby Bruce, especially today, without makeup, wearing simple, form-fitting jeans and a ragged old Petroglyphs Provincial Parks T-shirt. This woman was not what Simone had been expecting. Perhaps she had been worried she'd be working with an arrogant, self-centred perfectionist. Instead, Evie was normal. That fact threw Simone off her game a little.

"You're nervous because you're not exactly sure what an intimacy coordinator does. Am I right?"

Evie nodded. "I've never worked with one before." She looked around at her dressing room, her eyes wide. "This is my first big role. I'm usually a day player."

This reaction wasn't new for Simone. A lot of her job entailed educating people, setting expectations. Even though this was a much bigger production than she was used to, it would start the same. "Have you worked with a stunt coordinator before?"

"Last year, we did a scene where I jumped onto a moving car."

Simone grinned. She had a starting point. "Good. I am no different. Well, except I coordinate intimate scenes. Stunts are intricate, involving a lot of moving parts, a lot of adrenaline, and you need to rehearse and know what everyone is doing, plus what you are doing to remain safe. A lot of the safety in what I do is keeping people's boundaries safe. Entering a scene where you'll be vulnerable, exposed both emotionally and literally, can make you feel intimidated and invaded. I'm here to make sure everyone knows your boundaries, what you feel comfortable with, and the same goes for the other actors in the scene."

Evie leaned forward, focused on Simone.

"It doesn't have to be today, but sometime in the next day I want you to think about this first scene with Ian and what your initial comfort level is." Simone leaned back on the couch. It was something hard and trendy, probably from Ikea. What would they put in her office? According to Jess, office space in the building was to be prized. And after seeing the tiny cupboard they'd shoved Jess into, she believed it. They were working on something for Simone. Not as spacious as this, but then she wasn't the star of a hit show.

To prepare for her job, Simone had watched the first season. It wasn't her usual fare. However, once she'd gotten past her snobbery, she'd binged all thirteen episodes. It hooked you because everyone knew someone like Abby Bruce, and you couldn't wait to watch the train wreck unfold. Had she been expecting Evelyn Harper to be like Abby Bruce? Perhaps in part. So many actors played a version of themselves on the screen. The two had in common only their charm and good looks, and even that similarity existed along a spectrum.

From what Simone could tell, this woman wasn't even wearing makeup, and she was gorgeous. Her thick auburn hair, though piled on top of her head, made her look sexy. The freckles, glasses, and just her general demeanour were disarming.

"No one told me I'd have homework." Evie grinned, revealing perfect white teeth.

"I promise you won't be tested on it."

"Good. Because I suck at tests."

"I spoke with Michael yesterday—"

"That must have been a joyful occasion."

Simone smiled. "He's certainly not a fan of mine." That was an understatement. Jess obviously liked stirring the pot. She was far too enthusiastic to introduce Simone to Michael, and after meeting him, she knew why. He saw Simone's presence as an intrusion.

"Michael's not a fan of anything, especially shooting delays."

Simone nodded, more of the puzzle falling into place. "Or rehearsals—"

"Or script revisions. Especially last-minute script revisions." Evie laughed, the sound short and delightful. "Last year we were shooting this really intricate scene. It took half the day to set it up and get everything into place, and just as Michael shouted 'action,' all the lights went because of a power failure." She tucked her knees into her chest as she laughed. "He went berserk, tripped over a cable and went straight through a backdrop. So the lights come on and there he is, ass up through a screen. It was…the highlight of pretty much everyone's year."

"He's promised me we'll have ample rehearsal time."

"Because of Cameron. He's over-the-moon excited about having you here. A lot of the producers are, so he's probably warned all the directors that they're not to mess with you." Evie leaned forward and lowered her voice. "Watch out for Michael though. It might appear that he's being cooperative, but if it comes to his shooting schedule or a better product, he'll pick his shooting schedule every time. He seems to think it makes him a better director."

Simone propped her elbow on her knee and rested her head on her hand, fully invested in hearing all the gossip now. "You don't like Michael."

"Does anyone?"

Simone shook her head. She couldn't say for sure. "You dislike him for what sounds like personal reasons."

Evie leaned back and picked up her fork. "I think he cuts corners. That's all." She took a bite of her salad.

Simone took that as her cue. "I'll leave you to the rest of your lunch. I just wanted to introduce myself. I didn't mean to intrude."

Evie waved her off. "Having company is better than skulking in my dressing room shoving down organic kale."

❖

Simone spent the next few hours meeting the rest of the cast. Will Stagg welcomed her the most by far. They talked for over forty-five minutes about the Me Too movement and why it was a long time coming. Will adored the old studio system for all its marvellous contradictions. Several biographies—Paul Newman, Claudette Colbert, and Clark Gable among them—lay in various piles around his dressing room, which reminded Simone of her mom. Granted, she preferred French film to English. Simone had grown up watching Danielle Darrieux and Annie Girardot—French legends. Simone favoured the musicals from the 1930s. Because of the Great Depression, they seemed so desperate, as if they were forcing themselves to smile, forcing the gaiety. Actors languished under the studio system, especially women. MGM once suspended Elizabeth Taylor's pay because she'd had the audacity to get pregnant.

And yet, here they were, almost a hundred years later, and things only appeared to have changed. Nothing much had. Women were still beholden to men for parts. For all the women who had spoken up about how powerful men in the industry treated them, hundreds more had stayed silent. Unless they actively put more women in charge, gave them equal power, the power differential would continue to happen. The Me Too movement created the illusion of a reckoning, much like the backdrops from classic movies—a facade to give the illusion substance. Things would get better now. Well, women had been saying that for thousands of years. Each time they made headway to be equal, they were squashed back down, and for the life of her, she couldn't understand why. Did men want power that much? Did women scare men?

Being emasculated—whatever the fuck that meant—by women wanting agency?

After speaking with Will, Simone hoped that at least some of the crew was on board. So far most of them seemed willing. Ian Davies had been polite, but very standoffish, and she couldn't fathom why. After all, from her understanding of how they planned to unfold the new season, she'd be working with him and Evie the most. It might take a few episodes to build the trust she was hoping to; however, she was confident they would get there. What they were doing was important, and the results would speak for themselves. The more the industry pushed big productions to accept the work she did as standard, the better things would get, and not just for women.

By far, her most interesting meeting had been with Evie. Abby Bruce was not a likeable person. She got away with being a bitch because she was beautiful. Like in real life, beauty excused a lot. Giving those same looks to Evie, who was likeable? Devastating. Simone wasn't worried. She had no problem separating her personal and professional life. Beautiful Evie might be, but Simone wouldn't be tempted to cross the line. At this point she felt they would work together well.

By the time she left the studio, she was emotionally drained. Talking to people could wipe her out faster than running a half marathon. And she still had two apartments to look at. While she'd been working, the second place had responded to her, and she'd scheduled an appointment to see it.

The first apartment was much closer to work than the other, only a few blocks north of the studio, which meant she'd be able to walk. She was pinning all her hopes on this one. When it turned out to be a huge dump, she felt completely let down. It had also smelled strange. Had the last tenant died there? She got the creeps the second she walked into it. No wonder it was so cheap.

The Lyft to the next one took almost half an hour. Each minute she hoped equally not to fall in love with the place. But, of course, she did. The second-floor apartment in a quaint neighbourhood overlooked the Humber River, and she would be able to walk to Bloor West village for groceries. It had no smell, and she'd met one of her neighbours, who'd seemed normal.

A two-bedroom, it turned out to cost only a fraction more than a one-bedroom. But the bathroom absolutely sold Simone on the place. The bath had one of those claw-foot tubs and a giant bay window that overlooked the backyard and green space. She could escape the noise pollution of the city, and judging by her first day, she'd need to.

She walked downstairs, where the landlord stood waiting—a petite Portuguese woman in her early seventies with bottle-brown hair curled tighter than a loaded spring, and thick, oversized glasses that kept slipping down her nose.

She nodded at Simone with a knowing smile. "You're in luck. The place was taken as of this morning, but their credit check didn't work out." She eyed Simone's clothes, which, if she'd paid full price, would have set most people back an entire paycheque, and rapped her knuckles on the banister. "Something tells me I won't have that same problem with you." She turned around to lead Simone into the downstairs apartment. "Although you never know these days."

The parlour was like stepping into an episode of I Love Lucy. Everything screamed mid-century modern, perfectly preserved, as if it had only recently been purchased. Plants took up most of the surfaces, holding the light in the bay window.

"I remember when things used to be simple. You sized someone up, and if you liked 'em, you gave 'em the keys. Now there's all this hubbub about credit checks and reference calls and profile scans. I have a girlfriend who has her son go through Google to make sure they aren't weirdos before she even starts the credit check. I'm Estela, by the way."

She pulled out a stack of papers and thumbed through them until she found two, then handed them to Simone. "You're better off filling this out here and giving it to me. Chances are, I'll have several emails waiting for me. If there's one thing that has improved since I started this, it's that there's no shortage of people who want the place."

Simone took the papers and began fishing for a pen in her bag. "How long have you been doing this?"

"Well, my husband—God rest his soul—it was really his thing. I didn't touch this stuff until he died, and by then all the kids were grown and moved out. So that would've been in…1988. Huh. So a lotta years. Things change. I don't have as many places now. I sold a few to my son. It's too much to look after." She made it sound as if she ran a nefarious business, like dealing drugs or human trafficking.

"How long have you lived here?" Simone took an offered seat on the couch. By the look of the paraphernalia surrounding the chair Estela plopped into, she spent a lot of time there. A pair of bifocals sat on a pile of books, ranging from biographies to cheesy spy novels.

"I moved in after my husband died. We had a large place on Gladstone near the chocolate factory. My boys helped me renovate it, and we turned it into three apartments. I didn't need all that space. Now it has families in it. As it should be."

Simone signed at the bottom of the page and handed the papers to Estela, who pulled on her glasses that were hanging from a chain around her neck. "Give me a day to check out your references and credit." She patted Simone on the knee. "I have a good feeling about you, but I have to do it anyway." She pointed to something halfway down the page. "It says here you're an intimacy coordinator. What is that?" Estela frowned, wrinkling her forehead and shifting her perm forward. Simone could only imagine all the thoughts going through this woman's head right now. When taken out of context, it sounded like she instructed people during sex, giving advice. Now there was a job Simone never wanted.

"I work on movie and TV sets. I'm like a stunt coordinator, except I help coordinate and choreograph the intimate scenes."

"Is that so? This is an actual thing?"

"If I can help it, yes."

Chapter Six

From the right angle the place could be a trendy café just before opening. Cameron stood behind the bar—using it as a stand-up desk—on one of the temporary sets for the show. The set department had transformed an old storage area into a café. If he pivoted more to the left, he could pretend he had taken over a coffee shop and was the only patron. The illusion broke down somewhat on the right facing wall, as that led to the rest of the unfinished room now housing grip equipment.

With his head bent, concentrating on script revisions, he thought he heard someone enter the set. Cameron had been told that he could've easily been in his late thirties or early fifties and that a mop of brown curls and a boyish grin were the two things that struck most people when first meeting him.

"Hey, Cameron. You got a second?"

He looked up from his laptop and grinned. "Evelyn, you found me." Cameron rarely worked in his office, many suspected because he didn't ever want to be found. The harder to find, the harder it was to come to him with problems. That's what Jess said anyway. But it wasn't quite that he wanted to hide out. He found it hard to be creative in the same space every day. Before fame, Cameron favoured cafés instead of an office. Such a setting allowed him to write with multiple distractions, which eventually became a necessity. He couldn't beat it for people-watching, and in turn it gave him great inspiration.

"How did the shoot go the other day? For Entertainment Weekly? That's big." He had no doubt she'd look gorgeous in it. Cameron had hired Evelyn only partly because she was a knockout. He couldn't understand how she'd gone so long without getting something better than the two-bit parts she'd had most of her career. Then he started working with her. She wasn't difficult to get along with. She was professional, a bit of a protectionist—but what good actor wasn't? Evie wasn't demanding. Cameron knew she wanted growth and job security, like everyone else. A director credit on your resumé helped with both.

"It went well. Only took a few hours." Evie shrugged. "They styled me to within an inch of my life, and even then, I'm sure they'll airbrush any flaws."

Cameron laughed. It was an unwritten rule that actors would have to promote the show. Most were fine with that assumption. Many thrived on the attention. Evelyn, he could see, was one of the few who fled the spotlight. Perhaps that was why she hadn't made it bigger sooner; she self-sabotaged. She loved performing. He could see it in her work and every time he visited the set.

Anytime the topic veered toward something personal or private, she shied away. And who could blame her? Why should the general public have so much of her? In the past the line between private and public had appeared more solid. Now, with social media, that line had not only blurred but become almost nonexistent.

Evie wandered over and leaned on the counter. "How are the girls?" Cameron had twin girls who were four going on thirty. The two demons raced around wreaking havoc any time they were on set. Last year they'd managed to find a can of red paint.

Once the girls were done, the set looked like they were shooting a horror film.

"They're starting school this year." He spoke with the same intonation one might use when speaking about winning an award. Excitement and anticipation.

"Oh, man. I don't envy their teachers."

Cameron laughed. "They've been warned." He'd had kids late in life and sometimes wondered if that had been the best idea. He loved his girls. He would give his life for them if asked. But they were tiring. Maybe because they were twins, they egged each other on, or he didn't have the stamina to keep up? Whatever the reason, he was glad he spent most of his time on set. His wife, of course, had a different opinion. Just last week she'd accused him of hiding out here, using it as an excuse to dump her with the girls. His wife, Steph, was fifteen years younger, he reasoned. She had the energy to run laps around them if she chose. Steph could defuse a situation faster than a bomb expert. To say they were both overjoyed the girls were starting school was an understatement. He was happy that the majority of their frenetic day would be spent with someone else in charge.

Cameron Buck had gotten his start working for one of the biggest Broadway producers in the 90s. He once said it was pure luck that handed him the job. He'd been walking down the right sidewalk at the right time. This producer was throwing a fit because his current assistant had called in sick because she had the gall to get pneumonia three weeks before opening night. In frustration, he threw his coffee from the loading dock onto the street. The half-full quad shot—two on the top, two on the bottom, extra-steamed, extra-hot-milk, macchiato—hit Cameron in the side of the head and spilled now only slightly steaming hot milk and espresso down the front of his one good dress shirt.

The train from Missouri had pulled in earlier that morning with Cameron on it, and in less than twenty-four hours, he had a job and even a crappy apartment with five other roommates. The producer had hired him, but not because he was ashamed he'd hit someone during his tantrum. Cameron's reaction had gotten him the job. He had caught the cup before it hit the ground, leaving a quarter of the contents of the former coffee, and rushed up to the loading dock to hand the drink back with a simple, "Here's your drink, sir." Anyone who knew Cameron understood that he was being sarcastic, but the producer was oblivious.

Cameron liked to cite that story when talking about his humble beginnings in the trenches. He spent two years in servitude hell, doing everything from fetching ridiculous drink orders to watering the man's plants when he went away on business. Now look at me, he liked to say. He was in charge of his own show. Most of it was luck. He had a knack for being in the right place at the right time. His next job, the job that rescued him out of that hell, had come when the producer was late for a meeting. There was talk of turning one of his shows into a sitcom. Cameron happened to be working on a script he was trying to sell around town. While they waited for the producer to arrive, Cameron got up the nerve to pitch his own idea. The executive producer liked the concept and gave Cameron his first real break.

No one could say that Cameron wasn't a good writer, or that he didn't deserve to be discovered. Luck had gotten him the jobs in the first place, but his work ethic and talent had let him keep the jobs. Once he was writing, even if he was the lowest of the low, he impressed people and moved up the ranks quickly. From there he progressed to bigger and better shows, eventually becoming head writer. For a few more years he worked in that position on some popular shows, others not so popular. Behind those jobs, Cameron was always working on his own scripts. He longed to work for himself, not someone else. And once Cameron finally made it to the top with his own show, the first of many, he realized someone else was always in charge. Even if he ran the show, studios, money people, and ratings committees were always getting in his way of true autonomy. Until streaming. That's when he started his own production house, with his own money, and completed whatever project he wanted without any interference. Then he could sell that project as it was to a streaming service. It was the perfect way to make a show his way.

And that's how Social Queen had come about. It was the first time he'd ever gotten a chance to be the one calling all the shots, a hundred percent. Money people? Fuck them. It was his money. He could spend as much or as little as he wanted. Censors and ratings?

It was streaming. He could do and say anything he wanted. Hiring? He got the final say. He never had to worry about putting a second-rate actress in a part because her dad had invested ten million in the production. Nope. This baby was all his.

He looked down at the script changes he'd been sent earlier. He knew why Evelyn was here and also understood he couldn't give her what she wanted.

"I wanted to talk to you about directing one of the episodes this year. Last year you said we could circle back around to the idea this season."

He steepled his fingers as she talked. Using his two index fingers, he pointed at her as he said, "And do you remember what we talked about? Why we'd circle back?"

Evie nodded. "I directed a film this summer. In Estonia."

"Estonia? That's great! That's wonderful." Cameron shifted some of the notebooks and paper around on the counter, almost like he was purposely acting as if looking for something. He finally put his hand on a book that had been in front of him the whole time. "Here we go." He flipped it open and scrolled through a couple of pages. "We're doing fifteen episodes this season. Two more than last year, which is great." He placed the notebook on the counter and leaned over, realizing what he was going to say next would kill Evelyn. Though he wanted to keep his talent happy, he also wanted to make a great show, and he didn't think Evelyn had what it took to direct. He just didn't know how to let her down easy. Last year he'd hoped it was just a whim, so he'd put her off. Now he realized it might not be so easy. "It's great that you're getting out there and gaining experience. Send me the film. I'd love to have a look at it." And she seemed so damned hopeful. "I can't provide a definitive answer right now. I gave a lot of the episodes to Michael because he knows the cast and crew." Her mouth tightened. "And promised a few more to other directors last year." Evelyn nodded. "We'll talk about it in a couple weeks. How about that?"

"Sure." She didn't look happy. No doubt, she wanted an answer now. But she wouldn't like the answer he'd give her now.

"A few weeks," she repeated.

"And in the meantime, send me that film."

Evelyn didn't say anything else. She gave him a thumbs-up—something she did only, he'd noticed, when she was pissed—and turned to leave.

Cameron returned to his script changes. As of right now, they were already behind schedule.

❖

A half-empty mojito glass perspired on the patio, a dark ring of wet concrete easing outward. Evie lay on a chaise lounge, still in her work clothes, stargazing, well, gazing at the sky. The only star visible was Polaris. Every few minutes the blinking lights of a jet would flash past. As a child, Evie remembered seeing the Little Dipper and Orion on her backyard deck. She'd grown up in Etobicoke, which was west Toronto. Her mom still lived in the same house, and for the life of her, she couldn't remember if the stars were still visible. Etobicoke had been pretty suburban in the 90s. Not like today. The light pollution reached farther each year. Before long all the surrounding cities and towns would look the same—a dark-blue blank slate.

It matched her mood.

She heard the door to the patio slide open. Shane sat on the lounge next to her, picked up the glass, and took a sip.

"Don't judge me." Evie generally didn't drink on workdays, but today had been a crap day. She'd come home and found a half pitcher of Shane's mojitos in the fridge. This wasn't her first glass.

"No judgment here. Just enjoying my handiwork. I was going to pour myself one, but you seem to have changed my mind on that."

Evie turned around to face him up right. "That sounds like judgment."

"Hmm. Does it? To me it sounds like concern. Day not go well?"

"What makes you say that?"

Shane checked his watch. "Well, it's almost midnight, and you're still up. That's for starters. And then there's also the missing half pitcher of mojitos."

Evie sat up and turned. "Is it almost midnight? Shit. I have a five a.m. call tomorrow."

Shane looked up at the monotone sky. "I can see how you might lose time, enchanted by the beautiful vista on display." He put his arm around Evie and hugged her close. "Tell me what's up. You'll feel better getting it off your chest, and then I'll tuck you into bed."

At this point she'd get only maybe four hours of sleep. That would make for a rough day tomorrow. The thing was, Shane was rarely wrong about these things. She usually did feel better sharing her problems with him. And she'd eventually tell him anyway.

"I spoke to Cameron today."

"Ahh. Let me guess. He blew you off."

"He said he couldn't give me an answer right now. And that sounds like a no, right? My mom used to do that when we were kids, when she didn't want to agree to something but also not let us down. She used to give us a maybe. And that's what today felt like. A maybe." She pulled away from Shane to face him, full rant on now. "The thing is, I know I'd do such a better job than Michael. He's…he's…" She looked away to the building across the street.

"He's safe."

"Yes," she nearly shouted. "He's by the book, and it pisses me off. He could be getting so much more out of every single actor, but it's like he doesn't give a shit. He wants to get it wrapped as quickly and as under budget as possible."

"And how many episodes would you say he directs in total?"

"Last year he did all but three."

"And which three didn't he do?"

"The first and last two."

Shane leaned back, clasping his hands behind his head. "Sounds to me like Cameron uses Michael to keep the show on budget, gives him the straight-forward episodes, and saves the more important episodes, the ones that need a little more finesse, for better directors. That leaves you vying for three episodes, and I guarantee you Cameron didn't get where he is, running his own show, if he didn't promise certain things to people. I think you just have to be patient."

"I hate being patient."

He took Evie's hand and squeezed it. "I know. From what you've said, Cameron respects you. It's possible this has nothing to do with his faith in your ability to direct an episode and everything to do with him having other obligations to people. If you wait him out, you'll eventually get your chance."

"I feel like I've been waiting forever. I'm thirty-three—"

"That's not what IMDB says." Shane quirked an eyebrow. "Telling lies, are we?"

Evie swatted his arm. "My agent shaved those years off. I had nothing to do with it." She took the mojito from his hand and sipped. "The point is, I've been sitting on my ass for the past decade doing nothing. I need to start moving forward, or I'm going to…"

"Stall out? That's ridiculous. Look at where you are." He spread his hands to show the view of their neighbourhood, which, at that height, wasn't insignificant. They could see High Park from their roof-top patio, as well as the lake, if they leaned out over the side a little. "At least three billboards around the city have your giant face plastered on them. What more can you want?"

Evie frowned. What more did she want? Shane was right. She was starting to sound like one of those spoiled brats who'd gotten a million gifts at Christmas but was still wondering where their fucking pony was. But she wanted that fucking pony so bad. "Is it so wrong to want more?"

Shane gave her a side hug. "It's not wrong. Just greedy."

Chapter Seven

Jess flipped through the schedule on her tablet waiting for Simone, who wasn't late, but Jess preferred early. That way you were always on time. It was their first day of filming. Most of the crew had been on set since 4:30 a.m., Jess included. She hadn't fallen asleep until well after eleven, which meant she was working on only four and a half hours of sleep. Too goddamn little for this kind of day. It always took her a week or two to get back into the ridiculous sleep schedule she demanded of herself during production. In bed by nine, up at four, on the set before five. It didn't always work out that way, because sometimes they were still filming past her bedtime. Not, incidentally, when Michael was directing. That should endear him to her, yet it didn't.

Originally, they'd scheduled the balcony scene between Ian and Evie first, but according to Simone, she needed more time to work. She had requested it be later in the week, so the actors had time to rehearse and review the scene in a more meaningful way. Jess had been in the room when Cameron had gotten the phone call from Simone. It was during a production meeting, so Michael had been there too.

Jess hated Michael. Usually, hate was too strong a word, but in this instance, she felt perfectly fine using it. When she thought of Social Queen, she envisioned a certain aesthetic and temperament to the production. Michael didn't fit that ideal. He was rude, even when things were on time. He couldn't create a great show, even with this paint-by-numbers formula they had going. He catered to the budget and schedule, everything and everyone else be damned.

His expression when he found out he had to rework his schedule would be a ray of sunshine during the dark nights of filming. It had endeared Simone to her, and so she didn't mind waiting a few extra minutes for her.

As it turned out, she didn't have to wait long. Simone rushed through the door minutes later, perfectly put together, as if she were going out for lunch on a patio with girlfriends rather than heading into work for what would probably be a gruelling fourteen-hour day.

How could some women just embody femininity? With her own curly mop of hair and dismal fashion sense, Jess always felt out of place next to women like Simone. She wasn't even an actress, for Christ's sake, yet she looked like she could be one, or even a model. She had that sculpted dancer's body that Jess had always envied among her classmates at school. Not that it occupied all her thoughts. Jess wouldn't have gotten as far as she had if she let thoughts of inadequacy drag her down. If anything, her job let her see what the rest of the world didn't—how human most of these women really were. Some weren't even that pretty without all that makeup and hair. And a lot of them weren't that nice off camera either. Knowing that everyone was flawed gave her confidence.

Simone checked her watch. "I'm not late, am I?"

Jess smiled. "Nope. Perfectly on time." She pointed the way ahead. "We found you an office. Like most in this building, it used to be something else. I hope you're okay with a few stairs. There used to be an elevator in that part of the building, but it doesn't work anymore. Easier to just block it." Jess took off at a good pace. She still had several more things to do before shooting got underway. The click-clack of Simone's heels followed them down the hallway. She hoped for Simone's sake she'd brought more sensible shoes. Judging by the size of her purse, she hadn't.

Jess led Simone through a maze of corridors and up some stairs and down more hallways before reaching one final staircase that appeared to lead into darkness.

"I doubt I'll ever remember how to get back here, let alone find my way back to the entrance of the building," said Simone as they mounted the last of the stairs.

"It is a bit of a trek. Unfortunately, it was the best I could do. Most of the space is production or storage."

"I'm grateful for the space, truly. I'm more worried about my sense of direction."

Jess sorted through a ring of keys until she found the right one and stuck it in the lock. "The first two weeks I worked in this building, I kept getting turned around, found myself out on the loading dock more times than I care to mention." Jess opened the door to reveal a neat little square of an office. "It has a window, which is more than I can say for mine." It was about half the size of Jess's office, containing a desk with a laptop, two chairs that appeared mildly comfortable, and a small window that looked out over the train tracks. Behind that loomed the compact grouping of large skyscrapers that made up Toronto's downtown core.

Jess flipped on the light and placed the key on the desk. You're welcome to come back down with me now, if you're worried you'll get lost. Just remember that you're in Tower B. You can't confuse it, because there isn't a Tower A."

"Strange." Simone opened the top drawer of her desk and placed her purse there.

"It burned down in a fire sometime around the second world war." They stood for a few minutes in silence, taking in the small room. Jess wasn't sure what it had originally been used for, but based on the state of it when she'd found it, a place to store forgotten stuff. Exposed brick, some of it cracking in places, peeked out from the wall. Unlike the rest of the building, which had been renovated over the years and had most of the original brick covered with drywall or paint, this place appeared untouched by time.

"Is there a place to get coffee around here?"

Jess smiled. A simple question that she could answer. "I'll show you to the…I guess it's a cafeteria. We do fifty percent of our filming in the building, so they designated a general spot for catering. It's not fancy. However, if you're hungry or need a caffeine fix, they have a coffee station and baskets of fruit and snacks that you can grab whenever you want. Lunch is served at 12:30, and then we're back on set at 13:30." Jess pulled out her tablet. "Most of what you'll need to know is on the call sheet. After I show you where the coffee is, I'll take you onto set."

"What are they filming first?"

"The scene after Abby confronts Sophia's teacher, when she picks her up outside the principal's office. That means the next scene we'll shoot today is the dinner scene. If the kids are in, they tend to shoot all their scenes together because of time constraints due to labour laws."

"I imagine they can be on set for only a few hours."

"You'd be surprised. It's not how long they can work, which is eight hours, by the way. It's the breaks. Drives Michael ape-shit. For every forty-five minutes in front of the camera, they have to take a ten-minute break."

"I guess there's that old adage. Never work with kids or animals."

"It's not so much the kids on this show. Mia and Oliver are great. It's their parents Michael hates dealing with. You'll see." She didn't want to say too much and spoil the show for Simone. Watching Michael throw a fit—which happened only on days when the kids were in—was a great introduction to working on the show. Most of the time everything was fine. The crew were good, everyone worked well together, but when things went tits up, it got interesting. Last year there was a blizzard during one of the location shoots, and no way could they make the massive amounts of snow work for the scene. At one point Michael grabbed a shovel from one of the grips and began scooping snow off the road like he was digging for gold, in a frenzy to get the scene done. By the time he'd cleared a few metres, his hair and clothes were disheveled, and sweat was pouring from his hairline. It didn't even matter. They had to call it and finish shooting another day.

"I get the impression not many people like Michael. Why does Cameron hire him for so many of the episodes?"

"Because he stays on budget. Cameron could give a fuck if people are happy, as long as the show is running smooth and coming in under budget."

❖

Evie shifted back and forth on her mark, ready to shoot the first scene of the season. This time last year she'd felt a mixture of excitement and anxiety. She found it interesting how fast things became mundane. This all seemed so normal, and it shouldn't. It wasn't normal. The clothes she wore belonged to someone else, yet she now had to pretend that not only did she own this look but also the entitlement and attitude that went with it.

That she could slip in and out of someone else's life so easily had always amazed Evie. She wasn't sure what had prepared her for this ability, but here she was. A group of grips stood behind a lighting setup, several flag-stands ready if needed. Her face heated: she didn't know a single one of their names, Evie had always been terrible with names and even worse at small talk.

Most of the time nobody came near her, probably out of fear that she was one of those actors. She'd once worked with an actor who insisted that everyone look anywhere but at her. She'd had only the tiniest of parts on that film, so she too was considered beneath this woman. The whole time, the only thing going through Evie's head was how lonely it must be to isolate yourself from the people you work with daily.

Part of the fun of being on set was the back-and-forth banter. They worked such long hours, sometimes it was the only way to make it through a hard day. If you removed yourself from that, you were removing yourself from the fun of being on a set. And sure, she loved acting; she loved what she did. But very few people could say they did their job only because they loved doing the actual work. No one said that. She wasn't even sure humans were meant to be like that in the first place. They were social to a fault.

She looked back down at her script. She'd memorized her lines in a frenzy, waking up early this morning in an alcohol haze, dry-mouthed and tired.

"Well, well. This is a first."

Evie turned at the sound of the voice. Will stood behind her, dressed as Ben in jeans and a tight T-shirt. She quirked an eyebrow in question.

"Don't you usually have your lines memorized the second you get the script?"

She flipped her book shut and set it down on the desk next to her. "They're in my head, but I'm not exactly sure where." She shrugged. Evie rarely worried about memorizing her lines, which usually took her only a few minutes. After years of serving in restaurants, she had an amazing memory.

Will smiled as if he got the joke. She wasn't sure why, but he was competitive when it came to these things. She decided to change the topic. "How was your summer? Do anything interesting?"

"I went canyon jumping in France." He grabbed Evie's arm and squeezed. "Oh my God. It was amazing. They give you this, like, flying-squirrel suit to wear, and below is the Bourne Gorges."

"You jumped off a cliff?"

"Evie, it is so amazing. You're like flying, and all around you are these beautiful, fucking gorgeous mountains. It's incredible. You have to try it sometime."

"No thanks. And I wouldn't share that story with Cameron."

"Why not?"

"Are you kidding? We signed a contract that said we wouldn't do anything crazy with ourselves."

His face fell from the recent euphoric glow. "No, we didn't… did we?"

"For the insurance company. Don't you remember? We're not allowed to do anything stupid with our bodies. What would've happened if you ended up with a broken leg or worse?"

Will looked over at the crew. Cameron and Jess, heads bowed, talked with the new intimacy coordinator. "Even on our own time?"

"Yes. Didn't you read it?"

Will shook his head. None of this surprised Evie. Usually she worked with Will. A professional, who got along with everyone and didn't cause any problems, he always came prepared. However, he definitely wasn't the smartest person she knew. He reminded her of all those jocks she'd gone to university with. They'd been loved in high school and coasted on their good looks, gotten away with being general clowns in class, but once they were in the real world, those antics didn't get them far. They had to reinvent themselves. They had to start taking things seriously because no one cared if they looked good or not. Some, those who, beneath that bravado, were actually smart, did all right. The others, the ones who had only their looks, usually didn't make it far.

Evie had been a bit of a strange duck in high school. She was beautiful, which meant she was popular because that's sadly how high school worked. But she tended to get along with a lot of different groups. She hung out with the dance theatre group, the AV club group, and the group who tended to not do much except exist to look good and shop.

"Hmm," said Will. "You think they've seen my Instagram?" He checked his back pocket. "Crap." She could see him searching the crew, presumably looking for the PA who'd set his phone aside for him. She turned back to her script.

"There they are." Cameron was guiding Simone their way. "I'm glad you're both here. I realize I introduced you all yesterday, but did you get a chance to chat at all? I'm sure Simone is looking forward to scheduling some rehearsal time this week."

Will waved at Simone. "We did. We had a great chat yesterday. I'm really looking forward to working with Simone this year. It's really refreshing to see that, as an industry, we're finally moving forward and making real positive change."

Simone beamed at him. "I'm very happy you feel that way."

Cameron clapped Will on the back. “You’re right, Will. And I’m sorry to say that I didn’t have Simone working with us last year.”

“Jen,” Will called to a PA walking past. “Excuse me a moment. I have to do something real quick.”

Cameron clapped his hands together, beaming. “Well, I’ve got some calls to make. If you’ll excuse me.”

“Hello again.” Simone smiled. She appeared uncertain, perhaps even nervous. Her gaze shifted to the soundstage and the chaos surrounding them. Grips and electrics rushed past making last-minute setup changes. “Is it always like this?”

“The noise?”

“The people.”

“Pretty much.”

Simone looked horrified. “Not when you shoot intimate scenes?”

“Of course not. No. It’s a closed set, which means only a handful of crew is there.”

Simone nodded. “Today, I mostly plan to observe. I would, however, like to schedule some time with you and Ian. I’ve learned they plan to shoot the balcony scene Friday, and it would be good if we had time to run through it before then.”

Evie nodded before Simone even finished speaking. “Sure. I think I have time later today, if we get through these two scenes quick.” Evie dreaded this new experience. She didn’t want to do it, but Cameron was so gung-ho, she needed to appear like a team player. Even Will seemed more on board with it than she was, although she wasn’t sure how much he would be working with Simone. In theory, Evie thought it was a great idea for Simone to be there too. In fact, this type of coaching should be mandatory. It was the actual practice that was giving Evie issues.

CHAPTER EIGHT

As soon as Simone entered the room, all conversation stopped. Evie and Ian sat on a child's bed in a room that appeared like it belonged to a little girl. Soft purple paint covered the walls with pink butterfly decals arranged so it looked like they had flown out of a toy box in the corner of the room. The bed appeared simple but girly with a headboard shaped like a crown. Instead of a plush carpet, traces of gaffers' tape from previous shots broke the illusion that they were actually in a little girl's room.

It was the only space available to them to rehearse. They could have gone to her office if she could remember how to get back there. Again, Simone sensed that she was welcome but not. Cameron and Jess had been very supportive, making sure she had everything she needed, but the director and some of the actors less so.

She'd spent most of her day on set observing. The two scenes they'd shot were with the two child actors of the cast, and Simone was happy to see everyone was looking out for them. They'd had to break twice for ten minutes, according to regulations, and each time someone on set had called time. As for the two young actors, they were more professional than some of the crew members. The assistant director had to quiet down some of the lighting crew for being too loud in between takes. She later found out from Jess that two brothers were always the ones causing the problems.

Social Queen was definitely not the level of productions she was used to. While it didn't go perfectly smooth—the woman playing the teacher kept forgetting one of her lines—it was much more organized than her usual jobs.

Everyone had their place and knew what they should be doing at any given moment. Simone felt out of place doing nothing. Her work would come later, and part of that work would be navigating the different personalities and egos on set, so in essence, she wasn't just standing around. She was researching.

The next scene, a family dinner scene, was on the same soundstage as the first set. It always amazed Simone how they created this illusion of completeness. When watching the show, you would never know that the dining room didn't in fact connect to the kitchen or the living room, but to the master bedroom by using a fake wall. Everything was crammed in like a jigsaw puzzle you wanted to fit together but didn't have all the pieces, only some that looked similar. They obviously made it work because the house presented as whole in the edited project.

By the time shooting began on this scene, Michael had thrown several unveiled dirty looks her way. He kept having a PA come over and ask her to move out of the way. It didn't matter where she stood; eventually she would be asked to move. Well, that suited her fine. Simone had never met a more stubborn person than her mother, and most of that stubbornness had gone to her middle child, who could stand her ground against anyone. And if she had to dig in and play dirty, she had prepared for that as well.

Ian and Evie sat on the bed next to each other, and by their facial expressions, they'd been called in to await punishment. They looked like an odd couple. Ian wore black jeans and a tight T-shirt, with about a day and a half's worth of scruff growing in. He hadn't been on the call sheet that day, only in for some last-minute fittings. Evie still wore her makeup and wardrobe from her last scene. She looked like an expensive doll next to Ian's scruffiness.

"It's amazing how they can make it look so real. I feel like we're upstairs in someone's house."

Ian snorted and leaned his arms back on the bed. "Not exactly the spot to rehearse a sex scene."

"This isn't what this is for." Simone paused. Everyone was too rigid. "I know it's easier said than done, but I want you to relax. Take a deep breath…" Simone mimed the action she wanted them to take. "And then let it all out, along with all the tension in your shoulders." She pulled up a child's stool and took a seat across from Evie and Ian. It was a twin bed not far off the ground, yet still they towered over her.

She watched the two actors take a deep breath. Evie looked over at Ian as if making sure he was also doing the assignment, not just her. Simone had felt a tension in the air the moment she walked in. True, she'd never been part of a project this big, and she also hadn't come in midway. Usually she was hired at the beginning of a movie. Everyone here had already established relationships with one another. They'd worked an entire year together, so Simone found herself in the uncomfortable position as the outsider. She had to gain their trust so she could do her job.

"I want to just talk. We're not going to rehearse. Only talk. I want to hear about your thoughts on this scene. Your honest thoughts."

Evie looked at Ian. Obviously they were having misgivings about this scene, but would they share them with Simone? Right now she wanted to get them on her side, to see her as an ally who would advocate for them.

Ian and Evie exchanged a look that Simone interpreted as consent of some sort. "Evie is uncomfortable with the position of…" He looked up at the fake ceiling, which currently held several lights that sat dark. "The simulated sex."

"Something about the idea of being bent over a railing bothers me. I know why they put this shit in shows because it's sensationalist and it sells, but come on." She looked over at Ian again, who laughed, which eased the tension.

"Neither of us has ever had sex like that—"

"Nor would I want to. It's…" Evie shook her head, struggling for her next words.

"It puts you in a vulnerable position," Simone said. "You're giving up control, and that's very hard to do, especially when it's with someone you're not actually intimate with."

Evie leaned forward. "Yes. I guess. When I first read the script, I didn't think much about it, but as I get into the mindset of actually doing it, I'm having a massive amount of anxiety."

Simone nodded. This was good. This was exactly why they needed her. Was it more important to have this scene in the show? To be sensational? Or was it more important to respect women? Simone wasn't there to police the way they ran their show or even critique it. She was there specifically for the actors.

"Now we're getting somewhere. We should discuss boundaries next." They spoke for over an hour. As time passed, Evie and Ian clearly became more comfortable talking about their misgivings and frustrations. By the end of their session, Simone had a clear idea of what should be done. Now she had to consult Cameron to see if it was possible.

❖

Simone stood at her new kitchen sink, her shoes kicked off and left near the front door. She'd learned her lesson about appropriate footwear, something that, perhaps, should have been self-evident before, seeing as how she'd worked on movies before. She had spent most of her day standing, which wasn't what she was used to. It also explained Jess's expression when she first arrived, which seemed to be a mixture of disbelief and pity. Now the thought of even putting those heels back on made her think about chucking them out the window and never wearing them again. She would be more sensible tomorrow.

Looking into the backyard, Simone thought about something Evie had said today that had thrown her a little. When she'd mentioned feeling vulnerable about getting into the position for the scene, Simone's thoughts—instead of listening to what Evie was saying—were focused on something entirely different. Something indulgent. Something inappropriate for the moment. As satisfying as it was to indulge in those thoughts of Evie, obviously she didn't remember Simone as the woman from the club, so she saw no point in pursuing her fantasies. She ought to wipe them from her mind, which of course was easier said than done.

Perhaps she should've gone back to her Airbnb first. Estela had given her the keys a half hour ago, and she'd let herself in to take a look. Her Airbnb rental wasn't up until the end of the week, which was good because this place wasn't furnished. She wouldn't need much—she didn't intend to entertain—but she would need a place to sleep and to eat, and the kitchen would need pots and pans, as well as other essentials. Simone sighed. Right now it all seemed like a lot to do on top of her ridiculous work hours.

The two-bedroom used to be the upstairs of an old house. Sometime down the line the owners had knocked out a few walls to create an open-concept kitchen connected to a living room. A balcony off the living room gave a great view of the street in front of the house. The window above the sink looked out onto a backyard full of green. A vegetable garden bordered the far wall, several flower gardens sprinkled throughout. Near the back an old shed slumped against the fence and what looked like an arbour with grapevines interlaced along the top. It was perfect.

Simone had already picked her room, which had a giant bay window and, like the kitchen, a view of the backyard. Less noise this way. The house wasn't on the main street, but it was tucked only one house in from the corner. In a city this size, traffic noise would exist regardless of the hour.

Someone tapped on the door. "Hello?" Estela poked her head in. She carried with her an oversized spider plant with spiderettes so long some reached the floor. Simone rushed to grab it before the woman toppled over.

"A home always needs plants." She wore a floral dress that reached past her knees and lime-green crocheted slippers. Her dark brown, uniform hair looked like the kind you got from a home dying kit, with pins holding her curls tight against her head.

"Thank you." Simone set the plant on the kitchen counter.

"Will you move in this weekend?"

Simone nodded. "I might have a few things delivered during the week, if that's okay."

"I'm home most weekdays, except on Tuesday mornings, when I visit my granddaughter, and Friday afternoons, when I visit Hugo. Some people think it's strange that I still go see my dead husband, but it gives me comfort. And to them I say…" Estela waved her arm in a common gesture that punctuated her string of Portuguese.

Simone laughed. In her late twenties she'd dated a woman from Brazil and was aware of their more colourful swear words. Translated she'd said, "Up yours." It reminded Simone of her mother, who also had a creative way of stringing French words together to make her own profanity. But her absolute favourite Portuguese swear word, which Adriana had used often, was the most bizarre. She would shout it whenever anything pissed her off. Whether it was a driver who'd cut her off or someone calling to clean her ducts, she would shout it at the top of her lungs. Simone couldn't help but laugh because it was so ridiculous to go around telling people to unshit themselves.

"Exactly. Who cares what other people think?"

Estela nodded, stepping tentatively into the apartment. "Come. I'll show you how the air conditioner works." Of course she led Simone to the other room, the one Simone had designated as an office. Below the window was a long, white, sleek-looking piece of plastic. Simone had never needed an air conditioner in her places in Montreal. The closest she'd come one summer was buying a portable fan, which had sat in her closet for at least four years now. Her loft had ceiling fans, and she could open the floor-to-ceiling windows that overlooked the St. Lawrence, which always got a good breeze flowing through the place. In her opinion, the buildings in Montreal were better designed. Like in Europe and

South America, the architecture took into account that occupants would need light and good air flow. She wondered, having seen most of what Toronto had to offer in the way of architecture, if anyone had thought of that here. A place that wore its humidity like a badge of honour ought to have better architecture to counteract the weather.

Estela picked up the remote on the windowsill and showed Simone the on button. "You press this once, and it turns on." Simone was genuinely curious if Estela thought she couldn't have figured that out on her own. "To turn it colder, press the big blue arrow, and for less, use the small blue one. To turn it off, press the off button once." She handed Simone the remote. "Now you try." Yep. Estela really did think she needed a tutorial for an on/off switch. Simone humoured her.

Estela clapped her hands together. "Good. Now, I make dinner. It's at seven." Estela waved, already turned to leave. Did this mean Simone was supposed to attend? She hadn't planned to stay much longer. She'd only wanted to take a few measurements and get an idea of what she'd need in the way of furniture. Of course, she had everything she needed, back in Montreal. She'd rented her apartment fully furnished, so it might seem uncouth to collect some of her furniture while her tenant was still living there. She could probably find a decent used bed frame and have a mattress delivered. As for a kitchen table, she could go to Ikea. She was loath to shop in that place. They made cheap furniture that, like fast fashion, had no place in her life. However, it came unassembled, which made transport easy.

She might also have to consider a car. She'd never needed one in Montreal, where it was easy enough to get anywhere on bike or transit. Her neighbourhood was remarkably walkable, yet the neighbourhood here wasn't so bad. She was only a three-minute walk to Bloor Street, which gave her access to the subway, restaurants, cafes, and small grocers that she liked. But the studio was on the other side of the city. Transit, during peak hours, took a little over an hour. She could bike, but that still took fifty minutes and meant she'd be biking thirty kilometres every day. If she got a car, it was half an hour during rush hour and only twelve minutes otherwise.

How long did she plan to stay? She had a contract for one year working on the show, with an option to renew, depending on how it went. She could be there for several years. How long was she willing to live a makeshift life? Was it better to plan to stay and make her life comfortable now? She could always sell everything later. Or should she assume she was here for a year and make do with the bare minimum?

She had initially left to get out of her headspace while also pissing her mom off—if she were being a hundred percent honest with herself. But Toronto was not Montreal. Could she even make a life here?

Chapter Nine

For the first time in months, the sun had risen without the oppressive heat of summer. The air had a hint of fall. The leaves hadn't started to turn yet, but soon they would become a mishmash of yellows, reds, and oranges.

Simone stood fuming on the front porch of her new place watching Estela sweep the sidewalk. Methodical, she would start at the boundary of her neighbour's yard and, in a practiced upward motion, push the dust toward the street. She would do that three times, then shuffle back, sweep three times, shuffle back, sweep until the sidewalk in front of her house was free of any debris. Not that there had been much to begin with. Simone had seen her do this earlier in the week and suspected she did it every morning.

Estela waved at Simone as she passed. "Are you waiting for a lift?" Still in her house robe and slip-ons, Estela reminded her of her grandma, who would come down every morning and make herself a cup of tea, then sit in the front room doing the crossword puzzle from Le Soleil.

"Mattress delivery," Simone called. She checked her watch. If they didn't come within the next five minutes, she'd be late. And today was the one day she couldn't be late. They were shooting the balcony scene. She wanted to be there to support Ian and Evie, although she was very happy with how they'd resolved the majority of Evie's anxiety. Talking to Cameron to arrange a body double had been surprisingly easy. She'd expected pushback, mostly because of what she'd experienced with Michael on set. He was not a fan of her. Cameron, however, had been more than happy to make that accommodation. Once that had happened, everything had fallen into place nicely. They'd still get their shot, Evie felt a lot more comfortable with the scene, and the body double hadn't had any qualms. As she explained, it's what she did. She also apparently posed for art classes at night so was very comfortable with her body.

However, Simone still had to be on set and had been waiting nearly a week for this mattress to come. She had a bed frame, but no mattress. This afternoon she had to be out of her Airbnb and really didn't want to sleep on the floor.

Estela leaned her broom against the steps and ambled around the side of the house. She came back a moment later dragging a hose and began spraying down the slabs in front of her house. This, Simone had never seen. She stepped off the stairs, stopping next to Estela.

"What are you doing?"

Without stopping she said, "It keeps the dust down. The summer months are dusty. Broxa has allergies."

"Broxa?"

"My cat. He's shy. You didn't meet him when you were over. That's okay. He's also fat and lazy. He already has breathing problems, and I don't want to give him more. Vets are expensive."

Simone agreed. She'd never had pets as an adult—not enough time to look after them. As a child, however, they'd had several dogs, including one who liked to make friends with racoons. Her mother was always complaining about the cost.

"Every year, I think he's not going to make it, but winter comes and he's still here."

"How old is he?"

"Twenty-two."

"Wow. That's amazing."

Estela shrugged. "He eats like a king, has no enemies, lives the easy life. Stress is the big killer." Estela stopped spraying, shaking the nozzle of excess water. "Is your job stressful?"

"It can be. I don't so much as find the job stressful as the people I deal with."

"Quit now, before you get high blood pressure. That's what killed Hugo. Stress. He was always worrying about something. It didn't matter what it was. Tenants didn't pay rent? He'd worry. Tenants did pay rent, he'd worry. We also owned a furniture store, and he worried each day not enough customers would come. When enough came, he'd worry about the next day." She clutched her chest. "It builds up in here until one day. Poof." She made a gesture with her hand to go along with the word. "I wake up, and he's lying on the kitchen floor. Heart attack. Stress. Too much stress."

Simone placed her hand on Estela's shoulder. "It must be hard not having him around."

Estela shrugged. "It was decades ago. I think I've lived longer without him now, than I did with him. This is life. Everybody wants it to be so easy now. It's not easy. If it was, there wouldn't be poverty." Estela walked the hose back to the side of the house and wound it up, the squeal of turning metal loud in the morning.

Simone checked her watch again. She needed to leave now.

Estela came back around the house and patted Simone on the back. "Go." She shooed Simone away. "I'll make sure your mattress gets upstairs."

Simone was skeptical.

"I'll just have them set it inside your door. Unless you want it in the room?"

"I have a frame set up."

Estela smiled and spread her hands. "Easy peasy. You go."

"Here. I thought you could use this." Charlotte, the actress who played Abby's neighbour and best friend, handed Evie a warm coffee cup. "It's a chai latte."

"Mmm. Thank you." Evie moved over for Charlotte to take a seat on the stairs with her.

"Hiding out?"

Evie nodded and sipped the latte. She'd been camped out in a back stairway for the last forty-five minutes as they got the set ready for the balcony scene. She'd gotten out of makeup early and didn't feel like hanging out on set with everyone else. This place suited her mood. It felt isolated, safe. It drowned all the noise from outside traffic and the chaos from the set. The stairwell was a good place to sit and think. And as much as she appreciated the latte, she wasn't sure she could take Charlotte's bubbly chatterbox at the moment.

But instead of talking, Charlotte just took her empty hand and squeezed it. Evie was grateful for the moment of silence.

"I keep telling myself: this is what I signed up for. These shows are popular because they're full of sex. This is really why people watch them—to escape into a world where your kid's soccer coach is hot and wants to have illicit sex with you on a balcony overlooking your backyard."

"You think that's what people want in their lives?"

"Maybe it's what they think they want."

"Sure, these shows have lots of sex, but I doubt you signed your contract happy that you were going to shoot a lot of scenes where you had to get naked with almost strangers."

"That sounds a lot like porn."

Charlotte's laugh echoed through the stairwell. "And you don't strike me as the person who would be into shooting porn."

"I'm not a fan of being told my lady bits have to be on display."

"I don't blame you, honey. It's normal to get nervous. It's normal to hate this part of the job. It's why I pulled back from doing all those crime shows. Having to live in those dark places and be exposed like that, it eats away at you."

"And then you found this show." Evie squeezed her into a side hug.

"I'm lucky they liked my bit-part character and made me permanent."

"Luck had nothing to do with it. You're great and everyone loves you."

Charlotte's smile after hearing this compliment could've lit the entire stairwell.

Charlotte grew serious for a second and turned to Evie. "I know no one likes doing these scenes. That's not true. I've met a few people who love them, but they're exhibitionists. Immersing myself in the why has always helped me to really get into character. Don't look at it as Evelyn Harper pretending with Ian Davies. See it as Abby Bruce finally giving in to this all-consuming passion she's had for Colton Jefferies for the past year. Finally unleashing it because if she held it in any longer it would explode." As she spoke her voice rose until it filled the small space.

"That's…hm." It was a bit dramatic, but then, Charlotte was a bit dramatic. She wasn't wrong though. Evie had been approaching it from not only a technical point of view, but also as something she had to get through. Maybe coming at it as Abby Bruce would help. While at this point in the story she didn't think Abby was in love with Colton, she was definitely in lust with him. He was everything her husband Ben wasn't—confident, opinionated, strong, successful. She needed that strength to match her own because, if one thing was clear, Ben was not the right man for her. Even if they did have kids together.

The set was unnaturally quiet. Off to the side, Evie stood with her chai latte watching Michael give instructions. They were shooting the balcony scene, and to Evie's great relief a body double was standing in for the close-ups. Evie would take her place when the camera switched to her face but would remain almost fully clothed. Fully clothed meant a bikini bathing suit coloured to match her skin. Still, she appreciated that level of protection.

Michael was in one of his rare good moods. Ian strolled over and jerked his head back to Michael, who was now speaking with the camera crew. "I've never seen him so upbeat. You could almost use the word jovial."

"I wouldn't. It's taking a nice word and associating it with someone who doesn't deserve it."

Ian motioned to her latte, and she handed it to him. It was also Ian's favourite place to get a latte as well. She didn't mind sharing. They'd be kissing each other in a few minutes. Might as well have the same coffee breath.

"You think it's because you-know-who isn't here?"

Evie looked around the set. She hadn't noticed, but Ian was right. Simone hadn't shown up to set today. From the start, Michael had made it clear he didn't like Simone. Evie would've given her left tit to be a fly on the wall when he found out he had to use a body double. The blowup must have been epic. As it were, this week they'd been spared any of his outbursts, which was unusual. He'd usually had one by now. Maybe that's why he was in such a good mood. They had one more day of shooting, and the first episode was in the can without too many hiccups.

"Could be," said Evie. "Could be he finally got laid. Who knows with that guy?"

"It just proves the man truly is stupid." Ian handed Evie her latte back. "If Cameron says he wants an intimacy coordinator on set and makes a big show of how happy he is that she's here, then it's in your best interest to make her feel welcome."

"Unless it is just that, all for show, and Michael knows something we don't."

"That's not Cameron's style."

Stephen from makeup came over to fix Evie's lips. He pointed to her cup. "You done?"

"Is this you asking or telling?"

Stephen winked. "I would never boss you around." He held out his hand for the cup. "But if I have to fix your lipstick again, I'm making it neon pink."

Evie laughed. "I'm sure Michael would love that."

They all looked back at Michael, who, miracle of miracles, was actually laughing with the AD. Stephen shrugged. "Today's the day to find out."

"You live dangerously, Stephen."

"Always." He smirked as he backed away. She knew the smirk wasn't really for her. He had a huge crush on Ian but was too afraid to do anything about it. So he bided his time and flirted with Evie instead.

Once Stephen was gone, Ian turned to her. "I'm shocked you would insinuate that all someone needs to be in a good mood is to get laid."

"Why? Because it's inappropriate to talk about that subject?"

"No. Because it would mean you'd actually have to think about Michael having sex."

"Okay." Evie held her hand up in protest. "I hadn't. It was a random comment, and now you've taken it too far." She made a disgusted noise.

"I'm surprised she's not here though."

"Who?" asked Evie.

"Simone."

"She probably is, just not on set yet. Have you seen the office they gave her? It's practically on the moon it's so far from set."

Ian quirked an eyebrow, a move he was known for, which usually sent women into a tizzy. Quite a few men too. For Evie, he pulled it out only when he was teasing her. "You've been to her office? Getting some extra pointers, are we? What do they call that these days? Extra credit?"

Evie gave him a death stare. His remark reminded her of something Shane had said the night before. He'd called her out on the fact that she hadn't had a date in two years.

"And you know what that means. If you're not dating, you're not having sex. And everyone needs sex," Shane had said. He was one to talk. He played like he had it all figured out, but Evie knew the only thing he wanted was to find a nice girl, get married, have kids, and live the dream his parents never had. The last thing either one of them wanted to do was keep dating. It was literally the worst thing in the world and, as Evie had pointed out, not really an option for her at that moment.

"Who am I supposed to be going on all these dates with? My face is sitting on top of a giant fucking billboard in Dundas Square. What am I supposed to use as a conversation opener: 'Have you seen my billboard? Isn't it great?' And it's just going to get worse. After this season, every date I go on, if they haven't seen the show before then, they certainly will after, and they'll get a great preview of what my bare ass looks like."

Shane had dropped his coat onto a chair and come over and given her a big hug because he'd known her long enough to see through this charade of pithiness. Evie loved this quality about Shane. He always knew how to make her feel better, because this subject had been on her mind for a while now. The more she became known, with her face on magazines and talk shows, the less likely she'd ever be able to go back to her old life. It was no wonder actors tended to date their costars. Who else were they supposed to hang out with?

Ian nudged her back to the present. "Well, if you're not going after Simone, someone should. She's hot. And I'm saying that as a neutral party. I have my hands full. And you can't tell me you don't think she's hot, because I saw you checking out her ass the other day."

"Checking out. What are we, in the tenth grade? And who do you have your hands full with? Did you finally notice Stephen?"

"Stephen?"

"In makeup. He's been drooling at your feet since last season."

"The twink? Too young."

"You're going to break his heart."

"He'll live."

"So who is it?"

"Who?"

"The guy who's keeping your bed warm at night?"

"Well, it's not all night. Although…" He stared off into space for a second, a smile playing at his lips. "There was that one memorable night when we almost did make it go the whole night."

"Earmuffs." Evie covered her ears. "I don't need the details. I like the fairy-tale part, not the behind-the-curtain stuff."

❖

It was fake. She kept telling herself that, yet she couldn't look away. The pure lust on display had Simone fully mesmerized.

The set was down to the bare minimum of crew. Besides Simone, only the actors, Michael, and the camera operator were present. Simone had made it to set, but not before they'd shot the section of the scene with the body double. Simone would've liked to have been there from the start. However, she was happy to be here now.

Before the scene started, they'd had a brief conference with everyone to go over the choreography, where the camera would be, what the lighting would look like, and Simone was happy that, for once, Michael seemed to be on board with everything. Perhaps he was finally seeing that her role actually helped with production instead of viewing her as an obstacle. She would later probably realize that was wishful thinking, but for now everything was running smoothly. Beyond smooth.

The only thing stopping Evie from going over the edge of the set balcony was one manicured hand wrapped around the ledge holding her in place as she kissed Ian with such ferocity and desire Simone had to physically turn toward video village to remind herself that she wasn't spying on some illicit tryst between her neighbours.

More surprisingly, her heartbeat thumped as if she were the one Evie was mauling. And that thought excited her. She couldn't understand her reaction. She'd never had this response on set before since everything was usually so choreographed the action became mundane, steps to reproduce. Part of her job was to make it predictable for the actors so they would have no uncomfortable surprises. This scene was different, unexpected. And for the life of her, she couldn't figure out why.

Simone could freely admit she was attracted to Evie. You'd have to be blind not to find her attractive. The woman was gorgeous. But finding someone attractive and being attracted to them were two very different things, and Simone had to get her thoughts in check and focus on her job. She had to put her mind back in charge and not let the urges of her body take over.

"Cut." The shout jolted Simone from her thoughts. "Excellent. Let's set up for the reverse shot now, and then we'll move on to the next scene." Michael checked his watch. According to the schedule they were more than an hour ahead. If they got this shot done in the next ten minutes they might even go home early today. They had four more scenes to shoot that day, all of them simple setups in the kitchen set with only one wardrobe change. In her experience from the past week, those scenes rarely took them into overtime.

"What the fuck are you doing?" Ian's baritone boomed through the set. They'd repositioned to the beginning of the scene, with Evie bent over the balcony and Ian behind.

Simone, who had been checking her notes, looked up to see a strange man in khakis and a polo taking pictures of Evie and Ian on his phone.

Michael, who had been speaking with the camera operator, charged over. "This is a closed set."

The man, who barely looked old enough to drive, stammered, "I'm with promotions. They wanted a picture for Instagram."

Simone stormed over to the man. "This is not a scene that's going to be used for promotional material."

"Who let you onto this set?" Michael didn't appear concerned with anything else. He was now dumping time into his schedule, and nothing got Michael's ire up more than screwing with his schedule.

"The head of promotions approved it. She wanted something sensational to promote the new season."

"Get off my set." Michael looked around, presumably for someone to remove this man, but since only five people were there, including the actors, no one took charge.

"But I work here."

Instead of having the day get derailed further, Simone held her hand out for the young man's phone. "Let's go have a word with the head of promotions."

He clutched the phone to his chest and reached into his pocket and held out a card that said Set Pass. Michael's eyes almost bugged out. "Someone gave you a hall pass?" He grabbed the card and ripped it in half. "This isn't high-school fucking musical. Get off my goddamned set before I personally throw you out."

Simone motioned for the intruder to lead the way. His expression told her he wouldn't be long for this job if he honestly couldn't understand the pecking order. It was as if he had no self-preservation at all. When she got to the door she looked back at Evie, who was watching the whole thing with a deep frown. Ian had his arm around her, and someone had had the good sense to give her a robe so she wasn't standing there in a skin-coloured bathing suit.

Simone rapped on the door to Evie's dressing room. It had taken her all afternoon to sort out the mess with Stan, the young guy from promotions. His job hadn't even lasted the day, having been sacrificed to appease Michael. Simone hadn't made it back on set, but she'd heard that Michael's mood never improved. They had only one more day, and for the next episode they would get a new director, which could be good or bad, depending how you looked at it.

Evie opened the door. She was out of wardrobe, still in the process of removing her makeup. In the background, music played on a small speaker sitting on her makeup table. She dried the ends of her damp hair, still wrapped in a towel.

"I just wanted to check in and make sure you were okay."

"I'm fine. I assume they're not using any of those photos." Evie motioned for Simone to come in.

Simone shook her head. "I made sure they were all deleted and that the trash on the phone was emptied. Everything's gone."

"It's just a shock that they would think of something so crass to promote the show. I don't consider it that kind of show. And now I'm wondering if other people do."

"There was a lot of miscommunication on this point, that's all. Once Cameron got involved, they worked everything out. I'm not exactly sure how much of a scapegoat Stan was, but I have a feeling this wasn't all on him. No one had informed other departments outside of production that the set was closed. Why they thought a shot from that particular scene was a good one to use, we're still not sure."

"It makes it look like porn." Evie flopped down on her couch, throwing the towel onto the back of a chair. In her jeans, T-shirt, and wet hair, she looked younger and more vulnerable than her counterpart Abby Bruce. "Right? I'm not overreacting, am I? I mean, I know Michael was pissed, but it had nothing to do with them shooting me bent over a railing half naked. He was just mad they were on his closed set. What an asshole."

Simone took a seat in a chair opposite Evie, resisting the urge to take her hands to lend comfort. She was here professionally, and that felt like crossing a line, even though it didn't stop the urge.

"You're not overreacting. This business, and the world in general, has spent hundreds of years telling women their feelings are irrational, so men don't have to deal with them. I don't want this comment to come across as some feminist-rage bullshit, because it's not that. What you feel is real, because you feel it. Ask yourself why men can say women don't deserve to be in positions of power because they get too emotional at work, when we both know that's not the case. Today, the only overly emotional person on set was Michael. He got angry, and he apparently is always screaming at someone. That's emotion. Yet it's okay for him to do it. If a woman had directed this episode, any woman, it doesn't matter, she wouldn't have reacted like that. You know why? Because women have been conditioned their whole lives to express their emotions differently than men. So many studies show men are actually more emotional at work than women. My job is so important partially because, for too long, women's thoughts and feelings have been dismissed. We've been told to suck it up. If we don't like it, get out of the workplace, find another job. The reality of our lives doesn't allow for that viewpoint anymore. The world has changed, and men are trying desperately to keep up, and they're failing." Simone couldn't help herself. She reached over and squeezed Evie's hand. "Don't ever doubt your right to feel what you do."

Evie laughed. "Did that feel good? To get it out?"

Simone let go of Evie's hands, sitting back. She hadn't expected Evie to dismiss her comments like that. What she'd said was true. And it made it even worse when other women couldn't see that truth.

Evie had fallen into this cool-girl trap. She had the real power, and she didn't even see it.

Chapter Ten

The town of Watershed, Indiana had little to offer except a movie theatre that showed only one movie a week and a diner still playing the same music it had when it had opened over sixty years ago. What it lacked in utility, it made up for in charm.

"If you thought the heat was oppressive in Toronto, welcome to twelve degrees hotter." Will spread his arms as if he were shooting a scene at a carnival—announcing animals as they stepped onto the big stage. A few crew members laughed, but most ignored him. They were too busy searching for shade.

The Cedar's Inn was the only motel in Watershed. What had once been a stark-white stucco had faded to grey as the dirt from decades of rainstorms dulled the effect somewhat. They'd bought it out for five days, and then they would head back to Toronto for the last day of shooting on set. The small parking lot of the double-story motel was packed with SUVs and crew milling around waiting for room assignments. Jess had disappeared into the manager's office twenty minutes ago.

With a book open on her knees, Evie settled under the shade of an impressive oak at the far end of the lot.

"Do you mind if I share your shade?" Her sun momentarily blocked, Ian towered over her before joining her against the oak. He flipped up the book she was reading. "American Predator. Glad to see you brought some light reading. What's it about?"

"The hunt for one of the most brutal serial killers in US history."

"Gruesome. How can you read that? It would give me nightmares."

Evie shrugged and hugged her knees closer. "I find it fascinating how broken some people are. This guy would hide what they called 'kill kits' all around the country, with money, weapons, and tools for disposing of bodies. Think about the foresight it would take to set all that up. Most people have at least one hobby, and I find it fascinating to think that some people's hobbies are killing and hiding people."

"That's a really fucked up way of looking at it."

"But not to them. That's how they get their enjoyment. They're broken, and I love reading about all the theories of how people think they became broken in the first place."

Ian shuddered. "Hard pass."

"What did you bring to read?"

Ian held up a photography book called On Second Glance: Midwest Photographs.

"You brought a picture book. How cute."

Ian swatted her hand away from his book. "There's some really great inspiration in here. I want to see if I can capture some of that while I'm down here. If I have time."

"I didn't know you were into photography."

"Big time. My gramps got me into it when I was a kid. Gave me my first camera. Nothing special. Just a Polaroid camera from the 80s. He used to develop his own film in a darkroom he'd made in his basement. I spent a lot of time there in my teens. Now everything's digital, which kind of ruins the fun."

Evie smiled. "I'm glad to know your hobby is much more wholesome than killing and hiding people."

"Does it mean we can stay friends?"

"Only if you promise not to take pictures of me."

Ian stuck out his hand, and Evie shook it. "Done. I take only landscapes so you're in no danger of ending up on my darkroom wall."

"And you just made it creepy," she said as she nudged him with her shoulder, smiling. She'd missed this banter. Ian hadn't joined the cast until the fourth episode last year, but they became fast friends almost as soon as he had. As Ian had pointed out after they'd gotten to know each other a little better, she didn't share her true self with many people. He said he could relate. It was sometimes hard to trust people in this business.

Amid a rustle of bodies and murmurs, Jess finally exited the manager's office with a small box and her trusty tablet. "Okay, listen up, ladies and gentlemen." She began listing names, two at a time. The majority of the cast and crew would be doubling up. The only people who had their own rooms were Evie, Ian, Will, and the director. It was the only way to fit everyone into the motel. Apparently, Watershed was not a huge tourist destination.

Ian helped her up from the ground, and they ambled over toward Jess. "It'll be good to get out of this heat," Ian said.

"I can't wait to change these clothes. I hate flying." At that moment Evie looked over at the nearest SUV as the back door opened and a pair of long, shapely legs gracefully stepped out. Evie scrolled up, locking eyes with Simone, who didn't appear to be fazed by the heat one bit. A bright blue sundress that stopped mid-thigh and was held up by two thin straps encased her torso. Try as she might, Evie couldn't maintain eye contact. Her gaze roved back down Simone's body, stopping at her strappy heels, but not before pausing at the bodice for several seconds.

Ian leaned over and whispered, "You're such a lech."

"Shut up." Evie had to physically turn herself around to pull her gaze from Simone. It was strange because it wasn't like she hadn't noticed Simone was pretty before. Okay, pretty was the wrong word. Beautiful was more appropriate. It was hard not to notice someone like Simone. Today, however, was the first time Evie had felt an attraction, an intense attraction that had her insides thrumming.

Thankfully, Jess called Evie's name before she started drooling and making an absolute ass of herself. "You're in room two-eleven."

Evie accepted the key—not keycard, that's how far in the boonies they were—and hitched her purse higher on her shoulder. She willed herself not to turn back around and instead beelined for the stairs to the second floor at the end of the building.

She was on the very end, and from her vantage point on the second floor, the view of the countryside appeared impressive, which wasn't saying much. The production team had chosen Watershed because of the quaint one-strip downtown that looked straight out of a movie from the 50s. The storyline for this episode had the family travelling for Abby's eldest daughter Sophia's soccer.

In the first season it was established that Sophia was a gifted athlete, so even though she was only eight on the show, she played with girls who were much older. Ian played Colton Jefferies, Sophia's coach. In this particular episode, Abby and Ben get into a fight about how much of their lives Abby is sharing on social media—she's turned the trip into a sponsor event for a number of things—and for once Ben has had enough. He's worried that Sophia won't enjoy the game as much if she sees it as a way to make money. Once Ben's left, Colton finds an interesting way to ease her loneliness.

From the second story of the motel, Evie could see the strip, which was within walking distance. The tip of the movie theatre was the most noticeable, as it was the tallest thing in the small town. Evie fumbled with her key, once again seeking out the bright blue below. When she did finally spot her, Simone was watching Evie from within the crowd. Her breath caught. There was something powerful, something magnetic about the pull she felt deep within her. She shook it off and turned away. As several people had pointed out to her recently, it had been a while since she'd indulged in some of the more fun aspects of being a single adult. She chalked her reaction up to her longer-than-usual abstinence, putting it out of her mind so she could focus on the days ahead.

❖

Evie groaned as she flipped through the absurdly large menu. The Cedar's Inn didn't have a restaurant but was conveniently located next to a Cracker Barrel. Fifteen minutes earlier she'd heard a knock on her door, only to open it and find Ian leaning against the door frame holding two vouchers he'd gotten from Jess. "Let's get fat together." He smirked.

He hadn't been joking. Travelling outside of Canada had not featured large in her upbringing or even early adulthood. Evie's parents' idea of a vacation was stuffing her brothers and her into a minivan and driving to the east coast to visit family at their cottage in PEI. And until this summer—which she'd spent in Estonia—her most ambitious trip abroad had been to Cuba one Christmas for one of those all-inclusive vacations with an ex.

Evie leaned over and whispered, "They have one salad on the entire menu."

"Welcome to the midwest." Ian devolved into an almost evil laugh. "Oh, just wait."

They were soon joined by Will, who for some reason had dressed up for dinner. Instead of the jeans and T-shirt he'd been wearing earlier, he was now in what Evie's dad liked to call frumpy casual—dark dress pants and a button-up shirt with the sleeves rolled to just below his elbows.

"Oh, my Lord. Well, isn't this excitin'." Their server, a pregnant woman with large hair and pale pink lips, stepped up to their table with several menus under her arm and a pitcher of water. "We've all been watchin' your show. We've never had famous people here before."

Will grinned. Evie knew from earlier encounters that this was his favourite part of being an actor. "We're honoured to be the first," he smarmed. Evie and Ian exchanged looks.

Their server tittered as she handed Will a menu. "My name is Pam, and I'll be your server today."

"Pam. Did you know that's my favourite name?" Will looked over at them. "Right, guys? I've mentioned this before."

Ian held up his menu to hide his face from the rest of the table and mimed barfing onto his lap. Pam, meanwhile, had practically melted into Will's. Evie suspected Will might've had a chance with her. The wedding band and the very noticeable baby in her belly said differently.

Pam swooned as she took their drink orders, then pranced off to fetch them as if they were the only table in the restaurant.

"Stop flirting with the server," whispered Evie.

Will waved her off. "It's harmless."

"I've seen what harmless looks like to you. Enough."

Ian poked his head over his menu. "We still have five more days here. Let's not alienate everyone just yet."

Evie banged her head against her menu at that thought. She'd have to find somewhere else to eat if she was going to survive five days here.

"Can we join you?" Evie glanced up from her menu to see Jess and Simone, who was still wearing the blue sundress from earlier. Evie smiled and willed herself not to let her eyes drift downward. She focused back on the menu instead.

"Of course." Ian pointed to the two empty seats beside him and Evie. "We just ordered drinks." He handed Jess his menu. "I already know what I'm having. I don't even know why I look at the menu. It's always the same thing."

"You've been here before?" Jess asked.

"I grew up here. Well, not here. I grew up in Portland, Maine. It was my dad's favourite restaurant. Every year on his birthday, we'd go. He loves anything fried."

Jess opened her menu, eyes wide as she scanned the pages. "Who doesn't love fried stuff? What's good here?" Evie couldn't tell if she was being sarcastic or not.

"My dad always got some form of fried chicken. I can't really say if it's up to your standards though. My dad's other favourite restaurant is Taco Bell. I think I was in my mid-twenties before I realized that Taco Bell is about as Mexican as a hot dog."

Simone opened her menu, scanned the pages, and then quickly shut it and placed it next to her place setting.

"Why is the gravy white?" asked Evie.

"Beats the hell out of me."

The restaurant had filled up quickly, mostly with crew members on the show. By the time Pam came back to grab their order, a small line had formed at the door. Simone was sorry Jess had talked her into coming, insisting this was part of the fun of going on location. She would've been happy to get out of her clothes and curl up in bed with a good book. Everyone else looked comfy in casual wear. Evie was in an oversized sweater, which had slipped, revealing the thin strap of a tank top underneath and yoga pants. She seemed determined to blend in as much as possible. Yet it was impossible. Even with minimal makeup she stood out. Her freckles and messy bun just made her more approachable.

When Pam came back to take their order, she appeared more harried than she had before. "Sorry 'bout the wait. We weren't expecting so many people tonight. I think word's gotten out." She pulled a pen from somewhere in her large hair and said, "So what can I get you this evening? I'll put a rush in to get it out here faster."

"Please don't go to any trouble on our behalf," said Evie.

"It's no trouble, Miss Harper."

"Don't mind Evie. She hates being fawned over." Will grinned. "I, on the other hand, love it, as you may have been able to tell."

Pam laughed, a big whooping laugh that got the attention of half the restaurant.

When Pam came to Evie she said, "I'll just have the salad, please, without the bacon, and the dressing on the side."

"That's just her starter." Ian grabbed Evie's menu. "You can't eat just a salad for dinner. That is so unhealthy."

Evie's eyes widened. "It's a hell of a lot healthier than Grampa's country-fried breakfast."

"Pick something else."

"Okay. I'll also have the country vegetable plate."

Pam plastered a smile on her face. "You get four sides with that. Which ones would you like?"

"What are my options?"

Pam began listing every side they offered, none of which were vegetables.

"Oh, for fuck's sake. She'll have a burger with fries," said Ian.

Evie took his chin between her thumb and forefinger and pulled his head toward her. "I am a grown woman, and you do not get to order for me." She motioned toward herself. "This is my body, and I get to choose what goes in it. If I'd wanted a burger, I would've ordered one." To Pam she said, "Please bring me a salad and a plate of vegetables. I don't care what kind of vegetables they are, as long as they aren't fried."

Ian held his hands up in defeat. "I'm just trying to look out for you."

Evie arched an eyebrow. "Apologize or stop talking."

Ian nodded his head. "You're right. I'm sorry."

"Thank you."

Pam stood a moment longer, obviously undecided on what to do. "Is that all I can get for you? Anyone need a drink refill?'

Simone sat back, impressed. If you'd asked her yesterday or even earlier that day what she thought of Evie, she would've had a completely different opinion. At first she thought Evie was playing the game, letting people dictate to her. This Evie didn't take shit from anyone, and if possible that made her even sexier.

Within a minute Evie and Ian were back to their old selves, teasing and laughing so much that when Pam came back, she made a comment about them being an old married couple.

Ian leaned his head on his hand and gave Evie an adoring look. "Sadly, I'm the wrong gender. Evie here only likes the—what did you call them?"

Evie swatted his arm.

"Babes. That was it."

"I did not use that term." Everyone looked over at Pam, forgetting for a moment that they were no longer in Toronto, where that comment would have been lost for its insignificance. Here, in a small town, it could land any number of reactions.

Pam smiled. "Oh. My husband's best friend's sister-in-law is a lesbian. And I'm pretty sure my eighth-grade gym teacher was one. Watershed is a small town, but we're very welcoming and open-minded." The way she sounded out the word lesbian, over-pronouncing the B, made it sound like she didn't use it much, even if she did claim to know a couple.

Simone didn't catch what Evie did to Ian under the table after Pam left, but it made him jump a touch out of his seat. "It was fine. Her husband's best friend's sister-in-law is one. You're in good company." Evie gave him a look that could've been a novel only Ian could understand. This was going to be an interesting week, and Simone wasn't sure she was ready for it.

CHAPTER ELEVEN

Cut. Let's do it again." Scott Bloomgren stood under a giant umbrella, shaded from the unrelenting sun that for the past day had done nothing but cause problems. Two grips were in the emergency room because of heat stroke, at least a dozen extras had quit, and casting was replacing the actress meant to play the opposing team's coach due to severe burns on her nose and shoulders.

As soon as Scott spoke, the stillness and quiet turned to controlled chaos as the scene was reset for another take.

"At least it's not Michael. Could you imagine what he would do being a day and a half behind?" Ian whispered at Evie. Today they were filming the game sequence, which was bound to be the most difficult, as they were working with more than a dozen ten- and eleven-year-olds in the scorching heat.

Evie didn't answer. Instead, she pulled a fan from where she'd stashed it in a prop bag by her feet. "Why is it so goddamned hot? I know we came south. But not that much south."

A PA stopped by and handed both Ian and Evie a bottle of water. "Scott wants everyone to stay hydrated."

Evie felt like she weighed twenty times more than she had this morning. "I like heat. I love it. In fact—"

"Nobody likes heat. Warm weather, sure. Not heat." Will opened his bottle and chugged half of it. "This is what hell must feel like."

"Okay. Ready on set." Everyone quieted. Evie put the fan back in its hiding place. Will moved into position again on the bleachers behind them. "Roll sound."

"Sound rolling."

"Roll camera."

"Camera rolling."

"And action."

A dozen girls in shorts and shin guards flew onto the field. One tripped unexpectedly, and Scott called cut again. He reminded Evie of one of those amusement-park billboards where you stuck your head through a hole to get a new torso. His face didn't match his body. In Scott's case, he had the round, plump one of an infant, but the face of a fifty-year-old man, and he spoke in a soft, almost high-pitched tone. Most of the time he used a bullhorn to get his voice to carry. Today, for some reason, he had decided to project, and it wasn't working.

Perhaps it was because they'd gained spectators. At the edge of the field, out of view of the camera, stood dozens of them. Far more than yesterday. They'd been shooting at a hotel pool a few towns over. Today, word had gotten out, and since they'd begun setting up a little after nine in the morning, people had shown up to watch. Evie wasn't sure if it was the same people since the beginning of the day, but if it was, didn't they have jobs?

The sun was heading toward the tree line, and with every take they did, Evie worried they might have to cut for the day and continue tomorrow. It would put them behind another day. Evie wasn't sure what they would do if that happened. They'd done only a few location shoots last year and none as far away as this. Michael had been the director for two of those episodes, and none of them had gone over time.

"You think they'll cut a scene if they can't get everything?" asked Evie.

"Possibly. Or extend us a day. No one's going to like that because they can't guarantee the rooms or locations. Honestly, I'm not worried about it."

"Why not?"

"I've got other things to worry about."

"Like what? Your dinner order?" Ian hadn't been lying. They'd eaten at the Cracker Barrel three times now, and he'd ordered the same thing every time. Evie didn't care to see if he was going to order it again tonight. According to Google maps they weren't far from a Save-A-Lot, which Evie was hoping was a grocery store. She had a fridge in her room, so even if she had to live off fruit and veggie platters, it was way better than the alternative. The smell alone had invaded her senses, and every time she walked by, it flipped her stomach. And not in a good way.

"We don't all have a photographic memory, Evie. It takes me a bit to remember my lines."

"I don't have a photographic memory." It was true enough. Evie could read through a script a few times and know her lines and everyone else's. She'd had this discussion with Ian before, who found it infuriating because it took him hours of dedicated practice to reach the same spot.

A loud call came from video village, and a second later Jess rushed by, gripping a walkie-talkie in her hand. "We need some security over here. They're starting to push onto the field."

It was after five now, and the size of the crowd had doubled. They watched as several crew began setting up lights to the left of them. Apparently, Scott was going to push through, daylight be damned.

Evie stared down at the map on her phone. "Why does it make it look like it's so close?" It was well past sunset. They'd finished the scene not long after a few men had arrived from the local sheriff's department to provide security. Everyone had rallied because they were all hungry and wanted to get to dinner. Evie had declined to join them in hopes of finding a grocery store. However, she'd been walking for twenty minutes, and it still appeared as if she were in the middle of nowhere.

The motel was a little distance from the main town, but driving hadn't made it seem this far. The road was empty in both directions, coming or going into town. Not that she would've hitchhiked. Having been raised in a big city with the privilege of a great—although if you'd asked any Torontonian they'd deny it—public transit system, she'd never had to hitchhike. Also, her mother would have dismembered her if she ever did. They were reared on the horror stories of girls who'd gone missing on the highways back in the 70s and 80s. And she'd listened to enough podcasts about women, and a few men, who'd turned up killed by some serial killer to know it was dangerous and stupid.

So when she saw headlights heading toward her, she wanted to run for the brush on the side of the road and hide until they drove by. When the car whizzed past, she breathed easier but picked up her pace nonetheless. A few seconds later the vehicle—a white pickup truck—slowed, and when Evie looked back, it was making a U-turn.

To her right, the road dipped into a dry ditch of loose dirt and rocks. Beyond that was a wire fence running alongside the road lined by pine trees. Could she make it over the fence by the time the truck reached her? Not likely. The hot and heavy sound of a V8 came to idle beside her. The passenger window rolled down, and an unshaven man in his early to mid-forties propped his elbow up and leaned out. It was too dark to see the driver. "Where're you heading this time of night?"

Evie hated this part. While she was lucky that she'd never really experienced something like this back home, she'd dealt with it enough to know she had three choices. She could be polite but indifferent and answer his questions and hope he left. She could be rude and sarcastic and hope he got the hint and left. Or, she could ignore him and hope he got bored and left. Whichever one she chose, she wanted him to leave. Rarely did anyone get the hint.

Before she could even say anything, a woman's voice nearly squealed. "Oh my God, aren't you that actress from that show?" A middle-aged brunette and her boobs leaned into view. "You are.

Jay, look. Sarah was telling us about the shoot down at the school. What are you doing all the way out here?" The woman was talking so fast, Evie got only about half of what she was saying.

"Can we give you a lift somewhere?" Jay leaned farther out, propping both arms on the window. He glanced down at Evie's feet. Was he checking to see what kind of shoes she was wearing? She'd thrown on some old Chucks she'd had since university. Not a total idiot. Four kilometres into town in anything other than comfortable shoes? No, thank you. In fact, she was surprised she'd been recognized at all. Her hair was up in a messy bun. Rounded out with worn Levi's and an old CBC T-shirt, she wasn't exactly screaming famous actress.

Evie shook her head. "No, thank you. I like to walk."

Jay opened the cab door, revealing a smaller door to a tiny backseat in the cab. He motioned with his head for her to get in, and at that moment everything in Evie screamed for her to run. This was every nightmare she'd ever had coming to life. Perhaps it was the amount of true crime she consumed, but all of this felt so wrong. She backed up a few feet, edging toward the ditch running the length of the highway.

It didn't matter that it was a couple. Couple killers were semi-normal, the most famous of which had happened to live right in her own province. The truck had a camper shell, the perfect place to hide a body. The chances of anyone knowing what had happened to her would be slim. She hadn't told anyone back at the motel that she was heading to the grocery store. How could she be so stupid? She should've asked Ian to come with her, but he was still at dinner, and she didn't want to be one of those women who needed a man to protect her. Now her ego was going to kill her.

"It's not too safe walking along the highway like you are. Don't want anything bad happening to you."

Evie's heart skyrocketed into her throat. Why was she out in the middle of nowhere by herself? Then she remembered her cell phone, still in her hand, and held it up. "I can call if I get into trouble."

"You got signal out here?" Jay looked back at the woman. "That's impressive."

Evie glanced down at her phone. She in fact did not have cell service, something she hadn't even noticed because she'd been more worried about the maps app. Maybe that was why it hadn't been updating correctly. So here she was, out in the middle of nowhere with no cell-phone service and two possible serial killers about to abduct her. Evie took another step back, gearing up to take her chances against Jay. Now was her chance. Headlights from the direction of the motel were heading toward them, coming up fast. She had turned to run into the ditch as Jay turned to look at the lights when Evie heard her name.

One of the rented SUVs came to a stop in front of the truck. It was Simone. "Are you okay?" Evie didn't even hesitate. She strode over and opened the passenger door and got in and slammed the door. "Drive, please," she said. Simone took a second, staring over at her, face full of concern. Then she put the SUV in drive and sped off down the road.

Evie rotated to look out the rearview window. The truck pulled another U-turn, heading back out of town. She leaned her head back against the headrest, unsure if she'd been overreacting or had literally just been saved from certain death.

"What are you doing all the way out here by yourself?" asked Simone.

"Looking for the grocery store."

"By yourself? Why didn't you ask to borrow a vehicle and drive?" Wearing black shorts and a tank top that wrapped around her in an elaborate fashion, Simone was more casually dressed than Evie had seen her since they'd met.

"I can't drive."

"How is that possible?"

Evie turned off the air vents blasting cool air at her. The adrenaline rush she'd experienced earlier had chilled her, and she was actually looking forward to the heat of the night. "Just never happened. I've lived in big cities my whole life. Owning a car is silly, and I wasn't willing to go through all the hassle." She'd been telling people that for years. Only Shane knew the truth. She'd failed her G1, the first test to get your learners' permit. Her brother Wes had teased her to the point she didn't ever want to put herself through that torture again. The idea of failing had plagued her for years after. As the need for a license faded, she had let it go. Why did she need one? Why put herself through that pain again?

"You could've asked someone to drive you."

"I didn't want to be a bother. It didn't look that far on Google maps."

Simone shook her head, whispering something in French Evie couldn't translate. However, she had a good general idea what Simone was thinking because she voiced her next thought. "It's stupid. You're in a foreign country, and it may seem like it's similar, but trust me. There are many differences. You can't hitchhike on the highway." Her French accent became more prominent the louder and more worked up she got.

"I wasn't hitchhiking. I know better than that."

"Really?" Simone slowed and pulled into a large parking lot with so many bright white streetlights, in the dusk it could pass for day. "Too many people in this town know who you are, and they're curious. It's dangerous to go out on your own."

Simone wasn't lying. The amount of attention was scary.

"Toronto is a bubble. No one gives a shit who you are because, if they did, it would destroy their veneer of indifference."

"Not a fan of Toronto?"

Simone offered a lopsided smile and shrugged one of her bare shoulders. "Who is? Unless you grew up there?"

"Guilty. Etobicoke."

Simone found a parking spot and shifted the car into park. She leaned on the wheel as she turned to Evie. "Don't you think it's strange that the only people who like Toronto are the ones who want to live there?" The emphasis she'd made on want wasn't lost on Evie.

"It's an acquired taste. I'm sure there are lots of other great places to live. But my family lives there, all my friends. I'm not going to apologize for liking Toronto. It's my home." Evie had found that it wasn't living in Toronto; the sin was liking it. It assumed you believed that the city was truly the centre of the universe. She was sure that arrogance existed. It was an arrogant city, but it also could be amazing. She wished sometimes people could set aside their prejudices and see that fact. But it was unlikely she was going to change Simone's mind at that moment, so she didn't try.

In front of them, glaring in bright red, stood the sign for the Save a Lot. Back home, Evie preferred the tiny groceries along the street, compared with the sterile uniformity of big ones. "Was this where you were heading?"

Simone nodded and released her seatbelt. "I needed different."

"I'll be happy when we're home again." There was something unnerving about being away for the first time since the show came out. She hadn't expected this amount of recognition. Of course, her interview on the Late Night with Seth Myers had happened a few weeks ago, which had definitely gotten her a few more looks when she went out. Nothing too crazy because people truly didn't care back home.

"Do you want me to go in for you? You can stay in the car?"

Evie shook her head, unclipping her seatbelt. It was nice of Simone to offer, but getting out was more than just grabbing food. Evie needed to, not escape, but break free a little. She was feeling cooped up in the motel room. All they'd done since they got here was shoot, eat at the restaurant next door, and hang out in their rooms. She needed to explore a little. Besides, how could you say you'd been to a place if all you'd seen was the hotel?

"Are you saying that because you don't want to be a bother? I'm going in anyway. It wouldn't be a problem. I'd just pick up a few extra things for you."

"It'll be fine. It's a grocery store. What's the worst that could happen?"

Chapter Twelve

If Simone could've talked Evie into staying in the car, she would've. Evie was oblivious as she perused the produce section, looking spectacular in tight jeans and a vintage T-shirt. With her hair up, no makeup, and Chucks, she looked younger and more vulnerable than she probably was.

A thirty-something-year-old woman should be able to take care of herself, although now Simone wasn't so sure, having picked her up on the side of the road. What would've happened if she hadn't come along?

Several people had turned the moment she'd walked in, pointing her out. Now a few of them were following her at a distance. When she saw the phone come out, she walked over to Evie and whispered, "People are taking pictures of you."

"Oh, no. She's shopping for groceries." Evie turned and offered a sly, mischievous smile that actually set Simone's heart skittering. "Scandal."

"You don't mind your privacy being invaded like that?"

Evie shrugged and picked out a package of prepared hard-boiled eggs. "I'm out in public, and I'm not doing anything that's going to embarrass me if it's published." She looked into her basket. "I've bought pre-cut veggies and some hard-boiled eggs. I mean, that's a party just waiting to happen."

Simone scrunched her face up at the mention of hard-boiled eggs. "You can buy them prepackaged? That's disgusting."

"For protein."

"I'd rather starve."

"Well, that's extreme. You don't like eggs?"

"Hard-boiled in general makes me want to vomit."

"So no egg-salad sandwiches? Devilled eggs—"

Simone placed a hand on her arm. "Please stop. I will throw up if you continue."

"I didn't know that was a thing. Now I do."

"Excuse me?" A mother with a cart full of food and kids approached. "Could I possibly get your autograph? I never do anything like this, but I just love your show. I think it's really smart. And you're so great in it."

Simone looked up to see that several people had taken notice. Evie's smile, whether it was or not, looked genuine. "Sure. Do you have a pen?"

The woman fumbled in her purse and came up empty, a sad expression on her face that swiftly turned to determination. She pulled one of her kids out of the cart. "Robbie, go ask the man at the customer-service desk for a pen."

"I don't want to."

She nudged him toward the front of the store. "Be quick about it." Robbie trudged off at a glacial pace.

A queue was beginning to form in a lazy, haphazard way behind the mother. Simone worried this might get ugly if she didn't do something quickly. At one point a woman approached, and the mother of four physically blocked her by moving her cart into her path. No sign of Robbie.

Simone stepped forward. "We still have a bit of shopping to do. Why don't you come find us when your son comes back with a pen? We'll be around." She used the same voice when speaking with tech-support people—calm, light, and airy. She found it helped smooth the brunt of what she said, which could sometimes get colourful. She'd inherited a bit of her mother's inventive language skills. Without waiting for a reply, Simone guided Evie away from the throng of people now milling about in the produce section. She kept her hand firmly on Evie's back, pushing her toward one of the aisles. She tried not to look behind her, as if that would prompt them to rush at them like a group of brain-munching zombies, which was a silly comparison, because these were just people shopping for groceries on a Thursday night. Still, her heart was pounding.

"Are you okay? You seem really freaked out," asked Evie. They'd escaped to the cereal aisle, shelves filled with every imaginable thing you could think of to turn into breakfast food.

"Is that normal for you? Every time you go shopping?"

"Oh, God, no. This is definitely a first. Although I'm pretty sure the people in the back thought they were lining up for samples or something."

"This doesn't worry you?"

"What are they going to do? Stampede? We're fine. I'm sure this place has security if anything goes wrong." Evie picked up a box of Dunkin Donuts cereal. "I guess this is one way to streamline the process." She showed Simone the package. "Combine your coffee and cereal into one." She mimed vomiting, and somehow she made that action look adorable.

Simone decided she needed to relax. If Evie wasn't worried, then she shouldn't be either. She picked up a box of Twinkies cereal. "How is this even remotely healthy? It's candy." She turned the box on its side to check the nutritional content. "Sixteen grams of sugar." A few people from the produce section had followed them into the aisle. Simone looked down at Evie's basket. "What more do you need?"

Then the woman with the cart full of kids pushed her way through, Robbie trailing behind with a pen gripped in his hands. Evie smiled graciously as she took it and waited for the woman to hand her something to sign. "Do you have a book? or a…"

"Oh." The woman slapped her cart and looked around, then pulled up her purse and rummaged through it until she found a crumpled receipt. She smoothed it out and grabbed a box of cereal for Evie to use as a platform to sign on. More people had filed into the aisle, creating a blockage.

"Who should I make it out to?"

"Anne-Marie."

Behind them people were filling up the aisle as well, boxing them in. Evie grinned as she signed the receipt, never making it appear that she might be panicking, but when her eyes met Simone's gaze, fear appeared that hadn't been there before. As she handed the receipt back, people began to push forward, demanding Evie sign autographs for them as well.

"This is a bit unreal," Evie whispered. Her voice calm, she probably didn't want to appear worried, but she had gone rigid.

Simone couldn't let this situation turn into chaos. She clapped her hands twice, something she'd seen her mother do a million times, to get everyone's attention. "Hello. Ms. Harper would love nothing more than to accommodate your requests. However, we have a prior engagement we must get to. Please clear a path so we may pay and exit." She thought that request sounded concise, assertive, and authoritative, but the look Evie gave her had her second-guessing that thought. As soon as she'd said it, the crowd pushed forward instead of moving out of the way, and shouts sprang up from various places about it being unfair that only one woman got an autograph. A woman, Simone might add, who had thoroughly and completely disappeared after causing this mess in the first place.

The second someone grabbed Evie's arm, Simone's hackles went up. She began swinging her basket to create a perimeter of space between herself, Evie, and the crowd that was swiftly becoming an angry mob. "It is inappropriate to touch a person without their permission." Her anger made her accent stronger.

She gripped Evie's hand and began inching them out of the aisle. Where the hell was their security? Didn't everywhere have security these days?

As soon as they were out of the cereal aisle, Simone took Evie's basket and placed it on the ground next to her own, and they strode out of the store.

In the car Evie began laughing. "Wow. You really went for it in there."

The reaction surprised Simone. "I'm sorry if it was too much. I didn't want the crowd to get more out of hand."

Evie placed a light hand on Simone's. "Thank you. If you hadn't been there, I probably would've missed work tomorrow because I'd still be signing autographs for people."

"You just say no." Simone started the car and put it in reverse. She had no idea where they were going, but staying there any longer wasn't an option.

"I have a hard time letting people down." Evie pointed to the grocery store, still lit up like Christmas. "And a bunch of people really won't like me now."

Simone shrugged. "So what? Why should their opinion matter? Most of them probably have no idea who you are—no offence—and if they're willing to run people down for a signature from someone they don't know, they're not worth your time worrying over."

"You're probably right."

"Of course I'm right."

"On the upside, I get to tell Shane I was mobbed and almost died in a Save a Lot next to the Dunkin Donuts cereal selection. He'll get a kick out of that."

"Who's Shane?"

"My roommate."

Simone nearly choked on a laugh. "You have a roommate?"

"Yeah. Shane and I have lived together since university." The way she said it made Simone feel odd for asking the questions instead of it being the other way around. Why still have a roommate when you could afford to live alone?

"I mean, of course we can both afford to live on our own, but why? So we can come home to an empty place? We both work really long hours and therefore don't date much. It keeps us from being lonely. Plus, he's my person. He knows more secrets about me than any human on the planet."

They drove in silence for a few moments, the streetlights illuminating the inside of the car with an orange glow every few seconds.

"You asked me earlier if I minded my privacy being invaded. The thing is, I know this comes with the job. It's hard to be successful in this business without the fame that goes with it. I think it's interesting, though, that Abby Bruce wants nothing more than to be famous, and it's kind of the last thing I want. If I could have the success without anyone knowing who I am, I would take it."

Simone realized Evie was a rare actor. In her years of working with them, she'd gotten to know quite a few. Most were insecure to an almost pathological point. They craved attention and self-validation, and fame did a good job of fuelling that need. And here was Evie Harper, who was happy to do the work, or maybe it was the money, and leave all that behind. Not for the first time Simone's first impression of Evie was shattered. She'd bought into the hype of her public image. She had this reputation for being a party girl, something she'd seen at the club the first night she'd met her. Yet, from what she could tell, Evie didn't go out that much. She wore jeans and old T-shirts, and the look suited her. Evie had a girl-next-door quality—which was clichéd as hell—but true nonetheless. She was cozy and warm and welcoming, and the more Simone got to know her, the more she wanted to curl up inside and live and bask in the warmth of Evie's attention.

"So where exactly are you taking us?" They'd long since reached the other side of the town and were now heading through fields dotted by farms and the occasional dirt road leading away from the main one.

"You know? I have no idea, but we still haven't eaten. I thought maybe we might find something out here." It was looking like she'd made a bad call. They were in the middle of nowhere now.

Evie pulled out her phone, she had one bar now, and googled food. Everything that popped up was back in town except one little marker ahead of them. "This says something's coming up called Lumberjack's Bar and Grill."

"Sounds enticing."

They saw the lights long before they spotted the restaurant, which was small with a huge parking lot and outside patio. A massive sign with a lumberjack stood at the entrance, inviting people to come in for cold beer. "It kinda looks like a lumberjack built the place," said Evie, peering out the front windshield. The outside was made of rough slats of wood with a corrugated-metal roof. Evie leaned back in her seat. "I don't know. I'm worried what happened at the grocery store might happen here too."

"It could." They watched as a man with a long white beard and an American-eagle bandana covering his bald head walked out of the restaurant to his pickup truck. "But do you really think these are the kind of people to watch a show called Social Queen?"

Evie smirked. "You make a good point."

They got a seat on the patio in a far corner where no one paid them any attention. Evie began to relax a little. Simone didn't envy her. And such experiences would only get worse as more seasons came out and she became even more well known.

As they studied their menu, which consisted of a few deep-fried appetizers, a couple of sandwiches, and wings, Simone realized there was absolutely nothing here for Evie to eat. She watched Evie as her frown deepened the farther down the menu her eyes travelled.

"Why didn't you talk to Jess before coming here and ask specifically for there to be food that you could eat?"

Evie flipped the menu onto the table and leaned back in her chair. "Because it's my thing, and I didn't want Jess to have to work harder than she already does. It seemed silly."

"First of all, this is Jess's job. Well, partly. She would've gotten an assistant or someone to make sure we had better catering. And you may think this affects just you, but I guarantee you're not the only one concerned about the food. If you had stepped up and asked and made sure there was better variety—something no one else had the clout to do—there would've been a lot more happy people. Many of the cast and crew feel dissatisfied with the choices of food."

Evie shook her head. “I never thought of it that way.”

“You may not like fame, or want the notoriety that comes with it, and I understand that. But you also now have something you didn’t have before. Leverage. And you can use that, not just for yourself, but to make others around you more comfortable and happier.”

“I see your point.”

“I’ll talk to Jess tomorrow and see if she can do something to make sure healthier options are available.”

Evie waved her off. “That’s not your job. I’ll talk to her. You’re right. It should come from me.”

The server came over and took their order. Evie ordered sweet-potato fries, and Simone asked for a burger with fries. She wasn’t the one who had to shoot a partially nude scene tomorrow. After the server had left, Evie said, “I know absolutely nothing about you, except that you’re from Quebec somewhere, which is a huge province. So, tell me about yourself.”

“Wow. That’s a broad question. Got anything a little more specific?”

Evie frowned as if thinking about that request and then patted down her pockets. “Let me see what I can find.” She pretended to pull something out. “Okay. Here we go. How did you become an intimacy coordinator? Like, how does one become that?”

Simone dipped her head back, pushing her hair off her face. The night was still humid, and while a slight breeze offered respite, it wasn’t fully enough. For whatever reason, unknown to Simone, she decided to tell Evie the truth. Usually she gave a simple, vague answer that only half explained how she got to where she was but didn’t include any of the pain that went with it. “When I was five my father took me to see the Nutcracker ballet. It was the most beautiful thing I’d ever seen. I wanted to be Clara, up on that stage, moving my body as if it were magic. I studied for years. And I was good. One of my instructors said I had the same body as Galina Ulanova and that the only thing that would stop me from realizing my goal was to become lazy and quit.” She felt Evie’s appraising gaze rove over her as she said this, but also an anticipation of sadness, as if she knew what was coming.

"When I was seventeen, I auditioned for Les Grands Ballets in Montreal. They were performing the Nutcracker, and I wanted the part of Clara so badly I could feel it in every muscle and tendon." Simone shrugged her slender shoulder, looking over at a rowdy table to their right, unable to voice what had happened. She still felt the trauma and tragedy of a ruined career over one mistake, an avoidable accident. "My knee will no longer allow me to do what I love. But I loved ballet, and so I channelled that love into choreography. I went to school and learned how to be the best choreographer I could be. I was determined that if I couldn't be the best ballerina, I would do this instead. But during my first year after school it proved too hard to be around ballet, so I decided to start over. I went to McGill and took psychology and graduated with no idea what I wanted to do with my life. Then, about four years or so ago, an old instructor who I knew through the ballet world approached me and asked if I would be interested in working on a play as an intimacy coordinator. I'd never heard of this position before, but the more I researched it, the more I liked the idea. Within the first hour I realized this is what I wanted to do and have been doing it ever since. From there I worked on a small movie and have gone from project to project."

Evie was silent across from her. The server came and dropped off their drinks—a Coke Zero for Evie and an iced tea for Simone.

"I'm sorry," said Evie. "I couldn't imagine not being able to do what you love."

"Acting is the same for you, yes?"

Evie wiggled her hand back and forth. "I love acting, I do. But sometimes I'm not sure if it's the craft of creating the whole piece that I love or the actual acting. Part of it is that it's never just acting. It comes with so much more baggage."

"What doesn't?"

"True." Evie took a sip of her drink. More people were crowding onto the patio, but nobody seemed to be paying them any attention. Evie was thankful for that. "This summer I went to Estonia to direct a film. It was only a short, but it's a passion project for me. I've been trying to get Cameron to let me direct an episode, but so far he's blown me off." Evie rested her head on her hands. "Part of me is drawn to directing because I get to be around this world and help create it, without all the attention that goes along with acting. Ugh. Listen to me. I'm like the poster child for white-girl problems. You, on the other hand, can't even do what you love. I didn't mean to monopolize the pity party."

Simone laughed. She found Evie charming and so disarming. It felt easy sharing her pain. For so many years she'd held onto it, as if she'd locked it away in a tiny box in her heart and would bring it out only for special occasions when she was alone, to mourn her past. It seemed silly now to hold onto it for so long. "It was a long time ago. I've mostly dealt with it, especially in the last few years. What I'm doing now feels important, which is odd to say about any job in this industry."

"Because it's so stupidly superficial?"

"Yes, and what I do doesn't feel superficial. It feels needed."

Their food arrived, and they ate mostly in silence, watching the show around them. An ax-throwing tournament was taking place on the other side of the patio. Simone didn't believe that alcohol and throwing large, sharp instruments was a good combination. She also couldn't get the idea out of her head that this felt like a date.

When she was done, Evie placed her napkin on her plate and pushed it to the side. "Mind if I pry into your life a bit more?"

"Depends." Simone's tone matched the flirty nature of Evie's. This conversation was starting to veer into dangerous territory. Dangerous but fun.

Evie leaned forward, a gleam of mischief in her eyes. "On what?"

Simone didn't really hear the question, distracted at the moment by Evie's shirt. The wind had finally chilled the air somewhat, and her nipples were pushing at the taut fabric. Evie glanced down, then back up, and her smile widened. "Well, I guess I don't even have to ask now."

"You were going to ask if I date women?"

"And do you?"

Simone nodded.

"Yes." Evie pumped her fist in the air. "I have excellent gaydar." She plopped her head down into her hands in a move that was both adorable and sexy.

"I don't believe in gaydar."

"No? How do you know then? When you want to date someone, what do you do? Hope they make the first move?"

"I don't date much." That wasn't true. She didn't date at all, much to her mother's dismay. At one point it had gotten so bad she'd threatened to stop going to family gatherings because all she heard was questions about her dating life.

Evie nodded as if she got it. Work. Fame. These were things that would make it difficult for Evie to date, but it wasn't the reason Simone didn't date.

"It's a shame though."

"What's a shame?" asked Simone.

"You must have to fight them off in droves."

Simone shook her head, still not getting it.

"You're fucking hot, Simone. It's a shame to keep that all to yourself."

Evie's words travelled down Simone's body, igniting a tiny flame that had been smouldering for a while.

CHAPTER THIRTEEN

"Oh, wow. Did you see this? They have amchur powder." Shane's excited voice filtered through the cramped shelves of the tiny bodega. It was one of their rare Sundays off together, which meant they usually liked to explore the city. They'd started the habit years ago as most of their friends paired off and disappeared during the weekends. They'd made a pact then that they would spend the time together even if they were in a couple. There was nothing worse than having a day off and no one to spend it with. Today they were in a store off Bloor Street, not too far from their apartment, looking for ingredients for a catering gig Shane had agreed to take on.

Evie weaved her way through to the back and glanced over Shane's shoulder. "It looks like every other spice you have in the kitchen."

He pulled the small bag back in mock horror. "I'll have you know this is treasure. It's not anything I can use for the wedding, but I'm buying it nonetheless and making a mental note that this place is gold." He flipped it into his basket and turned back to the wall of spices. "So. Tell me about this new intimacy coach—"

"Coordinator, not coach."

"Oh my God, whatever. What's the difference?"

"Coach makes it sound like I have intimacy problems, and she's helping me work on them. She's like a stunt coordinator, but for intimate scenes. That's how she described it anyway."

"Doesn't matter what her job title is. Let's talk about the fact that you've mentioned her in pretty much every sentence that's come out of your mouth since you got back from butt-fuck nowhere. Has she seen you naked?"

"What?" Evie smacked his arm with the back of her hand. "No. That's an inappropriate question."

Shane placed his basket on the grungy floor and turned. Grasping her face with both hands, he tilted it up and said, "You once asked me if I exfoliate my dick, thus proving our friendship has no inappropriate questions. So. You like her."

"I mean, I don't not like her."

"Oh, what the fuck does that mean?"

"It means she's not something I'm going to pursue. End of story."

Shane added a few more boxes of spice from the shelf to his basket and continued through the store, Evie following. "You know what the end of this story is, right? You end up alone. What happens when I find my princess charming and go off into the sunset to make lots of babies, and you're still alone? I am not adding a mother-in-law suite to my basement so you can move in and become a nanny to my many, many children."

Evie stared up at him in amazement. "You've thought way too much about this. Also, you're over-estimating the number of kids you're going to have. You're looking for women in Toronto, and most of them don't want any children. Where is this magical princess who's willing to reenact a 50s musical with you?"

"That is the beauty of my search. I'll know she's the right one when she's willing to produce a litter for me." He flicked her playfully on the nose. "Stop changing the subject. This is not about me. It's about—"

"Evie?"

They both turned. Simone stood at the end of the aisle, her basket full of fruits and vegetables. Paired with her dress today were knee-length boots and a Burberry jacket tied and cinched around her waist. She reminded Evie of that last scene in Breakfast at Tiffany's when Holly goes looking for the cat down the alley.

"Simone. Hi."

Shane practically pushed Evie out of the way. "So you're the new intimacy coordinator on the show." He took her hand and kissed the top of it. "It's so nice to meet you. I've heard so much about you." Evie elbowed him in the ribs. "I'm Shane, by the way, Evie's roommate."

Simone smiled, seeming charmed. "I've heard about you. A chef?"

Shane turned to Evie and spoke as if Simone couldn't hear them. "She has an accent. You know that means she gets extra points."

"Shut up."

He peered into her basket. "What are you making?"

As if Simone hadn't heard any of that, she said, "My brother is coming for a visit, and he's feeling a little down, so I'm making him his favourite, beef stew."

"Sounds delicious. Are we invited?"

Evie turned to Shane as if she'd never met the man before. "Oh my God. You don't just invite yourself over to someone's house. Who raised you?" To Simone she said, "He's kidding, by the way."

"No, I'm not. I'm interested to see what you're going to do with those anchovies. Are they for the stew?"

"Yes. My grandma's recipe."

Shane looked over at Evie in childlike wonder and delight. One of his favourite things was passed-down recipes. He said they were always better than anything you found on the internet.

"You may come if you like, but I must warn you. My apartment doesn't have much furniture. I moved in only a couple of weeks ago."

"We're not fancy people," said Shane. "You don't need to impress us with places to sit."

After getting the address and time, they left Simone to finish her shopping while they continued their afternoon adventure. Outside, in the late-September sunshine, the air had crisped, letting everyone know that summer was over, and the cooler autumn weather was on its way.

"She is beyond hot. Hell, yeah, you're going to pursue her."

"I can't believe you invited yourself to dinner. It's the epitome of rude."

"You can thank me by being your most charming self tonight. I can't wait to see the beautiful babies you make."

They crossed the street in order to cut through a small parkette on their way home "That's not how biology works." Even as she brushed the thought off, Evie felt the storm in her stomach. She worried the more time she spent with Simone, the more she felt like a hormonal teenager. Even when she was a hormonal teenager, she'd never felt so out of control. She never got in too deep, and that's how she always stayed in control. Simone made her feel like she was in a car on the highway with no brakes or steering.

Shane had insisted on the tight black jeans and scooped-neck sweater Evie wore. She hadn't wanted to go too fancy. This wasn't a dinner party. It was a crashed family dinner, and Evie was surprisingly nervous, even with Shane next to her, who had always been her anchor. He squeezed her to him before knocking on the door. "Stop being so nervous."

"How can you tell?"

"You've been silent the entire way here, which means you're overthinking this situation. Stop it. We're meeting her brother. She's making us stew. There isn't anything else you have to make this about. And I'll be here for comic relief."

The door opened, and a tall, lanky man with curly black hair and Simone's smile and eyes opened the door. "Hello. You must be Evie and Shane. Come in." His accent was even stronger than Simone's.

Evie handed him the bottle of wine she'd brought. "I'm sorry if we're intruding on time with your sister."

"Don't be. When Sims told me she had people coming over, I was delighted. She doesn't always meet people well, and I'm happy she is settling. I told her change is good." He walked them up the stairway to the second floor. "I'm Gabriel, by the way. I'm not sure if Sims told you. She sometimes forgets her manners." This last bit he waited to say until they were in the apartment.

"You're the one with no manners in this family," she called from the kitchen.

The most amazing aroma filled the apartment, and Evie regularly came home to amazing smells. Shane beelined for the kitchen and began poking his head into various pots. "Feel free to kick him out. He can get a little too handsy."

"I'm just looking," Shane shot back. He lifted a pot lid and stuck his nose in.

"You look with your eyes, not your hands." She turned back to Gabriel, who had seated himself on the couch. The sparse apartment held only a small couch—no coffee table—a reading chair that looked like it had been plucked out of the 50s, and a simple dining table with four mismatched chairs. Evie chose the 50s chair. It was uncanny how much the siblings looked alike, from the colour of his light-brown eyes to his chestnut hair. He even had one of the same mannerisms as Simone. His mouth turned up in the corner on certain words when he spoke.

"Gabs, don't be rude. Make yourself useful and offer them a drink," Simone called from the kitchen.

He raised his eyebrows and turned toward the kitchen, humour and light mocking lacing his voice. "And am I not a guest as well?" He swivelled on the couch to face Evie. "I travelled thousands of kilometres, all the way from Quebec City, to be with my sister, and she accuses me of being a bad host in her own apartment. That hardly seems fair, does it?"

"You were here for work. Stop making yourself out to be a martyr and pour some wine. Can you tell he's the youngest?"

Gabriel smirked at Evie as he stood to retrieve a bottle of wine. "You'd think with how bossy she is, Sims was the oldest."

"She's not?"

Gabriel picked up a bottle of red and showed it to Evie. "Red okay?" She nodded. "Mani, our sister, is the oldest by two years."

"But with the way she acts, you'd think she was the middle child," said Simone.

"And where does she live?" There was silence as the other two exchanged a look. Evie knew that look well. She used it with her brothers all the time. How much to tell outsiders about your family? It didn't always mean anything bad. Sometimes it was easier to gloss over things than to explain an inside joke that had been around so long nobody could even remember how it started.

"Last I heard she was in Halifax. She doesn't like to share her plans with us. She's always been secretive like that." Gabriel placed a wineglass on the counter for Shane and handed the other to Evie. "I don't blame her. Our mother likes to stick her nose in everyone's business, so sometimes it's easier to keep that business to yourself."

Simone kept silent on the subject. She grabbed a towel from the oven rack and opened it, inviting the smell of fresh, warm bread into the apartment.

"It's surprising how much you've managed to get done. You've been here only a few weeks, and you already have so much furniture." Evie thought it best to change the subject. They were heading into uncomfortable territory, and it was too soon in their friendship and the evening to venture into uncharted waters.

"Our first apartment was mostly milk crates and garbage finds. The epitome of student chic."

"Remember that one apartment with all the couches? We had this roommate, Matt, whose dad would call him up at random times and be like, there's a couch on Cecil near Beverley. And he would go out and get this couch, even though we already had three in the apartment."

"That's how we ended up with the mice."

"Oh, God. I forgot about the mice. Remember the bat?"

Gabriel and Simone exchanged a look. "You two really aren't selling Toronto as a great place to live right now." Gabriel laughed.

"Why people want to live here is beyond me. It's expensive, dirty, loud."

"Work," said Shane and Evie in unison.

"Shane could work anywhere, but all the best restaurants are in the city. And there are a few places I could live and still work as an actress, but this is the best. Plus, my family's here. You'd feel differently if you grew up here."

"There are good things about it too," Shane said. "Try finding amchur powder anywhere else around here. We have nightclubs, museums, the waterfront, good restaurants. Everything's close. You don't have to own a car."

"There's High Park, and—"

"You don't need to sell me," said Simone. "I'm here for now. I'm sure it has its charm."

"Hiding in the sewers underneath all the garbage." Gabriel laughed.

Simone swatted his arm. "Come. Help me set the table."

"I can help." Evie stood and placed her wineglass on the kitchen counter. "Put me to work." Gabriel leaned back on the couch as Shane joined him with his wine.

The sun had set behind the houses, casting the neighbourhood in the last of the orange rays. Simone flicked on a light above the sink and opened a drawer next to it. This was the most relaxed Evie had ever seen her. She was wearing capri yoga pants with an oversized sweater, which hung off one shoulder revealing white, creamy skin. She had bare feet, and her hair was freshly washed and tousled to create messy waves around her face. Comfortable suited her. In the tight space of the kitchen, it was hard to think of anything but pushing her up against the counter. Evie wanted to explore her long neck, maybe that shoulder too.

"Hmm?" Simone had nudged her.

"The table is that way. Stop trying to undress me with your eyes and do this work you mentioned." Her brown eyes held humour and something else Evie hadn't seen before. Promise?

"I wasn't..." Evie took the utensils, thankful she'd gotten over her blushing phase years ago.

"Mmm." Simone turned her toward the dining-room table, her hands lingering on Evie's hips a little longer than necessary. Evie took a deep breath and stepped away. Apparently it'd been so long since she'd had sex, all she needed to get her going was a little innuendo and light flirting.

Simone handed her some placemats, which Evie distributed around the table. "Again, I'm sorry if we've intruded on family time."

"Nonsense. Gabriel is social. He loves people. If it were just the two of us, we would be bickering about his problems." Evie raised an eyebrow in question but didn't ask, not wanting to pry. "Or my problems, or Mani's problems."

Evie folded napkins, handing them to Simone. "Is that why you came to Toronto?"

"It's funny you should say that. Gabriel thinks so. I needed a change, to get out of my head and be somewhere new."

"And is it working?"

Simone paused as if she were really thinking about the question. "For now."

"The problem with running from your problems is that they follow you."

Simone nudged her chin toward Gabriel. "Too true." But she didn't say anything more. It was hard to have a private conversation in the apartment. Evie suspected that she didn't want to say too much in front of her brother. Now she was intrigued though.

At dinner Gabriel entertained them with stories of when Simone and he were little, the adventures they would go on in the woods behind their house. "She had this idea that we were going to find bees' nests and honey in all the trees and sell it."

"There was a Little House on the Prairie episode where Laura and whatshisface sell honey to get rich."

"Little House on the Prairie?" Shane asked. "That doesn't seem like your…thing."

"It wasn't, but it was the only English show we were allowed to watch as kids. And anything English back then was like—"

"Gold," Gabriel said.

"So what happened with the honey?" asked Evie.

"We found out she was allergic to bees."

"Oh, no."

"Oh, yes." Evie could tell Gabriel liked an audience. He was getting into his story with enthusiasm. "So Mani and I are rushing back to the house with her strung between us wheezing like our papa Phillipe taking a flight of stairs. Her hand is swelling to the size of a baseball mitt, and she's screaming, 'We forgot the honey. We need to go back.'" He collapsed back in his chair laughing. "Needless to say, we didn't become honey barons as she promised."

"So Simone was always the troublemaker?"

"Always."

"What a lie." Simone threw her napkin at Gabriel from across the table. "So, Shane, do you have any brothers or sisters who torment you?"

Shane pushed his plate—which had practically been licked clean—back and rested his elbows on the table. "Nope. Just me and my mom. Although Evie's become family over the years. She's like the pesky little sister I never had."

Evie rotated her finger around. "More like the other way around. Shane's my younger, annoying brother."

"Oh my God, by two months. Two months. I have more life experience. I've done more things. That basically makes me older."

"If by things you mean women?"

"It's not my fault you practically have cobwebs growing between your legs."

Evie clamped her mouth shut, pursing her lips. She could feel the heat rising up her neck and knew, without having to look, that her cheeks had gone bright red.

Shane slapped his hand over his mouth, clearly trying not to laugh. "I'm sorry, Evie." But he couldn't stop himself. The laugh burst forth, loud and boisterous.

Evie rolled up her napkin and swatted him on the head. "See? Younger, annoying brother."

Chapter Fourteen

The stairs leading from Simone's office felt longer today. Longer and steeper, as if she were descending from Jack's beanstalk. Perhaps it was the wine she'd consumed the night before? Or the lack of sleep she'd had? Either way, this was torture. She blamed Gabriel. She always drank more when he was around. Gabriel loved wine, all wines, but mostly a good Bordeaux, several of which he'd brought with him. Shane and Evie hadn't helped much, but because of Evie's early call today, they'd at least left at a reasonable hour. Gabriel had kept her up talking about their mom and what was happening with Marissa. Apparently now she wasn't speaking to him. He said he wanted to marry her. Simone was convinced it was the classic case of wanting something more because you couldn't have it.

Simone hadn't met Marissa, or even heard much about her, until this had all happened. She hated seeing Gabriel like this; however, she also hated being thrown in the middle. No doubt she'd get a call from her mother this week complaining about Gabriel and that horrid woman he wanted to marry. It put her in the worst spot. She usually sided with Gabriel since her mom tended to be unreasonable and chaotic—a side effect of living with her dad all these years—but she also didn't want to cause strife, so she had to listen and nod and agree with her mother only so she didn't stir the pot.

Halfway down she stopped to remove her heels, unlatching the clasps and hooking them under her fingers. At the bottom she stopped and ducked back. Ian and Charlotte were talking in hushed voices down the hall. Simone was not the type to eavesdrop, but something was off-putting about Ian's stance. He looked angry, while Charlotte looked near tears. She held back, waiting for them to leave so she could get to the set.

Charlotte's voice rose. "It's wrong. It shouldn't have happened." She wiped a tear away with the back of her hand.

"But it did." He grabbed her arm. "And it doesn't mean—"

"No." She pulled her arm back. "It's over. I'm ending it." She stormed off down the hall. Ian paced for a few more seconds, seething, breathing loudly before punching the wall and rushing off in the opposite direction.

Simone waited until she couldn't hear either of them before proceeding to the set. She was sorry she'd overheard their argument. She'd now think about what it meant when she didn't want to. Her first day, Jess had mentioned someone was trading sex for parts, and she now wondered if Ian had anything to do with that rumour. Simone remembered that Charlotte had been hired as a day player, but her part had grown to a permanent supporting role over the course of last season. Simone knew this was none of her business, and Jess had told her not to worry about it, but it was in her head, and it wouldn't go away.

On set, Evie's red hair stood out as a beacon amongst the shades of grey and dull browns. Up close the look was even better.

"How is it you look so put together this early in the morning?" Put together was an understatement. Evie was devastating. Her auburn hair, styled to frame her face in loose waves, glowed. Deep green, smokey eyes gazed out from under side-swept bangs. And the dress she wore stopped mid-thigh, revealing long, lean legs, the front dipping low enough to reach her waist.

"I have Cecilia and Justin." Evie primped her hair and batted her eyelashes. "Plus, I had only one glass of wine last night. I don't like to drink much when we're shooting. I wake up foggy."

"How is that even possible? I tried to have only one glass, but Gabriel kept topping me up."

"I covered my glass with my hand any time he tried."

Simone nodded. The movement made her feel like she had billiard balls rolling around in her head, weighing it down. Evie stepped close, steadying her with a hand on her back. Her fingers felt like an ice pack on a hot day. "I have just the thing for this," she whispered into Simone's ear, who dragged her gaze up from the skin between Evie's breasts to meet kind eyes. Evie guided Simone to her dressing room, and for a moment Simone's mind went to a place it shouldn't—to the hard love seat pushed up against the brick wall and all the things she'd like to explore on that couch.

There was a pull between them now, as if Simone had developed an extra sense and could feel Evie without even touching her. It was distracting as hell because, since the location shoot, she couldn't think about anything but Evie.

Evie picked up a pile of books on her love seat and moved it to a free space. "Have a seat. This won't take long."

"What are you doing?"

Evie had moved to a side table in the back and was mixing liquid from various bottles together. She opened her mini fridge and popped open a can of V8. "I used to work as a bartender. Hangovers are basically your body telling you it's missing fluids and certain nutrition. This drink makes sure you're hydrated and gives you back a lot of the potassium your body needs to feel better. Shane and I swear by it."

Evie handed Simone a glass with liquid tinged dark green. "It looks disgusting."

"It's not going to taste much better."

Evie sat on the coffee table across from Simone, the most eager look on her face. As if she'd baked her first cupcake and wanted Simone to taste it, even though she'd missed a few of the key ingredients. Evie reached over and squeezed Simone's knee lightly, which sent a dangerous shockwave through Simone's entire body. "I promise, it'll make you feel better."

Once she had her breathing under control, Simone took a sip. It tasted worse than it looked, like she'd taken dirt and mixed it with a protein shake and added something sweet, which was actually more suspicious than if it had just tasted like dirt. "It helps if you plug your nose. Like pisco."

"Like what?"

"A type of alcohol they make in Peru. It's from fermented grapes. First comes wine, then comes pisco, and if you ferment it even longer, it becomes industrial cleaner. Pisco is so strong they have special glasses that allow you to drink it without smelling it. Helps it go down."

"You are not selling this concoction."

"Well, I'm not trying to. I'm trying to cure a hangover. You don't have to drink it if you don't want to."

Simone contemplated that offer, she really did. But she didn't want the look on Evie's face to turn sour. She groaned, pinched her nose together, and tilted the glass up. She took three giant swigs and then put the glass on the table, unable to take anymore. "Is the purpose to make you want to vomit so you don't feel so bad?"

Evie laughed, and her hair brushed Simone's bare knees and sent a tingle down her thighs. "That's not its main purpose, no. Let me know how you feel in a few minutes." Evie helped Simone stand, pulling her up by her hands. For a moment they were inches apart. Evie smiled and tucked a strand of Simone's hair behind her head. "See? You didn't die."

"I didn't know that was an option."

"Come on. I have to get back to set. They're probably freaking out right now." She took Simone's hand and tugged her out of the room. Evie probably wasn't even aware of the effect she was having on Simone. She kept telling herself she was only being friendly.

"Do you know if Charlotte and Ian are a thing?" Simone blurted as a way to get her body to think of something else.

Evie immediately shook her head to say no but then stopped. "I thought he was seeing a man, but he's been very cryptic, and

I know he's bi." She scrunched up her face in this adorable I'm-thinking-real-hard way. "God, maybe that's why he won't say. And I can't remember if he mentioned a gender. I assumed it was a man, and he didn't correct me. But he didn't confirm it either." They entered the set, which was still in a state of chaos. Charlotte sat in her chair reading over her script. Her face perfect, as if she hadn't been crying a few moments earlier. "Why? You don't take me as the type to get into gossip."

"No. I don't. I saw them talking and was curious. She seemed upset." Simone didn't feel comfortable sharing anything further. It was unlikely that she was aware of the situation Jess had mentioned. Jess would want to keep something like this to herself until she discovered more because it had the potential to cause a PR scandal. Simone didn't necessarily agree with that approach. Women were being exploited, which meant the problem was already deep-seated within the show.

Evie opened the door to her apartment to the sound of pots crashing to the floor and loud swearing in Italian. When she entered the kitchen, Shane was picking up the scattered pots and stacking them on the long island that was full of food in various stages of prepping.

When Shane saw her, he rushed over and enveloped her in a giant hug. "Thank God you're home. I'm in so much shit."

"What happened?" Up close, the place looked even more of a disaster area. Every dish they owned lined the counters, used in some capacity. The sink overflowed with dishes. Spilled sauce, food scraps, and utensils covered the counters.

"I'm such an idiot. I agreed to cater this wedding. But I bid too low. I wanted the business. I also didn't want to pay for it out of pocket, and now I don't have enough money to hire prep cooks."

Evie stared, unable to form words. This was not the Shane she knew. He was good under pressure—a star, in fact. That's why he thrived in the kitchen. Chaos was his bitch. She wasn't sure what to do with a Shane who freaked out. "What do you need me to do?"

"I need help. Just simple stuff. Cutting up vegetables, washing dishes, that sort of thing." Evie widened her eyes, and Shane rushed over, taking her face in her hands.

"I know it's a lot to ask, and I know you just did a whole day of work yourself. But I'm desperate. I've already called people, and they're all working, or I wouldn't ask this." His hands pushed in slightly, forcing her cheeks together so that when she responded yes, she sounded like a squished puffer fish.

Exhausted but determined, Evie dropped her purse onto the couch and headed back into the kitchen. "So what are we making?"

"A carrot and ginger soup, tomato salad with whipped feta, baby greens, and crostini. Then for the pasta course, they'll have pappardelle arrabbiata with caramelized onions, kale, and mushrooms. For the main course I'm making braised beef short ribs, and then for dessert there will be four options." He started counting off on his fingers, but Evie had stopped listening.

"When's the wedding?"

"Tomorrow night. But I have a full shift tomorrow, and I want to get all the prep done. The soup is served cold, so I just need to make enough and refrigerate it. I can plate the salads at the venue, so they just need to be prepped. And I can finish the pasta and braised ribs at the venue because they have a kitchen. And it wouldn't be so bad except they added like thirty people last minute."

"I hope you charged them extra for that."

He gave her a look of pure disdain. "What am I? New? You know how much I spent on beef ribs for a hundred and seventy people? Let's just say, it was my share of this month's rent and leave it at that. I want this to go amazingly. I want them to tell their friends and hire me for their weddings."

"But not if you die in the process. You can't do a catering business on your own. You of all people should know that. You're always talking about how important your prep cooks are. And the line cooks and the servers. This is not a one-person job."

Shane squeezed her to his side. "But now, toots, it's a two-person job."

Evie groaned. "You're an idiot. You know that, right?"

"I believe I started my sales pitch with that fact."

Forty-five minutes later, they had the kitchen back in order, looking less like the cupboards had thrown up all over themselves and more like a catering kitchen should, when Shane's phone buzzed, announcing someone at the door.

"Oh, good. Did you finally find someone to come help?"

"I did. And you're welcome."

"What's that supposed to mean?" But Evie didn't have to wait long. A few minutes later, Simone breezed into the kitchen, with Shane and his huge grin behind her. He was playing matchmaker, the fucker, even during this time of chaos. They must have hit it off better than she thought because she wasn't even sure if she had Simone's number yet.

"Thanks so much, Simone, for saving my butt."

She grinned at them. "It's my pleasure. It looks like you have things under control. Based on your text, I was expecting a little bit more havoc."

"You should've been here half an hour ago. You would've seen the epitome of havoc in all its glory."

"She's exaggerating," said Shane and clapped his hands. "Okay, my little chickadees. Let's get to work. The first batch of soup is simmering nicely, so let's start prep on the salad. I need enough grape tomatoes cut for a hundred and seventy people." He handed them both a knife and pulled over a box with dozens of packages of grape tomatoes. "Remember to wash them really well first. I want them cut in half and placed in this bowl." He held up a gigantic metal mixing bowl and placed it between them on the island.

"Where did you get all this extra equipment?" Evie pointed to one of several tall soup pots on the stove. She didn't remember Shane owning any of this a day ago.

"I borrowed some stuff from work. Alejandro said it was fine. He thinks I'm catering my sister's wedding."

"You don't have a sister."

"Alejandro doesn't know that."

Later, as they sat on the couch taking a break, Evie said, "I'm sorry he roped you into this. And also, thank you for coming and helping out." Evie stretched her fingers. They were sore from holding the knife so tight.

Simone turned to Evie, her knee inching closer. "I meant it when I said it was my pleasure. I like Shane. He gave me some great pointers the other day to make my stew even better."

"Unsolicited constructive criticism is Shane's specialty. I don't generally cook, but when I do, Shane has thoughts."

Simone shook her head, laughter in her eyes. "It was completely welcome feedback. I love cooking, and to hear how to improve it only makes me happy."

"Well, then, you're a perfect match because I hate constructive criticism."

"Even for your craft?"

Evie laughed. "My craft? I love it. You wouldn't have been using that term over a year ago. I feel like this is the first time I've actually gotten a chance to use all the training I've done, and most of what I do is look pretty."

"Not true. I've watched the show. You're talented. Yes, you're gorgeous. But that isn't why they hired you. It's because you have the acting talent to carry an entire show. It's why your picture is up on the billboards around the country. Not Will's or Ian's. You don't think they're pretty? I assure you many women do, but they aren't the show. You are."

All Evie took from that was Simone thought she was gorgeous. She was stunned into silence, and for a moment she thought Simone might lean in. If she did, Evie wasn't so sure she couldn't resist kissing her. Evie dropped her gaze to Simone's lips. Red when she'd arrived, they were now a natural dusty pink, full and inviting.

But just as she was about to make a move, Shane popped his head into the room. "See. I've been telling her this for years.

Maybe she'll listen to you." He plopped down on the couch beside Evie and put an arm around her. "You're amazing at what you do, and the sooner you realize how talented you are, the better the world will become, because you will conquer it." He made both his hands into fists in front of them. "And once you conquer it, you will be its master, and everyone will bow down to you and you…" His voice trailed off. "I'm not sure where I was going with this. But you're one talented bitch, and you need to realize it."

"And scene." Evie punched him in the arm. "How long have you been up? You're starting to become incoherent."

"Since five a.m." He slumped his head onto Evie's shoulder. "You girls are the best. You saved my ass, and when I conquer the world and give everyone free pizza, you two will be the first to get theirs."

"Well, gee, thanks."

Simone stood. "It is late, and I should go."

Evie's heart sank. But maybe she should thank Shane. He might have saved her from certain embarrassment. There was a good chance Simone was just being nice and didn't actually like her. Working together after an awkward kiss would be uncomfortable, with an explanation mark. She stood as well. "I'll see you out." She looked back at Shane, but he was already snoring lightly on the couch.

"Thanks for coming. You saved my butt too, because I'd still be in there."

"I'm glad I came. If nothing else, I got a crash course in cutting technique." If you weren't holding the knife right, or your stance was wrong or your fingers were in the way, Shane would come over and instruct you on how to do it properly. Evie hated his lectures, mostly because she didn't care if she was doing it right. As long as it got done, she was happy and felt Shane should be too.

Simone ran a hand lightly down Evie's arm and squeezed her hand. "I'll see you tomorrow." She offered her a cryptic smile and opened the door to leave. Evie watched her walk down the hallway, certain she hadn't had a better night in years, and all she'd done was cut up vegetables. The woman could make work fun.

CHAPTER FIFTEEN

Jess was in the middle of chaos when Simone found her head-deep sorting through a pile of different coloured scripts.

"Do you have a moment?" Jess's office was in disarray, as usual.

Jess looked up, her hair escaping her once-tame bun. "I have a second, possibly half a second. What's the trouble?" She gazed around her office, as if noticing, for the first time, the absolute mayhem it had become. "I'd offer you a seat, but the script revisions have taken over."

"Revisions? This many?"

Jess pushed her hair off her face, blowing at it, as if that would help. "I guess it doesn't matter because you're going to hear about this soon anyway, but Charlotte is being written off the show. Please don't spread the news around. They won't be making the announcement until the next show."

"What? Why?"

"I don't know the specifics. I only know that I'm battling script-revision hell because, of course, she was in every episode this season. So now she dies in the next episode, which means a whole storyline gets abandoned, and the writers have to come up with something new to fill that time. What did you want to talk to me about?"

"It's interesting, this development, because I saw her arguing with Ian last week, and I remembered what you'd said when I was first hired."

This remark stopped Jess. "That is interesting. Extremely, because last year Ian got to direct an episode, and it so happens that the episode Charlotte started on was his episode."

"What do you think it means?"

Jess shrugged. "We can't really say for sure because we don't know all the specifics, but a lot of coincidences are involved here."

"Perhaps he offered her a bit part in exchange for sex. But then she got hired on as a regular, and he didn't want to keep up with the relationship, and now with her leaving, maybe he had something to do with that too? Maybe he's forcing her off the show?"

Jess held up a hand. "That's a lot of speculation with absolutely no facts to back it up. Let me do a little poking around to see if I can find out why Charlotte is being written off. In the meantime, please keep this discussion between us."

Simone nodded, but inside she was seething. If Ian was forcing Charlotte out because he was done with the arrangement, that was inexcusable. And so, she had to ask herself, was she going to sit by and let this event unfold, or was she going to do something about it?

Realizing this scenario wasn't anywhere near her job description, in fact, it wasn't even in the same postal code, Simone made her way down the hallway to Charlotte's dressing room. She hadn't had much opportunity to talk with the woman. She'd met her in passing, but since Charlotte was portraying a single mom going through a divorce, she didn't have much need for an intimacy coordinator on the show.

Simone knocked and waited to be invited in. She knew Charlotte was in there because she could hear the shuffling of papers. A few minutes passed, but the door stayed shut. Simone knocked again, thinking perhaps Charlotte hadn't heard her the first time. Still nothing. Simone turned to leave. If Charlotte didn't want to talk to anyone, it was her right, but when she entered the set, Charlotte was already on set speaking with the director. Who was in Charlotte's dressing room? And what were they looking for? Whatever the answer to those two questions, they held the key to why Charlotte was being written off the show.

❖

The apartment was dark, save for the light over the sink in the kitchen. Simone sat alone on her couch staring at her phone and dreading the call she was about to make. Outside, a siren wailed in the distance. While on set today, she'd received a voice mail from her mom asking what time she was arriving home for Thanksgiving. Simone had decided a few weeks ago that she wasn't going home for the holiday, as it was a long trip for such a short time, and in all honesty, she didn't want to be pulled into the middle of her family drama.

According to Gabriel, Mani wouldn't be home either. Not that he'd heard that from her himself. She'd called their mom a week ago to let her know that she couldn't get the time off work. Simone suspected another reason and had left a message for Mani but, not surprisingly, hadn't heard anything back from her yet.

Simone regretted waiting so long to tell their mom, because now she would feel the full force of her anger, as she was the second child to say she was skipping out on the family dinner. Simone lifted her phone, and the digital display said it was half past eight at night. She swiped up and dialled her mom's phone, hoping that she was now, as was tradition, at her sister's house for dinner and wouldn't pick up. Leaving a message on her mom's answering machine was much preferable to speaking with the woman in person.

As it would happen, no such luck. The receiver was picked up on the second ring, and her mother's thick Quebecois accent rang through the line.

"Salut?"

Simone froze. She was in for it now. She took a sip of her wine before speaking. "Hello, Maman."

"Ah, Simone," in French—"little kitten." She carried through for a full minute before Simone could cut into the conversation her mom was apparently having without her.

"Maman, I won't be able to come this year for Thanksgiving."

"Why?" The word was like a dagger, sharp and cutting.

"I have work. We're not getting the time off I'd need to come. I don't want to take a train all the way there for just a day."

"They're not giving you time off? What kind of work is this?"

"Work I happen to love. I'm willing to make the sacrifice."

"I don't understand how you can like work that will not let you at least celebrate Thanksgiving with your family. Are others going home for Thanksgiving?" Her mother had never understood what she did for a living, so it wasn't surprising that this news would upset her.

"I'm not sure. A lot of the crew are from the area, so they don't have to travel as far."

"Did he put you up to this?"

"Gabriel?"

"He says he's…" She paused for a moment, as if remembering the word. "Boycotting my Thanksgiving. I'm not even sure what that means, boycotting. My own children are abandoning me, and why, I ask?"

Simone pulled the receiver away from her ear. Her mother could go on for quite a while. She always did love playing a martyr. She took another sip of wine, considering how she would placate her mother. Simone could kill Gabriel. If she'd known he wasn't going, if he'd given her some indication when he'd visited, Simone would've called much sooner. She'd been putting off an unpleasant conversation, but now as the third and last child to cancel on their mother, this would be a great betrayal. It would be brought up every time they had an argument.

Simone took another sip of wine, savouring the complex flavour as she swirled it around her mouth. At thirty-two she had always obeyed her mother. She'd spent her whole life being loyal, doing what was asked, appeasing everyone. Well, she was sick of it. She was sick of being the good daughter, the one who always came through. She was finally doing something amazing, and she wasn't going to let her mother spoil it with one of her guilt trips.

She pulled the receiver to her ear and spoke loud enough to cut through her mother's tirade. "There is nothing I can do about it now. You will see me at Christmas. The show will be on hiatus by then. I will be home for part of that." And before her mother could launch into another tirade she said, "I'll call you this week. Say hi to Dad." And she hit end on the call. Two big breaths and another significant sip of wine, and she was feeling a little more herself.

She dialled Gabriel's number, and when he picked up, she didn't even let him get a word in before saying, "Boycotting? You're such an ass. Why didn't you tell me you weren't going home for Thanksgiving?"

"Boycotting? That was Mom's word, not mine. I'm not boycotting. I'm going to B.C. to have Thanksgiving with Marissa's family."

"Wow. That's a big step."

"I know. She invited me a few weeks ago, but I didn't say anything in case it didn't happen. Emile wasn't planning to give me the time off, and I wasn't sure I could get the money together for the ticket. Why is it so fricking expensive to fly across the country?"

"One of the great mysteries of the world. So you're going out to B.C. to meet her family? Are you nervous?"

"Uh, yeah. There's like almost a hundred people I'm supposed to meet. Okay, that's an exaggeration, but their Thanksgiving dinner is held at her parents' ranch-like thing, and over twenty-five people will be there for dinner, and they do another gathering for like a hundred people. She assures me everything's going to be fine. But if I brought Marissa home to meet our family, so much judging would be going on I'm worried they're all going to be judging me behind my back. What can I give her? I'm a stupid electrician. I don't even have a university education. They're all going to talk circles around me."

"First of all, never call yourself stupid. You're an electrician. And you worked hard for that profession. Don't sell yourself short just because you didn't go to some fancy school and get a useless degree. You went to college and worked your butt off and can offer a lot. If Marissa's family can't see you as the amazing person you are, they don't deserve you in the family."

The line was silent for a moment. "Thanks. I needed that."

"It's what I'm here for. Pep talks and disappointing mothers, my two strong suits."

"Oh, please. You're her favourite. That's why she's so upset. She's so used to Mani letting her down and not showing up, that it's expected. For the past six months, I've let her down so much, she was probably relieved I wasn't going because she knew I'd want to bring Marissa."

"I was her last hope."

"You're better off. The house is a little too crazy right now. Dad hasn't been doing so well. She found him in the basement in his workshop again." Simone refilled her wineglass, her hand shaking a little. This was a topic of conversation they rarely ventured into. Instead, they always danced around it. "He'd unplugged every electrical appliance in the house, including the fridge and chest freezer. I'm worried about her because she's not talking about it. I had to hear about this from Aunt Teresa." There was a pause as they both let this news sink in. "She's just holding it in. But he's not doing well. It might be time to start talking about getting her some help for him."

"You know she'll never go for that," said Simone. The possibility had been brought up every couple of years for decades, but nothing ever happened. Simone wondered what all their lives would've been like if her mom had gotten the help she needed for her dad.

"Eventually she won't have a choice."

"I hope it doesn't come to that." She didn't want to think about what it meant if her dad finally became too much for their mom to handle. It was a dangerous thought, so dangerous in fact that Simone lived much of her life in fear of it. It wasn't just the implications of what would happen to their family. It was the broader worry, the worry she'd had when she discovered the name for what made her dad pull her into the basement at six years old and tell her aliens were coming, and if they didn't hide, their brains would be sucked out. It was the worry that schizophrenia was hereditary, and Simone was at the right age for it to begin manifesting itself.

After the call, Simone refilled her wineglass and stood in her dark, empty living room. She hadn't done much more in the way of furnishing because she was afraid of what would happen if she set down roots. Hearing that her dad had gotten worse, and her constant worry about Mani made her feel like her future had finally caught up to her.

As Simone waited for her Lyft, she watched Estela rake the leaves in the small front yard of her house. Most of it was garden vegetables in the summer, but now everything had started to wilt. Many of the plants had already been pruned and made neat for the winter. With her back stooped and her arms wobbling, she pulled each pile of leaves toward her before bending over and placing them in a large paper bag open beside her. She looked too fragile to be doing this work on her own.

"Don't you have anyone to help you with that?"

Estela smiled and stopped raking for a moment. "My son says he'll do it. He doesn't like seeing me work so hard. But he has other things, and it gets done faster if I do it. Besides, I'm not dead yet, and work is good for you." She pulled off her cloth gloves and stuffed them into a pocket in her apron.

"If you need help, let me know. I can pitch in." It seemed only fair. After all, this was where she lived now.

Estela scanned Simone, a wry smile on her face. "In heels and a trench coat? You offer to help me do yard work."

"I have other clothes. I know how to dress for the occasion." This remark made Estela laugh, a deep, throaty laugh that set her whole body convulsing.

"I heard you are not going home for the holidays." Simone cocked her head to the side, unsure how Estela would know that. "The vents, they carry sounds." She stooped and picked up a few twigs on the ground and threw them into the bag. "You can come to dinner with me. We're going to my younger sister's." It wasn't so much an invitation as an order. Simone wasn't sure what to say. She'd planned to spend the night at home, maybe having a nice bath, a glass of wine, reading a book, although these fantasies always seemed better in her imagination. She worried she'd feel lonely on the day of and a glass of wine in the bath might turn into a pity party for one.

Before Simone could say anything, Estela waved her off. "You wouldn't be imposing. We like big family gatherings. You wouldn't be the only stray there, believe me."

"Stray?"

"Someone who has nowhere to go for the holidays. I don't mean it as an insult." That thought struck Simone. She hadn't thought of herself as a stray because she did have somewhere to go, except this year, she didn't want to be around her family. Come to think of it, it had been years since she enjoyed being around them. At some point, adult Simone had found she didn't have as much in common with them as she had when she was a kid. She'd ventured out into the world, and the values and ideals she'd grown up with had morphed from her experiences and now didn't match exactly. She loved her family, but sometimes she didn't like them. And that was okay. She still wasn't sure she wanted to take on someone else's relatives for the holidays.

"That's a very generous offer. Can I think about it?"

Estela nodded. "Of course." In the same breath she added, "We leave here at noon on Sunday," as if she already knew what Simone's answer would be.

CHAPTER SIXTEEN

Both Will and Evie were handed purple scripts at the same time. It meant two previous versions had gone through the writers' room. Blue meant one, green meant two, and purple meant three. It was rare to see a purple script. Will looked up at Evie with the same worried expression. Something major was going on. Evie flipped through several of the script's pages to see what had changed, and her gaze lingered on one line: "Abby flies to the window at the sound of an explosion. Her face is bathed in red light."

Will kept flipping through the script, but Evie had stopped. She knew what they'd done without having to go any farther.

"Are they serious?" asked Will. "Are they seriously writing Charlotte off the show? Why?"

Evie looked around to see if Cameron was on set. Why had they told them this way? There should've been a meeting. This had all changed since the table read yesterday, but based on the purple script, they'd known about this development long before yesterday.

"More important, why did they keep it from us?" Charlotte had been at the table read yesterday, quiet and withdrawn, which was totally unlike her. Why hadn't she said anything, and why had they put her through that ordeal when they knew she wouldn't be on the show much longer? Did they fire her? This was all too much. She had to find Cameron and speak to him.

"First positions." Michael was directing this episode. Evie found that fact oddly comforting. Now she had a person to fuel all her rage into. Not that it would help. Being mad at Michael rarely had a good outcome. It only made the day longer and more frustrating.

She moved to her first mark, a small cross with gaffers' tape at the head of the bed in her and Ben's bedroom. She was already dressed for bed, wearing pyjama shorts and a camisole. They had the air-conditioning cranked because of all the lights, so of course her nipples were pushing through the fabric like that creature breaking through that guy's stomach in Alien. From across the studio, she spotted Simone, who'd just stepped in as they shut the doors before filming. Their eyes met and held. Evie's stomach did a tiny flip when Simone's gaze drifted down the length of her body. On the way back up they stopped at her breasts. Evie's clit began to throb. Everything else in that moment fell away—the sound of the crew doing last-minute prep, Will mumbling his lines, memorizing them as fast as he could on the other side of the set, the lights as they were switched on one at a time. She lost Simone as each loud click brightened the set, throwing everything else into darkness. But she knew she was there, watching. And instead of making Evie self-conscious, the knowledge energized her. A PA came over and took the script from her hands. Cecilia from hair did a last-minute primp, and then everything went quiet, and she heard the familiar back-and-forth of starting sound and tape as they began to film.

Will came into the room and stood by the window, looking out onto a green screen, which would later be replaced with the backyard. "Did you know you could see right into the Barnhams' bedroom window? Makes you wonder what they can see."

Evie turned away from Will toward the camera on her right, making sure her face reflected a certain fear as she let her features play over the emotions of thinking what that window might have shown.

"Did you talk to Jen today about taking the kids on the weekend of the twenty-sixth?"

"Cut," Michael called.

"That line was cut," the script supervisor said. "The new line is 'Did you talk to your mom about taking the kids on the weekend of the twenty-sixth?'"

Will nodded. "Yep, okay." He went back to his first position mumbling the new line.

They did the start of the scene again, stopping on the next line change, then beginning again. Will kept messing up the new lines. This day would last forever. Until he had a chance to sit down and actually go over the script and memorize everything, they would have a tough go of it.

It took over two hours to get the scene done, even though it would amount to less than thirty seconds on the show. It was the first of the day, and Evie was already exhausted because she knew what lay ahead.

Simone approached as crew swarmed around the set, moving lights and tape and preparing to change to a new sound stage for the next scene on the call list.

"What a mess," Simone said. She placed a comforting hand on Evie's back. "Are you doing okay? I heard about Charlotte."

Evie gave her a weak smile. "I'm surprised. A little furious, but otherwise okay." She shrugged. What else was she supposed to say? She had no idea why or how this had happened, and until she had a chance to talk to Cameron, none of it would make sense.

Simone's hand on the small of her back was light but deeply felt. Only her touch seemed to matter. And at that moment she would give anything to be having this conversation in private. Not at all coherent, she kept focusing on what she'd like to do to Simone, and none of it was professional or intended for an audience.

"That's understandable. It was a sudden announcement."

"Announcement? They handed us a script."

"That's how you found out?" Simone turned toward Evie, keeping her voice low. "Why wouldn't they announce it at the table read?"

Evie shook her head, and the movement caused Simone's eyes to stray. Still in the thin camisole that left little to the imagination, Evie resisted the urge to cross her arms, even if she was cold. She liked Simone's attention on her. "It's being mismanaged because it's sudden. Whatever happened, I don't think they were expecting it."

A loud clang from the set pushed them apart. Simone cleared her throat, and her hand dropped from Evie's back. Simone looked around the set as if she'd forgotten for a moment they were surrounded by people. She pushed away, a tight smile on her face. "I'll look into it."

"You don't have to. I'm going to go talk to Cameron after I change." They both stared down at the flimsy outfit she was wearing. Evie laughed as she walked over to her chair and grabbed a robe, throwing it on in one swift motion and knotting the tie at her waist. "Somehow I don't think I'd get as much of his attention as I'd like." Evie liked Simone's dazed expression. She was definitely having an effect on her, and it gave her a thrill she hadn't felt in a long time.

❖

When Evie finally found Cameron—in a lounge chair in the reception area, his laptop on his knees—she had only a few minutes left before she was due on set.

When Cameron spotted her, he smirked. "Shit. I thought I'd found a good spot this time."

Evie took a seat next to him, now dressed in a light-coloured sundress, ready for her next scene. "Now isn't the time to be hiding, Cameron." She tossed the purple-paged script onto the keyboard of his laptop. "We deserved to hear what happened from you, not read about it in script revisions. That's some pretty poor judgment, and I'm surprised by how insensitively this whole situation has been handled."

The admonition had the effect she was hoping for. Cowed, he picked up the script and handed it back to her. "I'm not surprised everyone is upset. I was too when Charlotte asked to leave the show. It came as a shock, frankly, and you're right. I didn't handle it well. I wasn't prepared for it."

"Why is she leaving?"

"That she wouldn't say. All I know is that we've worked it out with her lawyer and agent. She had a good reason that I'm not aware of, but everyone was satisfied with the deal that was struck. So," he pointed to his laptop, "I'm in revision hell trying to rework a good chunk of this season's story. As you know, Charlotte was supposed to play a big role later on, and now we have to pivot and get someone new in to fill that spot." He leaned back, scratching at his hair, which looked scruffy. Every part of him was rough—his face, clothes, eyes. If he'd gotten more than an hour's sleep last night she'd be surprised.

"While you're here, I heard that Jason Phelps pulled out of directing episode nine, something about a movie shoot going longer than expected. And I wanted to talk—"

"Are you kidding me with this? I've got three weeks' worth of work to do in a few hours, and you're worried about directing? I don't have the time or the patience to deal with this right now, Evelyn. I told you, I would let you know when I made up my mind, and I haven't." He shut his laptop and stood, striding out of the reception area and leaving Evie feeling like she'd been shouted at by her dad for leaving the garage door open all night. Again, she was amazed that, with a few choice words, he could make her feel like a child. She would sit and strategize about how she would approach him, and then it would all go to shit the second she saw him.

Evie slumped back in the cushy chair, thankful for this moment to get her head back together. Her next scene was with Ian and Will and the kids. They were having a celebration dinner for Mia's character, whose soccer team had won a league award. Evie wasn't sure if even the writers knew what they were talking about, but she put her faith in them, because the only sport she knew even a little about was hockey, and that was only because she'd been dragged to her brothers' games and practices growing up.

A side door opened, and Jess emerged, a tablet and script tucked under one arm. "There you are. What are you doing sitting out here? We need you on set."

❖

It wasn't until later, when they'd finished filming for the day, that Evie got a chance to seek Charlotte out. She was in her dressing room, which she shared with Laura, who played Sophia's teacher.

A file folder box on a coffee table was stuffed with a few picture frames and some books, a travel mug, and a sad-looking spider plant. In front, on the couch, staring in dejection, sat Charlotte, still in hair and makeup from earlier.

Evie rapped a knuckle on the door jamb. "Can I come in?"

Charlotte seemed to shake herself out of whatever melancholy she'd been deep in. And it was here that her talent as an actress really shone. She smiled, brightening her whole demeanour, and for a second Evie could forget she'd seen her so sad a moment ago, because here was the bubbly Charlotte she was used to.

"Hi, hon. Whatcha up to?"

"Came to see how you were doing." Evie took a seat on the couch next to Charlotte.

Charlotte had changed into black pants and a light sweater with knitted wolves. It would've been worn in earnest in the late 80s but was now only for irony. "Well, as you can see, I'm packing up. I'm sure everyone's heard by now. I'm leaving the show."

"We heard, but not why. This is so sudden. I don't understand the reason. This show isn't the same without you."

Charlotte squeezed Evie's knee. "That's a kind thing to say, even if it is bullshit. You're the show, Evie." She turned now, all of the bubble dropped. "Don't forget that. You make this show, no matter how much they try to bring you down or shove you into a corner." She grabbed hold of Evie's hands. "You are a spectacular actress, and the only thing people are going to say bad about you is that it's a shame it took you so long to be discovered. You are the heart and soul of this thing. Don't forget it." A tear had formed at the corner of Charlotte's eye, and she quickly wiped it away.

"That's bullshit if I ever heard it, but I'll take it. Thank you."

Charlotte grabbed a Kleenex box off the table. "Shit. I didn't want to have this sappy good-bye with everyone." She blew her nose and laughed. "Now I'm going to look awful. I always fake-cry on shows because my eyes puff up and my nose gets all red."

"Is that why this was such a secret? I don't get it, why you're leaving. I mean…" Evie was at a loss. Sure, she sometimes got overwhelmed with everything and dreamed of what it was like before random people on the street knew who she was. But she wasn't actually prepared to walk away from all this. Not yet anyway. On the other hand, Charlotte had been at it a lot longer than she had. But why now? When she'd found a great show?

"My mom is really sick. She's in a home in Florida, and I want to take her out of there. She's only going to get sicker if she stays. It'll be cheaper if I'm looking after her anyway."

"Wouldn't it be better if she had medical care from professionals?"

Charlotte took Evie's face between her hands and shook it a little, laughing. "We don't have universal health care where I'm from. Remember, silly? Someone has to pay for those medical-care professionals."

This made even less sense to Evie. Why leave a paying job when she needed money? "This is ridiculous, Charlotte. Isn't there any other way than giving up your life, your career?"

"I know it's hard to understand. You've finally made it after working so hard to get here, and the idea of giving all that up is probably a crime in your eyes. I see your side of it, I do. For me, I've never needed the recognition. The first season set me up with a good bit to get me through this. I have some residuals from other projects. I'll be okay. It's more important to me that I'm with my mom. She's not going to be here much longer, and I want to spend the last few months or years she has there with her."

Evie nodded. She might not understand. Hell, she might not even believe Charlotte, but she knew this was all she was going to get out of her. There would be no big confession for why she was really leaving the show. Or, maybe Evie was off. Maybe she did have a sick mother in Florida and was giving up her career to spend the last few months with her.

Evie pictured her own mother in that position, but it was hard. Her mom was still relatively young. At sixty-five, she acted more like she was in her forties. She always had something on the go—friends, parties, events. She still worked part-time as a nurse, and any spare time was filled with activity. The idea of sitting around watching her mother wilt to nothing was a foreign idea to Evie.

"Can I help in any way? Clear the hall? Procure a paper bag to hide your hideously red and blotchy face?"

Charlotte's laugh was real this time. With her head thrown back and her shoulders shaking, she grabbed ahold of Evie's clenched hands. "I'm going to miss you most of all, scarecrow."

CHAPTER SEVENTEEN

If her mind hadn't been completely buried in the article she was reading, Simone would've heard the steps on the stairs long before she was jolted by the knock on her door. The long climb usually alerted her that someone was coming to see her long before they arrived. As it was, her heart was still in her throat when the door opened to reveal Evie in tight jeans, an oversized knit sweater hanging off her right shoulder, and black heels. She leaned against the jamb, hooked a foot around her ankle, and crossed her arms.

"That's some hike," she said. "So this is where you hide out?" Simone pulled her focus from Evie's bare shoulders to her eyes, which sparkled with humour.

"Are you here to talk about the upcoming scene with you and Ian? I haven't had a chance to go through it as much as I want before we discuss it."

"Actually, I'm here socially." She stepped in and dropped to a chair someone from props had brought up to make the place look less austere. The effect Evie was having on Simone was devastating. She was wearing a scent, something complex. Her presence filled the room, like her scent, invading every crevice.

She'd obviously come from hair and makeup, but they hadn't overdone it. She still looked like her Evie. Well, there was a thought. Evie was most definitely not hers, but it was interesting that she thought of her as two separate people, almost like she was Abby Bruce and Evelyn Harper. Today she was a mix between the two.

"I have one more scene, and then I'm heading out for the long weekend. I wanted to check in with you, see what you were up to. I assume you're going home for Thanksgiving?"

Simone propped her arms on her desk, crossing them. A large part of her was excited that Evie had sought her out. They'd been dancing around each other for the past few weeks, and she wasn't sure if they were friends. There was some flirting and a definite mutual attraction. Simone hadn't let herself think about it, because that attraction scared the shit out of her. This wasn't like usual. She couldn't have a few dates, lots of sex, and then bow out before things got serious. Simone suspected Evie wasn't a casual-affair-with-coworkers type of girl. Besides, whatever happened, it was already more serious with Evie than with any of the dozens of women she'd slept with in the past few years. The moment anything happened, it would immediately become something, and that's what worried Simone. She wasn't willing to let the potential time bomb in her head affect anyone else's life the way her dad's had, wasn't about to let this never-ending cycle of suckage continue.

"I'm not going home. It's too far for such a short visit. I plan to spend it with a friend." Up until that moment she hadn't decided to accept Estela's offer. In fact, it would be really easy to make an excuse and hole up in her apartment drinking wine and watching shitty TV.

Evie's face fell at the word friend. That was also unexpected. Simone wasn't sure why she hadn't just come clean and said her downstairs neighbour had invited her out. Perhaps because she didn't want to feel like the charity case she already was to have to get an invitation from an old woman who pitied her.

"Well, I hope you have fun. I'm glad you're not spending it alone." Evie stood and began to leave, then seemed to think of something and turned around. Her smile wasn't as bright as it had been when she first arrived. "If, for whatever reason, your Thanksgiving plans end early, my brothers and I usually grab a beer at Henry the VIII's. It's a pub around the corner from my mom's house. You're welcome to join us if you'd like." Evie was gripping the chair in front of her. She nodded and turned without saying anything else.

Simone couldn't explain why she was so sad at seeing her leave. She felt like she'd let Evie down, which was ridiculous. If she had gone home, she wouldn't have been able to join them anyway. Yet she wasn't, and she'd just lied about what she was really doing, making it seem more than it was. And that, realized Simone, was what was making her so sad. She was playing games with Evie. That was worse than flirting. It meant she cared what Evie thought of her, and that could only lead to trouble.

She collected her papers and stuffed them into her bag. She wasn't even sure why she was still here. She'd had a brief meeting with Cameron earlier, but after that she was done. Deep down she knew she'd been hoping to see Evie. Well, she'd done that. Now she could go on and have her fun-filled Thanksgiving.

Simone found something comforting about walking into another family's Thanksgiving. She felt no pressure to perform, to meet the obscure and sometimes ridiculous requirements of success in her own family. Married? Doesn't matter. Employed? Doesn't matter. Have an apartment above ground, not beside a highway or a subway? Doesn't matter. She could be unemployed and pregnant, living on a friend's couch, and it wouldn't matter because she was never going to see any of these people ever again. Except, of course, Estela, but Simone wasn't worried what she thought of her because Estela had probably already made up her mind about her the second she decided to rent her the apartment.

Thanksgiving this year was being held at Estela's sister's place. "She's younger, but you wouldn't know it by how she acts," Estela whispered as they entered a large foyer overflowing with coats and boots. "You'd think she came back from the dead the way she goes on about her aches and pains." Estela showed Simone where to hang her jacket and tuck her boots in. "Don't let her corner you at any point. You'll never hear the end of her hip-replacement nightmare."

During their ride over, Simone had learned the basics. Every year as far back as they could remember, the Pereira family had gotten together for Thanksgiving. Each year a different family member hosted. This way no one's feelings would be hurt and everyone got their turn, whether they wanted it or not. Estela usually hosted at her eldest son's house because her first-floor apartment wasn't large enough for the entire family.

Stepping into the living room filled with chatting adults and loud children of various sizes and ages reminded Simone a lot of being home. Only it was always her Aunt Camille's house because she had the most space and the biggest dining-room table. Her family did more of a potluck, and each brought a dish to share, which spread out the work of hosting an event. She suspected her Aunt Camille loved hosting people because it made her feel important. She was forever holding such events over her mother's head.

In the living room Simone met a variety of people with names she didn't even try to remember because she knew she never could. The house was full of wonderful smells and people laughing and talking. She felt homesick for what felt like the first time since she'd left Quebec a few months earlier. She'd been so busy working and navigating this new experience she hadn't had time to miss home.

Suddenly, she felt like she'd made the wrong choice. She shifted her gaze from one person to the next, everyone chatting and getting along, laughing, and took it back. Without Gabriel or Mani there, she would be ripe for nosy relatives. She'd learned long ago that it didn't matter how successful you were in her family, some choice in her life could always be used to make her feel inadequate. Here she appeared to be an unwrapped present, all new and undiscovered. The second Estela introduced her and mentioned that she worked in television, everyone's interest was piqued. When they learned she worked on Social Queen, she found herself in the middle of a rather large circle of Estela's relatives.

Even when they sat down to dinner, the questions kept coming, some of them easier to answer than others. "Is Colton Jeffries as hot in person as on the screen?"

"That's a stupid question. Of course he's as hot in person. The show is literally about people who get paid by advertisers to post about their lives because they're so hot. They wouldn't hire ugly people."

"His name isn't Colton Jeffries. That's the character Ian Davies plays." Simone couldn't remember the names of the women, but she was pretty sure one of them was Estela's daughter-in-law. The women sparred back and forth. The atmosphere was comfortable, and Simone was happy she'd come because being here took her mind off her family issues. She was sitting next to Estela, and every few minutes she would pipe in and share the backstory of what someone was talking about, gossiping like a schoolgirl. Simone suspected Estela liked having her here because it gave her an opportunity to show off her family. And thankfully all the personal questions were saved for family members. Until they came to dessert.

"So, Simone, do you have a boyfriend, a husband?" The woman sat at the end of the table, and from what Simone could remember, she was someone's aunt.

"She likes women. Stop trying to throw your son at every woman you see." Estela passed Simone a plate with a piece of crumbly pie. Okay, so the vents in her apartment really did carry sound well.

The woman shrugged as if the comment had slid right off her back. "I have a daughter. She works in a bank." The woman looked around the table. "It's a good job. She makes nice money."

Estela leaned in toward Simone. "Just tell them you're seeing someone. It makes the interrogation easier."

Simone turned and whispered, “If I was seeing someone, why didn’t I spend Thanksgiving with her?”

Estela raised an eyebrow. “That’s a good question. Why didn’t you spend Thanksgiving with her?”

“Because I’m not seeing anyone.”

“What about the redhead who came to dinner a few weeks ago?”

“She’s someone I work with.”

Estela shrugged and passed a plate of gloopy pastries to her left. The man, Filipe—Simone had met him earlier but couldn’t remember how he was related to the family—grinned at Simone and said, rather loudly, “You’re dating Evelyn Harper?”

“Who’s that?” someone halfway down the table asked.

“Abby Bruce. The lead in the show.”

Simone shook her head. “I’m not—” But the table had erupted, and no one paid her any attention anymore.

“She’s dating who?”

“The mom. The one on all the posters.”

“What’s it called when women like women? Lesbo?”

“That’s a lesbian, Mom. No one uses lesbo.”

“Isn’t that an island off France?”

“It’s Greek, and it’s Lesbos, with an s.”

Simone grabbed Estela’s arm, dreading the possible PR nightmare this conversation could create, not to mention it hitting the papers before she had a chance to talk to Evie. Estela patted her arm. “They don’t really care if you’re dating her or not. They have a new fun topic of conversation. They’ll move on before dessert is over. Don’t worry.”

“But it’s not true. What if someone repeats this story, and suddenly it looks like I’m going around falsely saying I’m dating the star of a show.” That would make her seem desperate for attention, and Simone certainly didn’t want attention in her life right now.

Estela shrugged. “Well, you can mention to her that they misunderstood. Get ahead of the story. Or,” and here she had a mischievous smile, “you could make it true.”

"What?"

"You're a pretty girl. Why wouldn't she want to date you?"

"But that's not—"

"What? She's not pretty enough?"

"But I don't want to date her." By now the conversation had drifted on to the best vacation places in Europe, and a debate between France and Greece as choices had erupted at their end of the table. Simone shook her head and dropped the subject, suspecting that Estela was winding her up a bit.

It was true though, right? She didn't want to date Evie. She didn't want to date anyone. Everything was too complicated to think about right now. Evie had invited her to have drinks that night with her brothers. Would she have invited her to dinner if Simone hadn't had something else to do? It was possible. Would she have gone? Did she intend to go out for drinks? She hadn't planned on it. When she left with Estela, she would go home and enjoy a nice glass of wine in bed with a good book. That's how she'd pictured herself at the end of the night.

Now, she wasn't so sure. She remembered the name of the pub. Henry the VIII. She could go and explain, as embarrassing as it was, the misunderstanding that had started at dinner. Give her a heads-up. It would be nice to hang out with people her own age. Sure, there were probably people her own age here, but they all had kids and acted like they were already old.

She still hadn't made up her mind by the time they said their good-byes.

CHAPTER EIGHTEEN

Evie placed the flowers in an ornate, blue glass vase, arranging a few of the prettier ones—she had no idea what they were called—to be visible from every angle.

"You didn't need to bring me flowers." Evie's mom, Linda, pulled a few white ones to the front.

"She had to do something," said Lucas, her younger brother. "She's useless in the kitchen."

"I didn't see you in there slaving away." Linda smirked. Evie smiled at her brother as if she'd won a prize, which vanished as her mom said, "He's right, though. You should learn to be a little handier in here."

"Why? I live with a chef, and most of my food on the show is catered."

"That's not going to last forever, you know."

The kitchen where they stood was bright, colourful, and modern, thanks to a renovation in the mid aughts. The length of the backyard was in full view from the kitchen sink. The maples dotting the lawn had changed colour for the season, creating a kaleidoscope of oranges, reds, and yellows. This was the house where Evie and her brothers had grown up, which made it odd to come back and see changes.

The aroma of turkey, always a comforting scent, filled the air, invading every room on the first floor. For some reason the roasting turkey smelled like home, full of memories. They'd spent every holiday together since she was a kid. She liked hanging out with her family and didn't realize how odd that was until she'd met Shane, who usually avoided his every chance he got. Before he'd started working in restaurants, Evie used to bring Shane with her to family dinners. He admitted that her family was nicer than his. However, he still didn't understand why she liked them so much.

She had what she thought of as a healthy rivalry going on with her brothers. They competed for everything: who had the best job, apartment, car, partner. Wes had won for years because he was the only one of the three to get married. After his divorce, Lucas and Evie refused to take pity on him. After all, their lives had been built around this competition. Surprisingly, Evie was rarely in the running as having the best life. Her job lost her points because she worked too much to enjoy the money she made, and she now had no privacy, which her brothers were quick to point out was a huge failing point of being famous. It was generally agreed that Lucas had the best job. A graphic designer for the provincial government, not only did he make decent money, but he also had a pension and wasn't overworked because, as he pointed out, the government was slow on change of any kind, which meant revisions took months, sometimes years.

Wes had the worst job. He worked at a bank as an accounts manager, which they all agreed was boring and lame. He had two adorable kids, which gave him points, but they were both under five, which lost him even more points because that was a lot of work. He shared custody with his ex, and even though they joked that should up his points, Evie could see it weighed on him. He truly loved his kids and missed having them in his life daily. Evie secretly gave him bonus points for being a great dad, definitely better than their own, who'd left and become nothing more than a card on birthdays.

The doorbell rang, and, the three of them, startled, turned to see Mark, Evie's stepdad, rise from the couch and place his newspaper in his spot like he was marking it as his. "Who could that be?"

Before he made it to the door, it swung open, and Wes entered. "Hon, we don't have to ring the doorbell. This is my mom's house." Wes stepped aside to reveal a tall, very well put together blonde in heeled boots that reached her knees. To Evie, she looked like she was trying too hard to impress. Then she turned around, and Evie's mouth popped open. It was Kristen Mason. They'd been friends in high school. She looked over at Lucas, who'd had a megaton crush on her, to gauge his reaction.

He didn't appear fazed. In fact, he didn't seem to recognize her.

Evie stepped forward, knowing she'd have to pretend to be happy to see her. Kristen had always been a little full of herself in high school, and from the look of things, nothing had changed.

"Kristen?"

She grinned and stepped forward. "Evie, can you believe it? How long has it been?" She rushed forward and pulled Evie into a great big hug. She smelled like cheap perfume and fruity hair product. What was Wes doing with someone so superficial? Trashy. That was the word that jumped out at her. But Kristen hadn't always been trashy. Bitchy, yes. Was this what trendy looked like in your mid-thirties?

Linda helped everyone off with their jackets. Apparently she knew Wes was bringing someone. This was why he didn't have the kids this year. It was a newer relationship, and they hadn't introduced her to them yet. Evie couldn't imagine her getting along with her niece and nephew.

The dining-room table was set and full of dishes and food. Kristen was barely eating hers obviously preferring to talk.

"I went into the bank to set up a new account. And who does that anymore? Most of it is online now, but I had questions and wanted them answered by someone who lives in this country, so I decided to do it in person, and there Wes was."

Evie cringed. This was not who she pictured with Wes.

"And you went to school with Evie?" Linda scooped green beans onto her plate.

"We were so close, and then after graduation everyone went their own way. Do you still talk to anyone from the group, Evie?"

Evie pushed mashed potato around her plate, wondering if Simone's Thanksgiving had turned out as bad as hers had. "Not really. I ran into Sarah at a club once. She became a dermatologist or something, a chiropractor? Something like that. But other than that, it's like everyone vanished."

"I feel the same." Kristen then proceeded to talk throughout the rest of dinner, telling stories of how awesome her life had been, which weren't all that interesting. At least she wasn't fawning over Evie about being on billboards everywhere. At first she thought Kristen might gravitate toward famous people. Now she just suspected that Kristen thought Wes was rich because he worked at a bank.

"I can't believe you still live in the same house." They were onto dessert now. Kristen had opted for a tiny sliver of pumpkin pie—because it looked the healthiest. "I used to pass by here whenever I came home to see my parents, but they sold their place years ago. Of course they're kicking themselves now. If they'd held onto it for five more years, they would've been able to sell it for so much more."

A look passed between Mark and Linda. Mark clearly had lost some battle because he was the one to speak. "We were going to wait until after the holidays. But since you're all here, now seems as good a time as any. We're putting the house up for sale."

Before anyone could interrupt them with objections, Linda jumped in. "We put an offer on a condo downtown."

"But this is your home," said Evie. "You've lived here for over forty years."

"Exactly. It's time to move on. We don't need all this space. What are we using it for?"

"Plus," said Mark. "With the market the way it is, we'll be able to buy a condo outright and have enough left over to do some travelling."

"What if one of us buys it?" Lucas asked.

"You have two million dollars we don't know about?"

"Two million dollars. Holy shit. This place is worth two million?"

Evie didn't have a childhood memory that didn't include this house in some way. The first time she broke her arm was climbing in the big maple in the backyard. In fact, if you looked hard you could still see the bloodstain from when she'd spit blood on the flagstone path along the side of the house.

Evie and her brothers used to sit at the top of the stairs and listen to their parents argue. They'd divorced when she was seven, and her mom had met Mark a year later. Mark had become her dad. He was the one who'd taken her to the hospital when she fell out of the tree. He was the one who let her borrow his car to practice in the parking lot of the Dairy Queen down the street. He was the first person she came out to when she was seventeen. And all of that weaved in and out of the walls of this house. It had changed over the years, gotten a facelift or tummy tuck or two. They no longer had bright-orange shag carpet in the living room or stencilled micro tiles in the downstairs bathroom. But the smell had never changed. It was like teleporting back to the nineties. Walking down the steep basement stairs made her think of that time she found Wes and one of her friends making out on the couch while watching Friday the 13th.

To her, that was worth more than two million dollars. Someone new would come in and rip out everything to make new memories, and then it would no longer be their house. The practical adult side of her knew her mom and Mark were right. It was ridiculous to hold onto a four-bedroom house in Etobicoke for just the two of them. They could do so much with that money. But it meant the end of something, and that's what saddened Evie. Not that she'd ever consider moving back home. The option no longer existed, and there was something final about that fact. It was like her childhood was ending, and now she really had to step up and become an adult, even though at thirty-five she should've considered herself an adult a long time ago.

She looked over at Lucas and Wes and wondered if they were as stunned as she was. She could tell Lucas was. He was always the last one to know. Wes seemed less surprised than the rest of them. It was possible Mom had consulted him before they made their decision. He was always good with numbers. They'd have to ask him when they went out for drinks after.

Later, as they cleared the table and did the dishes, Evie whispered to Wes. "She can't come drinking with us. Tell her it's for siblings only."

"Oh, come on, guys," Wes said. "We aren't doing that this year, are we?"

Both Evie and Lucas looked like he'd pulled out a light-saber and cut off their heads. "Of course we're doing it. It's tradition," said Lucas. He handed Evie a plate to place in the dishwasher. "And I agree with Evie. Siblings only."

"Weren't you friends with Kristen in high school?"

"That was a long time ago, and the last time I spoke to her was at graduation, where she wished me luck and shit. I think she was headed off on some vacation her parents had sent her on. I have no idea what happened after that."

"And surprisingly, after that monologue at dinner, we still don't know." Lucas laughed. "Ditch her and come. It's tradition. This is like the one time of the year the three of us get to hang out without anyone else around."

Wes rolled his eyes, but Evie knew they had him. Tradition was huge with Wes. Evie excused herself. She didn't want to be around when Wes told Kristen he wasn't going home with her.

Sliding into the booth at Henry the VIII was also a coming home of sorts. Evie had worked there on and off through university, mostly in the summers as a bartender and server. She still knew some of the staff who'd been there for what seemed like decades, and James the owner still ran the pumps a couple nights a week.

He was working that night, and he nodded and smiled at Evie and her brothers as they came in.

The place hadn't changed in decades. She knew James had bought it from his dad back in the late 90s and did a bunch of renovations. The only thing he hadn't changed was the name. They'd gone all out to make it feel like you were stepping into a pub in England. Everything was dark woods and low lighting, cozy booths tucked into nooks around the place. Behind the bar stood shelves of spirits and a long line of pumps filled with English, Canadian, and Irish beers.

After finishing a few orders he came over with menus. "Well, if it isn't the trouble trio. Drinks, or did Mark cook the turkey this year?" He dangled a few menus in front of them.

"Just the drinks menu. Our stomachs made it safely through dinner this year. And I don't think I've eaten that much all week," said Lucas, who looked like he wished he'd worn track pants instead of jeans.

The tradition had started after Evie turned nineteen. She'd felt uncomfortable drinking in front their parents even if it was legal, and so Wes had taken her to Henry the VIII after dinner to have a few beers. A year later—with a fake ID—Lucas had joined them. James didn't even blink the next year when he came in and was no longer Fred McMurrey but instead Lucas Dankworth. Not a name easily forgotten, nor necessarily fondly remembered, which is why Evie took Mark's last name when she started acting. Harper sounded a hell of a lot better than Dankworth.

"Drinks it is. Good to have you guys here. And Evie? Congrats. You've earned every second of it. Enjoy it." Evie ducked her head to peruse the menu. That was one thing she still found odd, interacting with people from before. In her head she'd divided her life in two: before fame and after fame. She hadn't had a ton of friends before she got the role. She and Shane had a small circle, and most of them had drifted away since university. Then there was her family, who thankfully didn't treat her any differently. If anything, she took more flack from her brothers than before.

Since she'd become famous she'd made friends with a few people, mostly cast and crew. She worried when the show ended if they'd still be friends, if she'd still get to see Charlotte now that she was no longer on the show.

She grimaced. This was the first thought she'd given to Charlotte all day, and that annoyed her. She was probably home now with her mom in Florida. Evie made a mental note to call her tomorrow and see how she was doing. The thought of her just picking up and leaving like that still worried Evie. Nothing about the situation seemed right.

She broke out of her thoughts when a hard-cover drinks menu landed on her head. "Earth to Evie." Lucas, still holding the drinks menu, an exasperated look on his face, waited for her.

"What?"

"What do you want to drink? We've only been asking for like five minutes."

"The same thing I always order."

"Still? But that's boring." Lucas turned to Wes as if he might get a different answer out of her.

"I thought fame was supposed to give you style and good taste," said Wes.

Evie laughed. "I'm sorry. You must have that reversed. If anything, fame subtracts taste and style from people. Almost like a debit. You get to be famous, but we will take every ounce of common sense and reasoning you have."

"So now that you're famous, you have zero style or taste."

Evie laughed. "Pretty much."

James stopped by the table. "What's it going to be then, folks?"

"I'll have a pint of Murphy's, please."

"That's like the cheapest beer we have."

"That's why she likes it, because it's cheap. You have money now. Buy something better."

"I like the taste of Murphy's, thank you very much. I'm not making you drink it, am I?"

Lucas rolled his eyes. Everyone knew changing Evie's mind once she'd made it up was like moving Mount Everest to the other side of the world. Impossible and pointless.

Evie could smell Simone's perfume even before she said hello, and her stomach did a tiny flip like she was on a roller coaster. "Hello. I'm sorry I didn't text beforehand. I realized I didn't have your number." All three of the Dankworth siblings turned to look behind James at Simone, who was dressed fit to kill in a form-fitting black dress, knee-high leather boots, and a dark green, vintage pea coat.

Evie stood first. "I'm glad you came." She was surprised she sounded so normal. It felt like something had lodged in her throat—maybe her heart.

Both Wes and Lucas turned to Evie, no doubt curious why she could invite someone to a "siblings only" event and Wes was expected to tell his girlfriend to go home.

"Guys, this is Simone. We work together. She couldn't go home for Thanksgiving. I didn't want her to be alone so invited her out with us. Simone, these are my brothers, Lucas and Wes."

As if the hint of an uncoupled woman was too much to pass up, Lucas's smile cranked up to overpower his face. "Simone. Are you another actress who works on the show?" He moved down the bench in the booth to give her room to slide in. She removed her pea coat and hung it on a hook beside her seat.

Simone laughed. "I would make a terrible actress. I'm the intimacy coordinator."

"What is that, like a therapist?" asked Wes.

James butted in to take the rest of their orders and retreated to the bar.

"No. I choreograph the intimate scenes on the show."

"Sex scenes," said Lucas. Evie kicked him under the table.

"Yes, but not just those. All intimate scenes."

Lucas gave Evie a what-the-fuck look. She leaned in and said as quietly as she could, "The last time you tried to hook up with a friend of mine, she ended up dating Wes. Cut your losses now."

"Which friend?"

"Kristen Mason? She just came to the house."

"I obviously dodged a bullet with that one."

"What are you two whispering about?" asked Wes.

James was back with a tray full of drinks. He handed out pints to everyone except Simone, who'd ordered a vodka tonic.

"We're lamenting your poor choice in women." Lucas took a sip of his beer, the foam briefly coating his lips before he wiped it off with the back of his sleeve.

"Kristen? She's great."

"She's kinda racist."

"There's no such thing as kinda racist."

"What are you talking about?"

"She didn't call to have her questions answered because she didn't want to talk to someone foreign."

"That doesn't make her racist."

"It doesn't make her a great person."

"You were friends with her in high school."

"Was. Have you seen me hanging out with her since then?"

Simone leaned across the table, which Evie couldn't help notice did wonderful things for her cleavage. "I feel I came in the middle of something."

"Wes brought Kristen Mason to dinner. I used to be friends with her in high school, and Lucas had a huge crush on her for years."

"Again, how did she embarrass you?" asked Wes.

"It was the beaver dance. Do the dance. Show Simone," Evie insisted.

Lucas frowned and looked down into his beer. "I don't have the teeth for it anymore."

"He used to do this dance to make fun of me for always showing up to things early. First day of high school he did it in front of Kristen, and she called him a moron. Completely crushed him. He wouldn't come out of his room for weeks."

"Oh, whatever. It wasn't as bad as all that. I propose demerit points."

"What for?"

"He's right." Evie sided with Lucas. "You went from being married to the sweetest person in the world to dating a viper. You lose points for that."

"You can't side with my ex-wife."

"We can and we did," said Lucas and held up his beer for a toast. "To Jen, the best ex-sister-in-law there ever was."

Wes didn't hold up his glass. "I'm not drinking to that."

"Suit yourself." Everyone else, including Simone, held up their glasses and drank to Jen.

Chapter Nineteen

"I don't understand your brothers or most of what any of you said, but I had fun tonight. Thank you for inviting me."

Simone and Evie stood outside the pub. It was later than Simone had planned to stay out, but she'd had such a good time watching them all verbally spar. It made her miss Mani and Gabs. "It's better than sitting alone in my apartment drinking wine curled up with a good book."

"That sounds good too, actually. Cozy, in fact." They'd agreed to share a Lyft ride since they both lived in the west end. Lucas had walked back to his and Evie's parents' place to sleep it off on the couch. Wes, who lived in the north end of the city, had opted to take TTC. He'd been teased for that too. Apparently he was a bit cheap and didn't like spending money when he didn't have to. Evie had joked it would take him hours to get home that way, and after having used the public transit in this city herself, Simone could see how that was possible.

A mist had descended into the city, creating halos around all the streetlamps and painting a glow on the multicoloured leaves. The pub opened on a side street, cocooning them in surprising silence, which enveloped the two of them like a hand holding onto something tight. Simone couldn't imagine Evie looking more beautiful. She wore jeans and a black bomber jacket and an oversized sweater, which had slipped several times throughout the night, revealing a red bra strap. This last detail would stick in Simone's mind most of the evening. She stepped closer, the vodka tonics she'd consumed earlier clouding her judgment. Her skin began to vibrate.

This was the way she'd felt in the club that first night. And not for the first time did she wonder if she should tell Evie or keep it to herself. It wasn't a secret, so she wasn't sure why she hadn't shared.

Simone snaked her hand around Evie's waist and pulled her closer. From the hunger in Evie's eyes when she tilted her head back, Simone knew they had the same thought. Her warm skin smelled like apple pie and cinnamon, and when Simone leaned closer, the floral scent of Evie's perfume surrounded her. Simone wanted to sink her hands into Evie's hair. But most of what she had in mind wouldn't be appropriate, even for a side street. Evie hooked a finger into the knot of her coat belt and tugged it loose.

"Hey. One of you girls call a Lyft?"

Startled, Simone jerked back and looked over at the man in the light blue Jetta. The cloud of desire vanished. Frustrated, she nodded.

Instead of sliding in on the other side, Evie chose the middle seat, clicking the seatbelt and gazing into Simone's eyes with mischief. She soon turned her head forward. As the car pulled away from the curb, Evie placed her hand lightly on Simone's thigh and left it there. The sensation sent a ripple along Simone's spine. Then, Evie's thumb began to move in slow circles along her thigh. A pleasant shiver shot through Simone. She peered over at Evie, who paid attention only to the road ahead of them, but a small smile lurked at the corner of her lips.

Simone leaned over and whispered, "What are you doing?"

"Enjoying the ride." Her hand parted Simone's coat, letting it fall open and smoothing Simone's dress farther up. Evie's fingers danced along the inside of her thigh, caressing the sensitive skin in some unknown pattern that had Simone gripping the door and resisting the urge to let her eyes close and her head fall back. What had started as a vibration of want now exploded, and all she could do was sit there in anticipation of what Evie would do next, which was add pressure. Her fingers began a slow climb up Simone's inner thigh, only to stop and descend, each time moving a little higher.

Evie leaned close to Simone's ear and said, "All night I've been thinking about nothing else but seeing what you have on under this dress." Evie's fingers brushed against her panties, and Simone bit her lip to stop herself from making a sound. She dug her nails into the plastic of the handle, causing just enough pain to wake her from this fog of desire she'd climbed into. She wanted this. Fuck, did she want this. But not in the backseat of a light blue Jetta with a guy listening to adult contemporary from the 70s in the front seat.

She was about to suggest Evie come up to her place when they stopped in front of her house. Sitting on the front porch was Gabriel, who stood as soon as the car stopped. At first Simone wanted to cry, but then panic welled up inside her. Gabriel was supposed to be in BC right now. What was he doing here?

Simone squeezed Evie's hand, which had thankfully retreated from between her thighs. "I'm sorry that I can't invite you up. Gabriel wouldn't be here if it weren't something really terrible."

Evie nodded. "I understand. Another time." She pecked Simone on the cheek and waved to Gabriel.

Simone stepped out of the car, taking a moment to regain her composure. She watched as the Jetta made a three-point turn and headed out onto the main street.

Gabriel came up beside her. "Did I interrupt something? I thought you went to Thanksgiving with Estela."

"And then I went for drinks with Evie and her brothers."

"Went well, I see."

Simone smacked him in the stomach. "We shared a Lyft. She lives a few blocks from here." She waved his next comment away with her hand. "Now, why are you not in B.C. with Marissa's family?"

❖

The Tuesday after Thanksgiving seemed to move as if it were in a stop-motion film. Michael was directing this episode, which meant the delays came with yelling and door pounding. Evie folded her script back as she walked onto set. She was still getting used to not having Charlotte around. They got only one script a week, but she could feel the changes. She was having conversations with other characters that she would've previously had with Charlotte, who was meant to be her best friend on the show.

She was early to set, which she liked. It gave her a chance to review the script without too many interruptions. Sure, she could go back to her dressing room and have total peace and quiet, but Evie thrived better in chaos. And being on set as the gaffers and props department sparred over space was always fun to watch. It calmed her, allowed her to focus, and she always memorized her lines faster that way.

Plus, being around people kept her mind busy and gave her less time to think about Simone, an activity that, if left unchecked, would become all consuming. The other night kept playing back in her mind. Simone's scent, her skin, the way she quivered when—see? This was why she needed to keep busy. It was no use thinking about what might have happened if her brother hadn't been waiting on the front steps for her.

Evie found a couch on the living-room set and took a seat, placing her coffee on a coaster beside her. She felt a little like she was in a friend's living room, even though it was supposed to belong to Abby Bruce. This didn't feel like home, mostly because her and Abby Bruce's tastes vastly differed. For one, she'd never own a leather couch. She abhorred the idea of cutting up an animal's skin to enjoy it as fabric. Also, too much red wasn't good for the soul. That was some grandma wisdom there.

"I heard she left because of Ian." The voice of Will Stagg rang out from behind the bulkhead.

Startled, Evie let her script drop to her lap.

"What happened with Ian?" Evie wasn't sure who the second voice was.

"This rumour's going around that someone is trading sex for day parts. Ian directed the episode Charlotte was hired for, and apparently she wasn't happy with the arrangement anymore and asked to leave."

"Are you kidding me?"

"And I know for a fact he's recommended a few other actors for parts."

Evie stood up. She didn't believe for a second this could be true. Who the hell was spreading these lies about Ian? She walked around the bulkhead to see Will and Susan, the script supervisor, sitting in director chairs.

"Who'd you hear that from?"

Will looked up and, for a second, appeared terrified to see Evie, then almost as suddenly, his face went blank and he said, "From Simone."

Evie froze. Simone was spreading gossip about Ian? That seemed totally out of character. Either she didn't know Simone as well as she thought, which, let's face it, she didn't. Not really. Or, Will had misheard something or misunderstood something, which was also possible. He was one of the biggest gossips on set. He always had his nose shoved somewhere it didn't belong.

The easiest and most direct way to find out was to talk to Simone herself. And that's exactly what Evie planned to do. She dropped her script onto the couch and headed for the door to the back hallway. Before she could exit, Jess stepped in her way.

"Can I have a word?"

"Um, can it wait?"

"This will just take a second. Have you talked to Charlotte about why she left the show?" Jess pulled Evie out of the doorway and off to a small corner. Work to set up the first shot of the day continued behind them.

"She said her mom's sick, and she decided to spend what time they had together."

Jess nodded and bit her lip. She looked down at her tablet, then back up again. "That's what I was told too. And then I found out her mom died three years ago. It turns out she had been on a show, which she left to spend time with her mother before she died."

"So you're saying at some point the story was true."

"At one point, yes." Jess leaned against the wall and crossed her arms. Her hair was still confined in a bun on top her head, indicating it was still early in the day. It usually broke free around noon and then became increasingly manic as the day went on.

"Why do you think she left?"

"Have you spoken to Ian about any of this?"

"Why would I speak to Ian?" Evie's stomach dropped. She'd hoped Will was just being Will and she could settle this all as a misunderstanding by talking to Simone. If Jess was involved, it was far more serious than she wanted it to be.

"It's my understanding that they might have been involved."

"Who said that?"

"Simone overheard a conversation that indicated they were more than friends."

Evie physically stepped back. How many people had Simone been talking to about Ian? She recalled the conversation they'd had the week before Thanksgiving about Ian possibly dating Charlotte, but she hadn't given it serious thought. Besides, Ian was free to date who he wanted.

"Judging by your reaction, you're not aware of any of this." Jess looked disappointed.

"I have no idea who Ian's dating at the moment."

Jess nodded. And Evie worried she may have added fuel to this fire.

"He's private. It doesn't mean anything bad."

"I'm sure it doesn't. I was just curious to see if he'd mentioned anything." Jess patted Evie's arm, as if to reassure her, which did the opposite, and walked onto set, her face buried in her tablet.

❖

From the bottom, the stairs looked like they went on forever. Having traversed them once before, Evie could attest to the fact that they did eventually end. Why had Jess given Simone an office as far away from set as possible? She had only an hour for lunch, and she'd squandered much of that getting out of her last outfit.

It felt harder this time, climbing a million stairs. Maybe because she was dreading what she would find out—that Simone was spreading rumours about her friend Ian. Not only to Jess, but to Will as well. She was willing to give Simone the benefit of the doubt because this was out of character. Or seemed out of character. They hadn't known each other very long. What if she'd misread Simone? She was wary of what she'd find out, because whatever was starting between the two of them would certainly stop. She couldn't date someone malicious. She'd learned her lesson the hard way a few years ago.

Juliette was a model and obsessed with fame. They met at some fund-raiser Shane had been catering. He thought it was a good way for her to meet industry people. And at the time, she thought she was lucky. Juliette was kind and supportive, and, as it turned out, a little too supportive.

They were still dating when she began working on Social Queen, and Juliette had started a rumour that Evie mistreated her costars, felt they were beneath her. Luckily a much more sensational story was doing the rounds that week, and Juliette's went unnoticed. Evie stopped dating after that.

Evie rapped a knuckle on the closed door at the top of the stairs. As she stood out there, waiting for Simone to open the door, Evie found it even more ridiculous that Simone's office would be so out of the way. What if she wasn't even in there, and Evie had wasted her time even coming up here. This was nervous thought. She was nervous, probably because if she didn't get the answer she wanted, this could change things. Instead of moving forward with something new, she'd be stuck with this weird longing. Her mind would be fully aware that she couldn't start anything, and her body would hold a vigil for all the sex she would not be having.

After a few seconds Evie heard Simone call that the door was unlocked. Evie poked her head in, ready to hold herself to convictions that she found difficult the second she spotted Simone sitting on a small couch, her legs crossed. One red heel lay on its side on the floor, while the other bounced ever so slightly on her foot. She wore a light blue dress, which brought her whole complexion to life. And the smile on Simone's face when she saw it was Evie made her grip the door jamb for support.

"I'm sorry if I'm interrupting."

Simone checked her watch and stretched, a lovely gesture that pulled the fabric of her dress tight around her breasts. God, Evie was in so much trouble. "If you are, it's a much-needed interruption. I've been lost for the last hour in a journal article that I'm not sure is more boring than it is arrogant." Simone moved over on the couch to make room and offered the spot beside her. "Is this another social call?"

Evie shoved her hands into her back pocket, not sure if getting too close to Simone would help. Simone sat up straight. "Ah. Something's up." She stood and retreated behind her desk. "Have a seat." Her smile had faded, as if she'd switched off a lamp in the room.

Evie chose the seat across from the desk and sat. Simone hadn't hung anything on the office walls, but the mostly exposed brick gave the place character. She'd added a plant, although it sat a little forlorn in the corner in need of water or more sunlight.

"I heard some stuff today, and it made me worry that perhaps…" Evie had made up her mind to find out what was going on. She'd thought about it all morning as they shot scenes but hadn't actually decided what she would say to Simone. Everything in her head made her sound like they were in the seventh grade. She started again. "A rumour's going around that Ian is trading sex for parts, and apparently it came from you. I wanted to hear your side of it first, before I jumped to any conclusions."

Simone leaned forward on her desk, intertwining her fingers. "Where did you hear this rumour?"

"Will and Susan were talking about it on set. And then Jess basically confirmed it. Apparently, Charlotte didn't leave because her mom's dying. She died a few years ago."

Simone nodded, looked thoughtful, but didn't say anything.

"Well?"

Simone stood and came around the front of the desk, half perching on top. "I'm not a gossip. I know this is partly what you're asking. But I haven't been going around talking about this."

"But you think Ian is trading parts for sex."

"When I was hired, Jess told me that she suspected someone was, yes. She became aware of it over the hiatus and wanted me to know. I saw something that looked very suspicious and took those suspicions to Jess. We decided that we didn't know enough to make any sort of accusation, and so she said she would look in to things, and it appears she is. That's the end of my involvement."

Evie bit her lip. Simone was obviously telling the truth. What irked her was that it appeared someone attached to the show was using women. Even more disturbing, it looked like it could be Ian, though she knew it couldn't be. There had to be some explanation. She would definitely talk to Ian, but he had only a few scenes in this episode, and they weren't with her.

Simone took the seat beside her. "I don't know how Will found out, but it wasn't me." She took Evie's hand and leaned forward. After a few moments she said, "I'm sorry about last night."

"Is Gabriel okay?"

Simone sighed. "I thought that by moving to a new province and city, I would get away from all my family drama. But no. The bullshit follows me wherever I go."

Evie checked her phone. She had only a few minutes left before she had to be back on set. "I want to hear all about your family drama, but I have to go. Come over to my place tonight." Evie stood and walked to the door.

"Don't you have a night shoot?"

"It was rescheduled for Friday. Yay." Evie waved her fist in the air to show her fake enthusiasm. "I'll make you dinner. I can't cook, but we have tons of leftovers from Shane, and I can reheat."

Simone joined her at the door. "I'm happy with reheated gourmet."

"Well, then I'm your girl."

Simone pushed Evie up against the door, pressing herself against her. Evie grinned. The pressure of Simone against her was having a devastating effect on her concentration. She could only focus on full red lips and the tips of Simone's fingers, which were playing with the neckline of her shirt. They danced over her collarbone and up her neck, pulling Evie's face toward her. Her heart was thrumming, along with other places. Evie jolted all over the second their lips touched, like she'd been shocked, or the time she went bungee-jumping and Shane pushed her off the bridge. It was surprising and exhilarating and a moment she never wanted to let go of.

She clung to Simone's waist, having ramped up to a hundred in what felt like an instant. Simone's hands were now inching up under her shirt, leaving heat trails along her skin. They were veering into dangerous territory when Evie's phone beeped. She pulled away and checked it.

"It's the AD. They want me on set."

Simone stepped away, smoothing the front of her silk blouse. "I will see you tonight."

CHAPTER TWENTY

The bass could be heard even from several floors down, and as the elevator doors opened, Evie froze. Only two apartments were on that floor, and the other one belonged to a couple who lived in Costa Rica during the winter. They'd left two weeks ago.

The door was already open when she arrived and found it full of strangers. She spotted Shane instantly, who rushed over, pulling her into the hallway.

"Why does our apartment resemble Sneaky Dee's on a Saturday night?"

"I thought you had a night shoot."

"That's not an answer."

A server wearing a black vest and tie popped his head out. "Hey, Shane. Where's the extra ice?"

Shane looked up to the ceiling. "You'll find four coolers along the north wall full of ice." Shane looked about as good as he did the time he'd mistakenly eaten a cannabis cookie at a friend's house. Sweat poured down his face. It had pooled at his armpits, and he was emitting a rather musty smell, like a cloth left in a damp place too long.

"What is going on?"

"Our venue fell through, and I didn't want to lose all the money and time I'd put into this event, so I offered up our place.

Do you know how much they're paying us to use this apartment for a night?"

"And we're going to have to spend that on fines and cleaning up the place. This is so absolutely fucking illegal. Not to mention I had a date. You said you were going to be working until like three in the morning."

"I will be. Only now I'll be here. Wait. Who was your date with?"

"Who do you think? Simone is on her way over here. I was going to heat up leftovers, woo her by the hot tub overlooking the park. It was going to be romantic, and I'd finally brush away the cobwebs you keep pointing out are collecting dust between my legs." Her voice had been escalating for the last half of that sentence until she was full-on shouting in Shane's face.

"You don't need anything special. That woman is wooed." Shane pointed behind her, and she turned, knowing that Simone was standing at the elevator and had probably heard the entire freakout.

Shane pulled out a wad of cash, and Evie became instantly worried about what he had gotten himself into. "Take this and get a hotel room for the night."

"I don't want to go to a hotel room." She leaned in to whisper. "That's tacky as hell. I want my own fucking place."

"Well, you have to stay in a hotel because you can't stay here." Off her look of pure death he said, "Your night shoots go to like six in the morning. I thought you'd be gone, and I'd have plenty of time to clean the place before you got home."

"Were you even going to tell me?"

"Of course. Just after the fact. It's easier to ask forgiveness than permission." Shane kissed her on top of the head and left her alone in the hall with Simone.

"What happened?"

Slowly, Evie turned to face Simone. She'd gone home to change and was now wearing tight black pants, heeled boots, and her pea coat. It was like she'd stepped out of Vanity Fair. Evie hadn't even had a chance to change her clothes from work. She shrugged and pocketed the money.

"He's turned our apartment into some sort of dinner club." She made up her mind that she wasn't going to let Shane ruin her night with Simone. She took Simone's arm and turned her back toward the elevator. "So, our plans tonight have changed a little. I'm going to take you out to dinner. I know a place that's quiet and intimate." Not as quiet and intimate as she'd originally planned, but it beat going back to a hotel by herself and sulking over room service.

Evie gripped the rail of the elevator as the digital readout indicated they'd passed the fiftieth floor. She'd been here only once before, with Shane, and hadn't had the courage to look out the window. The restaurant was located on the seventy-second floor, but if she sat somewhere in the middle, she could pretend it was much lower to the ground.

The issue was the elevator ride. The building swayed the higher it got, and that was nowhere more noticeable than in the elevator. What if it stopped and they were stuck dangling sixty floors above Toronto? Two other couples shared the elevator with them, and neither looked resourceful.

Simone took a step toward Evie and whispered, "You okay?"

"Heights. They're not my friend."

"Then why'd you pick this place?"

"Because it's really nice and exclusive, and I wanted to impress you." The elevator jolted and swayed. "And now I'm rethinking my idea of impressive." She'd asked Shane to call ahead and pull some strings to get them in. It was the least he could do. She'd also asked him to grab her a better blouse, so at least she didn't look like she'd come off working a double shift at some cheap bar and grill. Now she was wearing a top that revealed too much skin—which tended to happen when you left wardrobe decisions to Shane—so in addition to feeling like her stomach had invaded her throat, she was freezing.

Evie felt the warmth of Simone's body behind her as she reached down and took her hand and held tight. "Only six more floors and we're there," she said.

After a few more sways and one final jolt, the door pinged and opened onto an open-concept floor surrounded by windows. Beyond, the Toronto skyline stood as if it had dressed to be inspected. The sun had just dipped below Lake Ontario, casting purple and orange hues across its waters. The buildings cast shadows that reached out like arms enveloping the dotted lights lit up in building after building. It was, in a word, impressive. And it was meant to be. The restaurant was exclusive and expensive for a reason. Not just anyone was allowed to dine there. They catered to the ultra-rich, the kind of people who thought keeping a condo in Toronto was a business expense even if they used it only once or twice a year. They were much more interested in yachts and private jets that could carry them to the very ends of the Earth at a whim.

The first time Evie had eaten here, a man in a dark suit and even darker tie had come around and asked that all cameras and camera phones be turned off. If the idea of being unavailable for two hours was too much, the man offered to pay for their meal, and they were asked to leave. A few did. Evie had been expecting something exciting. Instead, a short man in a simple suit, which probably cost twice her monthly rent, came in with several guests and sat at a table by the window. The event was anticlimactic, and she couldn't understand why anyone would want to take pictures of the man. She later found out he owned most of the real estate along the Mexican Riviera. It was probably a publicity stunt to make him feel more powerful than he was.

The two couples ahead of them had reservations and were whisked off to their tables by servers standing by to do just that. When they approached the host, who looked like he'd stepped out of an Armani ad, he greeted them with an air of demur.

"Do you have a reservation?" He asked as if he enjoyed making people who didn't ride the elevator all the way back down.

"My friend Shane called. He knows Anthony."

The host shook his head imperceptibly, a tight smile forming that told them this was not how it worked here. The establishment had rules. Rules they were clearly breaking. Evie turned to Simone, whose expression still looked as serene as when she'd stepped off the elevator. It said, I belong here, and she appeared as if she easily could. Evie, on the other hand, was still wearing tight jeans, even if they were black and, for her, rather expensive. She still felt out of place. Before she could apologize to Simone, a man strode over to them.

"Ms. Harper, we're so very happy to have you this evening. Right this way, please." He gave the host a side glance as he picked up two menus and escorted them to a table in the middle of the south wall of windows. As they strolled through the tables, a meandering path no doubt meant to show off their new guest, a few people looked up, but the majority paid them no attention. Evie was once again grateful to be in Toronto, where most people could give two fucks if you were famous.

At the table, Evie chose the side that was least likely to make her throw up from vertigo. Hard to do in a restaurant specifically designed to showcase the skyline.

The man who'd rescued them from the insufferable host handed them each a menu. "Here you are. Your server, Stephanie, will be with you in a moment. If you have any questions or concerns, please direct them to me. Enjoy." He was smooth, obviously management, tasked with knowing who people were at a glance.

"I guess fame has its perks. I thought the host was going to call bouncers to escort us into the elevator."

Evie snorted. "People like him shouldn't have that kind of power. Besides, it's only the people who run restaurants and clubs who give a shit. They want people like me here to post about it on Instagram and TikTok." Evie picked up her menu and slid her finger down. "Unfortunately for them I loathe social media."

"Do you ever think it's ironic that you play a woman who has figured out how to weaponize social media when you have so little interest in it?"

Evie smiled and placed her head on her hand and gazed at Simone. She adored this woman. She had a way of getting to the root of something in an instant. "I've never liked social media because it gives control of how you're perceived to other people who are under the illusion that you have full control. Anyone can skew and repost anything I post. They can warp my intentions. I can never know ahead of time what consequences a certain post will have, and so I'll never have control. Abby thinks she has control because she feels in charge of social media, but really, she's stuck in this cycle where her life now fits this mould, and she has to continue in that mould or she breaks the illusion."

Simone smirked and crossed one leg over the other. "Yes. You have thought a lot about it."

They ordered wine from Stephanie, who was tall, blond, and low-key professional. If she recognized Evie, she made no attempt to show it. To her, they were valued guests, the same as everyone else in the restaurant. Evie appreciated that attitude.

After she'd left, Evie said, "Tell me more about you. What's your family like?"

"Ugh."

"Sore subject?"

Simone shook her head and took a delicate sip of wine. She stared out at the lake and buildings below. "I came to Toronto hoping for some distance to get perspective. My family is…loud. They are loud about my choices, about who I date, when I date, what I should be doing with my life. They don't like that I'm a lesbian because my mother thinks I'll never have a child, not even considering that I might not want children. They are in my life and my business too much. So here I am." She spread her arms. "In another province to get away from all that, and who is sleeping on my couch? My little brother, who didn't have enough guts to tell my mother he had other plans for Thanksgiving and went home only to find she'd tried to set him up with someone when he already has a girlfriend. Only they don't like his girlfriend."

Evie took Simone's hand, which had been waving frantically as she punctuated her sentences. "It sounds like you've set some boundaries that your family isn't listening to. You've taken the first step, which is the hardest part. Setting boundaries with your family is almost impossible. I find it hard to do too."

"I didn't mean to rant. I love my family. They have big hearts. They just don't always know how to…step back. The one thing I do miss about back home is the stars. Here, and even in Montreal, you don't see anything except the North Star."

"I know what you mean. My mom and stepdad Mark used to take us to this cabin up north for two weeks every summer. At the time I hated it. Being stuck in a cabin with your whole family with only one bathroom is more than any preteen girl should have to endure. But what I remember most are the stars. It was like stepping into the Milky Way. At night the whole world became the sky. It's the most beautiful thing I've ever seen."

Simone turned her head toward the view while Evie looked down at her napkin. "I've met Gabriel, and you have an older sister?"

"Mani. I worry about her. She hasn't been in touch for a while. She drops off sometimes, and no one hears from her. And then all of a sudden, she'll be in a new city with a new job and everything's fine." Simone placed her hands on the table and said, "Enough about me. Seriously. I'm bored with me. Let's talk about you. For instance…what was your first paid acting job?"

Evie didn't even take a second to think about it. "It was for a commercial. I was twenty-four and right out of university. My parents had tried to convince me for years to do anything else, and I thought this would be the moment my career took off and they finally saw that I could make a living from acting." Evie's laugh bubbled out.

"Do you remember the cash man? That guy who used to buy gold for cash? I was one of his backup dancers." She stopped talking for a moment, trying to breathe through her laughter. When she could focus again, she said, "When the ad came out, it was so bad I didn't even tell my parents about the job. Luckily it's only ever appeared in the middle of the night or during infomercials. But for years, every once in a while I'd see it come on, and there I am in the back doing high kicks with four other girls in leather miniskirts."

"Is that the guy who ended every sentence with 'Oh, yeah'?"

Evie nodded, unable to speak she was laughing so hard. "Impressive, right? Can you imagine if anyone ever finds out it was me? The potential shit storm of that thing going viral used to keep me awake at night."

"But not any more?"

Evie shrugged. "It's embarrassing, sure. And if my greatest credit to date was Handmaid on The Handmaid's Tail, then I'd probably still be worried about it. But now that I'm on the other side," she shook her head, "I don't know. Sometimes I miss the scrounging. Everyone hates auditioning. It's the worst part of acting. You're basically on a nonstop rejection high for weeks, and then suddenly you'll get some rando part where most of the time nobody knows it's you because you're either dressed like an alien or wearing hoods or wigs or whatever. But you get to know the other actors. You have company in your misery, and now I feel like I'm missing out on something. Which is stupid. I made it." She threw her arms out, indicating the restaurant. "The cheapest thing on this menu is the Caesar salad for thirty-two bucks. It's literally a charred romaine heart with some sauce dribbled over it and a crouton on top, and the price doesn't faze me. I feel like it should, you know?"

"You like the craft, not the fame. I get it. I'm not famous, nor have I ever wished to be, except maybe when I was six, when I wanted to be a fairy princess. Not everyone has wings and a tiara. That might have made me famous." She smiled and looped a strand of hair behind her ear. "I can't imagine what it's like to go into a grocery store and have half the customers almost maul me because they think I owe them my autograph."

Evie had almost forgotten about that incident. Instead, she remembered sitting on the patio watching Simone and really seeing her for the first time and how beautiful she was. It was her kindness that had gotten her out of not one, but two bad situations that night. “The moral of that story is that I should never travel, unless you’re with me.”

Simone quirked an eyebrow. “If it’s somewhere warm, I can get behind this idea.”

“I’d love to go somewhere warm with you. Hell, I’d love to be…” Evie stopped because she didn’t want to finish that sentence and sound sex-crazed. “Let’s just say I had big plans for tonight. But as it is, I don’t even get to sleep in my bed.”

“I would invite you over to my place, but the couch is full with Gabriel, and when I invite you into my bed, it will be when I can take full advantage. And I don’t want my brother sleeping on the couch in the other room when I do.”

Evie rested her elbows on the table and leaned forward. “We have similar goals. I haven’t been able to think straight since Thanksgiving. I have this fantasy—”

“Have you had a chance to look at our menu?”

Evie looked up. Stephanie stood at the end of the table, waiting, a polite smile spread across her lips.

“Can you give us another moment, please?” Simone asked. They both waited until she left. Simone rolled her finger. “Keep going. I want to hear about this fantasy you have.”

“Let’s just say, I cannot wait to get you alone.”

CHAPTER TWENTY-ONE

Monday morning, ten minutes before the table read, Simone was in her office going over a few notes she'd made. She wanted to be there to see how a few of the scenes would play out and talk with Cameron about one issue in particular.

She hadn't seen Evie since their date, but they had been texting with increasing frequency. She had just gotten a message a few minutes ago and had to place her phone on the other side of her desk. She was hot and bothered, and beyond frustrated. Their plans to get together that weekend had been thwarted not only by Gabriel, but Shane as well. Gabriel had shown up on her doorstep almost a week ago and refused to leave. He'd cancelled going to B.C. with Marissa for Thanksgiving because their mother had talked him into staying at home for the holiday. How she'd managed that, even Simone didn't know. And now, Marissa wasn't speaking to him, and he was depressed. He'd taken leave from work and refused to move off her couch. So this weekend she'd held a mini intervention and took him out to cheer him up and managed to get him to go home and try to patch things up with Marissa.

Then on Sunday, Shane had an emergency that Simone still wasn't clear on, so they hadn't had a chance to do any of the things they'd been texting about. But she desperately wanted to.

She had picked up her phone, ready to text her response, when the door opened, and Evie rushed in, panting, closing and locking it behind her. She was in a low-cut top, which would have given Simone, and anyone else within eyeshot, a good show, but she pulled it up, almost on reflex.

"Did you run all the way up here?"

Evie nodded, checking her watch. "I have only seven minutes until I have to be at the table read. But I wanted to see you. This texting back and forth is killing me." She ventured closer. She laughed at herself, heaving a huge breath and twisting her hair, which fell in soft waves around her shoulders. "Whew. That is a workout. I need to up my cardio game if I'm going to do that more often."

Simone stood, meeting Evie on the other side of her desk. "More often, hmm?"

Evie looked around. "It's quiet up here. One of the perks of having an office on the twenty-seventh floor."

"We're on the fourth floor, fifth at the most."

"Semantics. It's private." Evie moved closer, pressing Simone up against her desk. "And did I mention quiet?" She laid a gentle kiss on Simone's neck.

Before Simone had time to overthink her response, she pulled Evie in for a searing kiss, which left her light-headed and out of breath. Things escalated quickly, and before she knew it, Evie had Simone up on the desk, her legs spread so she could settle in between them. Evie's hands moved up her legs, pulling the hem of her dress up as they went, her thumbs running circles on her inner thighs as she did. Simone's hips began moving with the rhythm. God, she wanted those hands everywhere. Evie's mouth was on hers, and she'd never felt like this before. Never met anyone who could set her skin on fire.

When Evie's thumbs reached the seam of her thong, Simone pulled back. "This would be much more comfortable in a bed."

Evie rested her forehead against Simone's. "Logistics. Would you like to come over tonight? I know it's a school night and all, but Shane has promised me he'll be working late, and not at our place."

Simone grinned. "I'd like that."

"I can't promise dinner. But I know the entertainment will be right up your alley."

Simone tilted her head to the side. "Was that a double entendre?"

Evie took a minute to think about it and then laughed. "I hadn't meant it to be."

Simone shooed her out of her office, taking a good five minutes to compose herself before heading down the stairs herself. She wasn't sure she could survive tonight, but then again, she knew she wouldn't make it to the weekend without finally breaking the tension between them.

When Simone entered the conference room for the table read, there was a hush over the room. She met Evie's eyes and knew immediately that something wasn't right.

Cameron waved when he noticed her. "Ah, Simone. Great to have you join us." She was handed a script by an assistant at the door. Looking down, she could tell there had been revisions. "You're just in time to meet our newest cast member. This is Jake Ackers. He'll be playing the new neighbour."

Simone walked over and shook Jake's hand. He looked like he'd stepped out of an Old Spice commercial. Handsome, yet rugged, he had just enough swagger and smarm to turn Simone off completely.

"This is Simone Lavoie, our intimacy coordinator on the show. You'll probably be working with her a lot next season." Simone took a seat in the back along the wall.

Only the actors and director sat at the table. She flipped through the script, trying to gauge what had changed. Not much of the original script seemed to be left. They were introducing Jake as the neighbour who moved in after Charlotte's character was killed. God, why did people watch this stuff? But then, she couldn't take the higher ground on this one. She'd binged the entire first season the moment she found out she had the job. That first episode had her hooked from the opening scene. Perhaps it had something to do with it involving Evie, front and centre, in a string bikini.

"All right. Let's get started." Scott Bloomgren was directing this episode, his first since the location shoot.

Simone leaned back to watch. It was always interesting to sit in on a table read. This was her fourth for the show, and she loved how some of the actors really got into their role, acting it out. A few would read the lines with very little inflection, which kind of spoiled it if you were to ask Simone.

Evie always dove into her part. Though they were two different people, Evie transformed into Abby Bruce the way clouds morphed into pictures. She embodied Abby. Simone became excited to see what she would do next, which role she would take on because she had that spirit, that quality that allowed her to step inside a role and become that person. Not many actors had that skill level to make acting appear effortless.

"Ah, fuck. Sorry. That was my line." Ian flipped a few pages into the script and read his line. Simone watched him go through the process of becoming Colton Jefferies. Usually he came across as confident and composed, but today he appeared jittery and quiet. Perhaps he worried what this new hire meant for his job. If Jake was going to be working with Simone a lot next season, he was most likely the new love interest. That put Ian's job on the line.

Had Jess said something to Cameron? Were they letting Ian go because they'd discovered that he was in fact trading roles for sex? Cameron sat opposite Simone, his focus on his phone, the script unopened on his lap. It would be the easiest way to avoid a scandal—let him go quietly, and the problem disappears. Except the culture for it to happen again still existed. And that would never change unless these things were made public and got people talking about them. Awareness was the start. The #metoo movement might have highlighted a lot of the toxic practices within the industry, but without positive change to go with the new awareness, people would just continue as they had, closing their eyes to the abuse.

Simone didn't have any solutions. It was an uphill battle.

❖

"Were you—did you know he was hiring someone new?" Ian found Evie in her dressing room after the table read getting ready for a wardrobe fitting. He sat down on her couch, and then, as if he couldn't stay still, stood and began pacing the room.

She grabbed Ian's arm and pulled him to a stop so he would look at her. "You have a contract for two more years. You have no reason to suspect they're writing you off the show. It's possible you might both be my love interests next season. Abby does have a rather rapacious sexual drive. I imagine she could keep up with the two of you."

"Charlotte had a two-year contract as well, and look where she is. I know she didn't leave because her mom is sick. Her mom died a few years ago."

"How do you know that?"

"We worked together on a pilot that never got picked up, like a decade ago. Charlotte and I have been friends for years."

"So you're not dating her?"

"What? No. I'm dating Stephen."

"From makeup? The guy who you said was too much of a twink?"

"That was to throw you off. Worked, didn't it?" Ian got all dreamy for a second. "He does this thing with his tongue that I am on board for. Plus, we didn't want to make it seem weird because we work together, and there's always that power-dynamic bullshit that goes on when you're dating someone from work, even if we do belong to different departments."

"So you didn't have anything to do with hiring Charlotte?"

"No. It was a total surprise. She just showed up on set one day. I mean, not that I wouldn't hire her. Charlotte's a great actress."

On impulse, she threw her arms around Ian's neck and squeezed until he gasped. "I can't breathe." She pulled back, still grinning. "What was that for? Were you hoping for Stephen and me that hard?"

Evie shook her head. "It means I was right, and everyone else is wrong."

Ian took a seat on Evie's couch, crossing his legs. "Okay. You're going to have to explain that one a little better."

Evie flopped down next to him. "Oh, where to begin?" She filled Ian in on everything she knew. About someone trading sex for parts, about the fight Simone saw outside of Charlotte's dressing room.

"Wait. That's what they're basing this whole thing on? That I had a fight with Charlotte outside her dressing room? Of course. I was pissed she was leaving the show and couldn't give me a good reason why. We talked for years about landing a show like this, and now that she'd finally found it, she was leaving and was super cryptic about why."

"There was also the fact that the episode you directed was the one Charlotte was hired for, and it was only meant to be a bit part and then all of a sudden bloomed into a supporting role."

"I have no say in that. The writers made that call. And besides, I didn't hire her. Like I said, she just showed up one day. In fact, originally her part had gone to another actress."

"Huh. So she was replaced last-minute, and then all of a sudden her role becomes much more. Who hired her?"

Ian shook his head. He seemed much more relaxed now. "I assumed it was one of the producers. She'd mentioned that the woman who was supposed to do it dropped out, and she was friends with someone on the show."

"But she never said who?"

"Nope."

Evie bit her lip. They were back to Charlotte. She was the key with all the answers. Or however that metaphor went.

"This could really blow up in our faces. If this gets out, what kind of impact will that have on the show?"

Evie leaned back on the couch. Ian was right. A ticking time bomb was waiting to explode.

❖

An early afternoon thunderstorm had cut the power to the studio, and they'd sent everyone home early. This was a windfall for Evie because it meant she could go home and get ready for Simone's arrival. Was it strange that she was nervous? Because she was. And she had no reason to be. On her way home she'd had enough time to stop at Shane's restaurant and get some back-alley takeout so at least she would have something to feed Simone.

Maybe her mom was right. She should learn to cook. Here she was living with an amazing chef, and she hadn't picked up a goddamned thing from him. That wasn't true. She could make a mean egg scramble, although that seemed low-bar and hardly something you would offer a guest for dinner. The morning after, perhaps? Well, at least she had fifty percent of the date covered.

She'd placed the entire dinner in the oven—not the fridge—as Shane had instructed. She'd showered, changed into something that was comfortable, stylish, and didn't scream that she'd stood in front of her closet for half an hour worrying about what to wear. I mean, she had, but she didn't have to announce that fact with her outfit. Now she was outside on the rooftop patio setting up the heater the previous tenant had left behind. It just needed a new propane tank.

They had such a great view of the park and the lake it was a shame they could use the space only a short time of the year. Plus, it didn't matter what the weather, Evie's favourite thing about the patio was the hot tub. It had a trellis overhead with vines that provided a fair amount of privacy in the summer. Less so in the colder months, but it wasn't like she was throwing wild nudist parties or anything.

She had lit the last candle when the buzzer on her phone rang, announcing she had a guest. Her stomach instantly somersaulted.

She met Simone at the door, still buzzing with excitement. And as soon as Simone stepped into the loft, Evie's mind went blank. She'd changed from what she wore earlier. Instead of the tight knit red sweater she had on at work, she wore a low-cut, wrap-around dress. The dark blue really set off her eyes, leaving Evie stunned into silence.

As she took Simone's coat she asked, "Can I get you some wine?"

"Anything red, if you have it?"

"I live with Shane. We have an entire closet of wine."

Simone stepped close and took Evie's waist, pulling her near. "But first, you look beautiful. I don't know how you can work a whole day, be up since five, and still be as luminous as you are."

Evie melted. "Me? You're the stunner in this relationship." She paused and bit her lip. They hadn't yet defined what they were. To hide her discomfort, she turned to get them each a glass of wine. She'd selected a nice pinot noir from a vineyard in Prince Edward County that she and Shane had toured last summer, before her life exploded. Not that she wasn't enjoying some of the perks that came with it.

Simone stood at the floor-to-ceiling window looking out over the lake.

"The view is even better upstairs."

Simone turned, taking the wine, and quirked an eyebrow. "Your bedroom? I'm sure the view is spectacular."

"Give me some credit. I have a whole seduction plan going on." She tilted her head toward the stairway leading up.

Once outside, Simone caught her breath. The flickering candles around the seating area and fairy lights stringing the arbour above the hot tub made it seem like they'd stepped into another place, as if they were on a tropical island somewhere in Hawaii instead of Toronto in October.

"It gets chilly, but that's why we have the heat lamps and this." Evie picked up a tiny remote and pointed it at the seating area. Flames burst through the centre of what had looked like a table but was actually a modern-looking outdoor fire pit.

"Impressive." Simone turned to Evie and clinked her glass with hers. "You really do know how to seduce a girl."

Evie glowed. "Well, I don't think seduction was the main ploy here. It was more of a wooing thing." Evie set her glass down on the table. "I picked up some things from Shane's restaurant if you're hungry."

Simone placed her glass of wine next to Evie's. "I'm suddenly not hungry for food."

Chapter Twenty-two

Simone spent all day every day thinking about all the ways she wanted to undress Evie. For whatever reason, she'd never imagined it as sweet as this. Evie had gone to a lot of trouble to set the scene, when really all she had to do was show up.

Evie wore a loose camisole and a light silk cardigan, and when Simone stepped close, she could see that Evie wasn't wearing a bra underneath the camisole. She ran her hands along Evie's shoulders, pushing off the cardigan and letting it fall to the ground. "Do you think the neighbours can see us?"

Evie grinned. "I'm sure a few could, if they crane their necks far enough out their windows. Do you care?"

"Not in the slightest." Simone leaned in, brushing her lips against Evie's, and the friction sent shocks down her spine. She backed Evie up until she reached the bench running alongside the hot tub and coaxed her down into a seated position. Evie ran her fingertips up Simone's legs, and for a second Simone stopped; the feel of Evie's hands did spectacular things. She was already so wet that if she let Evie continue, it wouldn't take long, and she wanted this to last. She'd waited long enough.

"No." Simone stilled Evie's hands. "It's my turn, only I don't plan to tease you tonight." Simone sank into the cushion next to Evie and kissed her neck. Then she kissed the bird tattoo below her ear and ran her hands along Evie's collarbone, her touch featherlight. Evie tilted her head back, leaning against Simone as she lifted the hem of her camisole. Her hand playing with the taut skin of her stomach, she skimmed her fingers up until she reached the underside of her breasts and then back down to the button of her jeans, which she unfastened with one flick of her finger.

Evie moaned as Simone's thumb brushed along the sensitive skin just above her panties. Simone repositioned herself so that Evie fully leaned back on her. With one hand she began playing with the ever-so-soft skin under her breasts, while the other explored the area beneath the waistband of her panties.

Simone unzipped her jeans, giving herself access to the area she most wanted to explore. They both moaned when Simone discovered how wet Evie was. She slipped her fingers through her folds, and Evie's hips jerked.

She leaned down and peppered Evie's neck with soft kisses, rubbing the now-hard nipple with her thumb. Evie cried out. Her hips bucked, seeking, but Simone wasn't ready to let her go just yet. She wanted to play this out as long as possible.

Everything about this situation had her turned on. The sounds Evie was making as she found the right spots, the smell of her hair, the feel of her body pressed tight against her. If she wasn't careful, she might come from these stimuli alone.

As Simone worked her hard nipples with one hand, she slipped the other gently in and then out, brushing Evie's clit as she did. Simone kept it slow, even though Evie's hips told her she'd like it much faster. Simone loved this power, watching Evie writhe against her.

"Oh, God, don't stop," Evie said as Simone found a particularly delicious spot. Simone's own hips were moving in rhythm with Evie. They were both so close now. "Harder," Evie whispered, and Simone obliged. They were both rocked forward as Evie came, gripping Simone's arm when she needed her to stop, her breathing erratic.

When she was finally able to, she turned and kissed Simone hard on the lips. "You are magical. I'm still fully dressed, and I think that's the hardest I've ever come."

Simone grinned. She was nowhere near done. "Less for your neighbours to talk about."

"Let them talk."

"Perhaps we should go in. I feel like we're both a little too dressed for the next portion of the evening."

Evie hooked a finger in the loop that kept Simone's dress wrapped tight around her body and pulled slowly. The knot came undone, and the dress fell open, exposing a black bra trimmed in delicate lace. Evie planted a kiss on each breast. "I guess we can make a quick scene change. Follow me."

Simone followed Evie down the stairs and around a corner to another set of stairs that led to Evie's bedroom. "Even better views up here."

Trailers lined the road leading up to Bluffers Park. Seven of them in total. The show was filming on the Scarborough Bluffs that morning, but Mother Nature had other plans. A storm front had blown in last minute, and everyone was scrambling to see if they could make it work.

Evie's heart skipped at the sound of a knock on her door. She hoped it was Simone, but it was Jess. She poked her head in. "We're still waiting to hear if we'll be filming this morning. Just sit tight." Evie nodded and picked her book up again. She was reading The Devil in the White City, the true account of H.H. Holmes, a serial killer who lured women to his fake hotel during Chicago's world fair. She'd read it a few years ago but had come back to it because it was such a suspenseful read.

Her phone buzzed, and again her heart did a tiny flip. "Ugh." It was just Shane sending a salacious gif with a quick question about how it had gone last night. She turned her phone over. She'd talk to him later, unable to bring herself to gossip about something so new. For whatever reason she didn't want to spoil it by sharing with Shane, even though they shared pretty much everything. The first time he'd had a threesome, he'd called her to complain that he was never doing that again. Or the time he'd had sex with a woman who screamed like she was being murdered with a chainsaw when she came.

They never talked about the good ones, though, and that gave Evie the warm fuzzies because it meant Simone was one of the good ones, and she really didn't want to ruin anything by blabbing about it to Shane.

The door swung open without any warning, and Simone stood there, her hair whipped into an adorable windblown look. She looked momentarily sad. "Damn. Thought I might catch you in a state of undress."

Evie leaned back on her couch. "No such luck. But I have some time to kill if you'd like to help with that wardrobe change. I have a feeling we're going to be here all day."

Simone smirked and closed the door behind her, locking it as she did. "Well, as it turns out, I'm very good at zippers and buttons." She waved her fingers. "I might be able to help." She sat down on the couch next to Evie and leaned in for a kiss, lifting Evie's T-shirt to expose a red, polka-dotted bra. Simone ran her thumb over Evie's nipple, which immediately stiffened.

The knock at the door stopped them. "No. Why?"

Simone stood and unlocked the door. Ian entered, looking equally windblown, although less adorable in Evie's eyes. "This is madness if they think we can shoot. I'm sorry, but I do not want to expose my bare ass to that wind."

They were meant to be filming a beach tryst today, only the lack of sun—which hadn't stopped production before, it was amazing how creative they could get with close-ups and establishing shots taken on a different day—and gale-force winds had different plans.

"Scott's out there negotiating with the writers and Cameron to see if we can't rework the scene to include the storm."

"Can't they just move on to something else?" asked Simone.

"Scott likes to shoot his studio shots first and then do locations, so all we have left are location shoots, and all our permits are set for each day. If we scrap, we lose a whole day and will have to add it at the end somewhere, which means overtime for everyone and lots more money."

"So it's cheaper to wait it out and see if the storm passes than scrap the whole day," explained Evie.

She had shared with Simone that Ian hadn't hired Charlotte, nor had they been dating. They had decided that Jess should know as soon as possible so they could discover who had hired Charlotte.

Ian took a seat on the chair at Evie's makeup table. "I came to invite you both to my Halloween party Saturday night. Costumes aren't mandatory, but I strongly encourage them."

Simone looked between them. "I…don't have anything to wear as a costume. What are you going as?"

"The Roman emperor Diocletian, known for his persecution of Christians and some other stuff that was too boring to read or remember. It means I get to wear a chest plate and carry a sword."

"And this excites you?"

"Beyond measure. Every year I wear the same thing but go as a different emperor. Luckily there were so many I'll never run out. Last year I went as Caligula."

"And next year you'll go as Nero?"

Ian shook his head and scrunched up his face. "Have you ever seen a statue of Nero? Looks a little too much like Mark Zuckerberg for my liking. Creepy little pale dude. He always has this expression like he's trying to replicate human emotions."

Evie laughed. "We'd love to come. I'll see what I can dig out of my closet. Who's Stephen going as?"

Ian grinned. "My horse."

Evie spoke her line again, this time a little louder. The wind whipped around the giant umbrella they'd placed in the sand, but at least it was preventing her hair from strangling her.

"We're going to have to ADR all this."

Evie knew Ian was right. They'd decided to go through with the shoot. They'd set up blockers off camera to keep the wind at bay on the sides and then a giant umbrella behind them. At this rate, they could've faked it in the studio by bringing in some sand. For the amount of work they'd have to do to clean up the scenes and make them usable, it wasn't worth it, in Evie's opinion. But then again, she wasn't the director, so she wasn't able to make that call.

Scott broke for a reset, and they all scrambled for their trailers. Evie saw Cameron leave video village for the catering tent and decided to follow him. Maybe she'd get a chance to plead her case again. Even if he'd asked for patience, hers was quickly running out. She could direct better than half the directors he'd had on this season so far.

They were alone in the tent, which Evie was thankful for. She didn't need an audience for her grovelling. Not that she planned to. She wanted to be stealthy and slip in her ideas for making days like this work. Maybe then he would see that she could handle taking the reins.

He smiled when he saw her. "Some day we're having, isn't it?"

Evie nodded and grabbed a paper cup from the dispenser. "I feel like any second I'm going to get blown into the lake."

"Sadly, nothing we can do about the weather."

"True. Although at this point you can't even tell we're at the Bluffs. We could've located back to the studio and faked it with lighting and establishing shots. As it is, we're going to have to spend a few hours next week ADRing most of the dialogue." Evie shut her mouth tight, thinking she'd gone too far. It was one thing to know you were right, but not necessarily a good idea to shove that opinion in your boss's face. If she were a man, would she have that same qualm? Doubtful. She'd say what she thought and damn the consequences.

Instead of being angry, Cameron laughed. "Of course you're right. Scott is one of the most stubborn guys I know. If he sets his sights on shooting on the beach, he's damn well going to shoot on the beach, even in a hurricane."

And that's when Evie realized she'd never be good enough in Cameron's eyes to direct. He wasn't using reason to pick directors. It was the same good-ole-boys' club she and every other woman who wanted to break into directing were up against. It didn't matter how much they said it had changed. The statistics told the real story.

She decided to broach another subject before she took one of the forks on the fruit tray and stabbed him in the eye. Although, in hindsight, she didn't pick a much happier topic. "Shame about Charlotte."

"It truly is. I never thought when I brought her on that she would flame out so quick."

Evie paused at the bagel station. Did he just say what she thought he said? "Oh. I thought Ian hired her when he was casting for his episode."

Cameron shook his head as he poured heaping amounts of sugar into his cup. "The girl they'd hired was too mopey. Didn't have the right look." Cameron stirred his coffee, throwing the stir stick at the garbage and missing. "She will be missed," he said, walking out and leaving Evie alone in the tent.

A new gust buffeted the side of the tent, sending a stack of coffee cups toppling over onto the ground. Things had just gotten a little messier.

"This is all just massive speculation. How do we even know Charlotte was involved in this scandal in the first place? We're assuming that because she lied about why she was leaving the show, she must be involved." Jess shoved her hair back into its bun, taming the chaos with a small elastic.

"Well, there is the part where she was hired on as a glorified extra and then ended up with a much bigger part," said Evie. She,

Simone, and Jess were all jammed into Evie's trailer waiting for the next scene to be set up. The fact that they were still going along with this farce of a shooting day had Evie madder than she'd ever been, and she was ready to have heads roll.

"Are you telling me that Charlotte as an actress doesn't warrant a bigger part? Or that this never happens? Come on, guys. We're grasping. Charlotte probably has nothing to do with any of this."

After a knock on the door, Ian popped his head in. "It's just me." He was laden with snacks—bags of chips, croissants. He placed them on the dressing table and began pulling bananas and apples out of his pocket. "Don't worry. I didn't forget about you, Evie." He tossed her an apple. "Where are we at?"

"Jess thinks we're in Wonderland and that Charlotte has nothing to do with this."

"Maybe she doesn't, but I think Cameron's our guy. I bumped into Scott in the craft-services tent, and he said there's a standing rule that Cameron has final casting say. He can override any of your decisions. So I asked if he'd ever had that happen to him, and he said on this episode there's a woman he hired to play the store associate in the second act. Cameron replaced his hire with one of his own. Scott said it came out of nowhere."

"What's her name?" asked Simone.

Ian shrugged. "Leah, I think."

"Okay, but Cameron's the executive producer. Of course he has final casting say. That's pretty standard practice." Jess grabbed a bag of chips and ripped it open. "This is the second show I've worked on with him, and I've never seen anything suspicious." She crunched down on a chip. "I'm not saying it's not him. I'm only saying we need to be damn sure before we do anything about it."

"And what are we planning to do about this if we do find out?" asked Ian. "I mean, if we go to the press, what's going to happen to the show? The news could possibly tank it. And that's a lot of lost jobs for a lot of people."

"We can't just let him get away with it."

"I'm not suggesting we do, Evie. I'm just asking what our plan is."

They all looked to Jess, who had somehow become the de-facto leader of whatever this had become. She finished chewing the chips she'd stuffed into her mouth and said, "Right now, we're just collecting information. We need to find out who this hire is and, also, if any of the other directors have had similar experiences. We also need to keep this quiet. I don't want it getting out before we know more. Look what happened with Will. He now thinks Ian is trading sex for parts."

"Or he's trying to throw the scent off himself," said Ian.

"How would that work? He's never directed an episode."

"Easy. He grabs the ear of a director, asks for a favour. It happens all the time. This business was built on nepotism."

Someone knocked on the door. "Miss Harper, they're ready for you on the beach."

"Yay," she said unenthusiastically. "Time to get more sand up my lady bits."

Chapter Twenty-three

"Well, hello, titties." Shane whistled as Evie came down the stairs wearing a red-sequined dress with a slit that ran the length of her right leg.

She peered down at the ample display and readjusted her bodice. "It's a risk. The last person who wore this was probably closer to a B cup." Her red hair had been toned down and hung in soft, silky waves around her shoulders. As she slipped on elbow-length, dark velvet gloves, she asked, "Too much?"

"I guess it depends on a few things. Are you trying to make people faint when they see you? Or is it swooning you're going for?"

She struck a pose, turning to reveal that the dress was backless. "You don't know how hard it is being a woman looking the way I do," she said in her best Kathleen Turner voice.

Shane pinched her cheek like a grandma would. "Well, look at you, squashing eons of feminism just to impress a girl."

"I'm not bad. I'm just drawn that way. Ugh. Am I trying too hard? I almost went as Poison Ivy, but it's freezing out, and at least this way I get gloves and can wear a nice long coat. Plus, it isn't as uncomfortable as last year's costume."

"Nobody asked you to go as the Babylon Prostitute. No one told you to wear a corset that cinched your waist until you looked like a pencil—"

"Fuck the corset. It was the wig that did me in. The wires in it kept digging into my scalp."

"Think about how Marie Antoinette felt. She had to live in that thing."

"I'm sure they were more comfortable back then. They probably cost the price of a small country."

"Which is why they cut off her head, I guess. Spending too much on wigs and not enough on bread for the people."

"Yes. Let's blame the entire French Revolution on the woman. Not the inept king or any of his ancestors who spent fortunes on hookers and palaces and silk stockings."

"Fair point." Shane took a seat on the bar stool, readjusting his housecoat.

"It's weird that you're not working. You always work Halloween."

"Yes, well. That's why I asked for it off. I'm fucking exhausted." He let his head sink to the counter. "I can't do both my catering and my job. It's killing me. Or drinking me dry from the inside. I feel like I have this energy-sucking parasite inside me making me do all these things so it can eat my energy. It's horrible. I've started having weird dreams about it. Apparently in one I named it Fred."

Evie began to take the seat next to him, realized she'd never make it up onto the stool with her dress, and instead just leaned against the counter. "Wow. That's disturbing on several levels. Didn't you once tell me your mom used to name all the spiders in the house Fred? That way they never seemed to die. It was always the same spider. And if that's true, then somehow you've turned every spider in this place into an energy-sucking parasite, which terrifies me. I'm not going to live here any longer if it's true."

"No. All the spiders were named Frank. But that does give me pause. And I do have one question. How are you ever going to sit down in the car?"

Evie smiled sheepishly and began pulling up the dress. "You just have to bunch it up a bit. It's not noticeable if you're wearing a jacket."

"You girls and your fashion. Speaking of girls, I'm assuming you're doing all this for Simone?"

Evie couldn't help herself. At the mention of Simone, her face split into an Earth-shattering grin.

"I'm going to take that as a yes."

"She'll be here soon, and we're heading over together."

Shane waggled his eyebrows. "I see things are progressing. Are you falling nicely, or have you—"

"Too soon. Don't jinx it. I like her. A lot. And I'm worried that it's all going to disappear if I talk about it too much."

"Well, then we'll just ignore the elephant in the room. Where are you two ladies heading?"

"Ian's. And Ian, of course, being Ian, lives far away."

"Describe far."

Evie scrunched up her face, aware of her prejudice of the east end. "East of Yonge."

Shane threw up his hands in an overly dramatic gesture. "Oh my God. How will you manage to travel such a vast distance? Shall I get you luggage? Will you need a change of clothes to go those horrible ten blocks east of here?"

"It's farther than ten blocks, and you know it. It's like as soon as you have to cross Yonge, the Lyft is double the price and triple the time of anywhere in the west end."

"Why are you friends with him? Doesn't he know the east end is where the lepers live?"

As soon as the elevator opened, Simone's heart hit her throat. This was such an unusual reaction for her. She saw Evie every day. Well, most days. She couldn't understand why now she was getting butterflies.

Because this was different.

They were going to a party. Together. They were announcing to everyone who was there that they were a couple, even if they hadn't defined what that meant themselves. What surprised Simone the most? It didn't faze her in the least. It should. They were taking a step toward being serious that Simone hadn't taken in years, if ever. And she was being so cavalier. While other people were free to make their own choices, she'd never felt she was. Gabriel had told her a few years back that he didn't plan to put his life on hold because he was waiting to know whether he'd become schizophrenic like their dad. He had absolutely no choice in the matter. He couldn't do anything to prevent it, only treat it if he did get it, so he intended to live his life as if he weren't aware of the chances.

Mani seemed to be doing the same thing, or perhaps all her travelling was a coping mechanism as well. Running from herself. Once Simone knew, once she got through her mid-thirties, it would be less likely that she had it, and that would give her peace of mind. But she wasn't in the clear yet.

She stopped at the door and adjusted her wig. She'd decided to go as Cleopatra, which was a simple-enough costume to do last-minute. When Ian had mentioned he was dressing as a Roman emperor, she'd thought, what's better than that? An Egyptian pharaoh.

She wore a white, slinky dress, with eyes that would've made Elizabeth Taylor sit up and pay attention. She chose a simple black wig, more in line with Claudette Colbert's portrayal of the famous pharaoh, and carried a stunning sceptre that Jill from the prop department had helped her make.

Shane opened the door wearing a ratty bathrobe. "Wow. You look stunning. The two of you are going to make beautiful babies someday."

"That's not how that works," Evie yelled from somewhere in the apartment.

Shane looked thoughtfully at Simone. "No. But it should."

When Evie stepped around the corner, Simone's breath caught. For a whole second she couldn't breathe, immediately reacting to Evie and everything she'd put on display. "I thought you were going as a rabbit."

"I said I was going as Jessica Rabbit." Evie struck a pose, showing off the slit in her dress.

"From Who Framed Roger Rabbit. She's his wife. It's a sight gag in the movie too," said Shane. "Personally, I think it's a little cold to put the girls on display like that."

"Well, nobody asked you, Shane. They're my breasts, and I can share them with the world as I see fit."

Shane kissed her cheek. "You're right. I will leave you now. Go spread joy." He picked up a tablet from the counter and a mug of steaming tea and walked to his bedroom.

Evie checked the clock on her phone before slipping it into a slim, black clutch. "I arranged for a car service I use for events. I hope that's okay."

"You look…" Simone shook her head, unable to put what she was thinking into words. "You look like Christmas morning and a chocolate sundae all in one."

Evie pulled a long, black felt coat from a hidden closet near the front door. "I'm guessing those are both good things in your mind."

"Two of my favourite things, yes." Simone stepped closer and, taking advantage, stole a better look at the cleavage on display, which had her thinking maybe they could arrange a detour before hitting the party.

Evie lifted Simone's chin. "I see where your mind is going. We will have plenty of time for that later." She kissed her softly on the lips, careful not to mar either of their lipsticks. "I have so many plans for you."

"Enjoying the view?" Out on the balcony for some air, Simone had the perfect vantage point from which to observe the party. She hadn't been able to take her eyes off Evie all night. That dress should be illegal. No, it wasn't the dress. It was the way Evie filled it out. The fabric hugged every curve like it was painted on. The back, which was nonexistent, dipped so low that, if it went any lower, this would be a very different kind of party. And every now and then, when Evie turned to talk to someone else, the slit would open, revealing a long, slender leg that had Simone's imagination going full tilt.

So when Ian came up next to her and asked if she was enjoying the view, she had only one answer: "Best view in the city." That view was also why she was out on the balcony wearing next to nothing herself at the end of October. It was a great alternative to a cold shower. The fantasy currently running through her head, and she had several, was to find a dark corner for her and Evie and to take advantage of the revealing nature of that dress. She took a deep breath. The cold air felt good on her skin.

"It is pretty great." Ian handed her a drink that looked like it had a severed head sitting at the bottom. "They called it evil-dead punch. It's only a little boozy. I had them halve the alcohol content." He looked back at the rowdy party. "Just in case."

They both turned toward the city. The vista alone had probably added a million to the apartment. Behind them lay a straight, unencumbered panorama of the lake and the city stretched out like a game board. Unlike the condos flanking the lake, where having purchased a lake-view one year didn't necessarily mean you'd keep it, this building had no competition.

"It's not really mine. I'm just renting. Who knows how long a show will run? I've got a contract for another year." He shrugged. "And then? The love interests rarely last on these shows. Evie, though, she's got the world laid before her. All she has to do is not screw it up."

Simone nodded, not exactly sure if he was talking about her or some other pitfall.

The wind pulled at Ian's leather flaps. The getup certainly was flattering. Ian had the type of body that most people, not her, would drool over. Tall, dark, and muscly.

"Enjoy this. It never lasts." Ian took a sip of his drink, which Simone noticed wasn't the evil-dead punch. It looked like scotch or something else strong, straight, and on the rocks. "I mean, you always go in hoping, but after a decade or two, you know that everything has a shelf life." He finished off his drink and set the glass on a table next to the railing.

"You're not talking about the show, are you?"

Ian looked back over his shoulder. Stephen, from makeup, was dressed like Cupid and heavily flirting with a poor imitation of He-Man. Evie had mentioned they were dating, but perhaps not anymore. She wasn't sure she should mention anything, but then Ian spoke up. "Apparently we weren't exclusive. Which is fine, I guess." He leaned back on the rail, crossing his arms, which made his muscles flex in an almost comical way. "As soon as he said it, I realized I'm too old for that shit. I don't want to play games and fuck around. I want honest, down-to-Earth, no fuckery fucking. And now I'm not sure if I'm depressed because I thought we had something or because I realized I'm forty-two and have become what I never thought I would."

Simone watched Stephen pull his Cupid arrow and pretend to shoot He-Man. He looked like a caricature of a gay man pretending he didn't give a shit about anything yet was having the time of his life. But every minute or so, he looked around the room, as if searching for someone. "Did you tell him you wanted to be exclusive?"

"No. I just told him…" Ian shrugged again. "Whatever. I can't deal with the drama these days."

"Maybe he thought that's what you wanted. And when you reacted like you didn't care, he got hurt. Sometimes people act like they don't care when they're feeling upset. It's a coping mechanism. If they can pretend they don't care long enough, maybe it will come true. You should go over there and tell him how you feel before he has a chance to regret anything."

"You know, I came out here to kind of play the friend, where I tell you not to break my friend's heart, and here you are giving me relationship advice."

Simone hadn't thought she was giving that kind of advice. Who was she to give that? She'd never been in a relationship that lasted longer than three months. "Please don't take what I say seriously. I'm just winging it like the rest of you."

"Oh, that doesn't sound good. That sounds like the introduction to a painful breakup."

Simone shook her head. "It's not that." How could she even explain? Or should she? She barely knew Ian, and she hadn't even told Evie about any of this, although somehow talking to Ian was easier, almost like a practice run. "It's not that I don't want to date… hmm, how should I put this?" Simone took a sip of her punch and almost gagged. The taste, even watered down, was strong. "My dad has schizophrenia, and so I've grown up seeing firsthand how that's affected my parents' relationship. It's hereditary, so I might have it as well. Usually, you'll see signs around early to mid-thirties for women, so I've kind of felt like a ticking time bomb my whole life. I guess I've just been waiting to see what happens, because the last thing I want to do is rope someone in to deal with how hard it can get.

"I remember some nights when my mom would sit up in the living room awake waiting, just in case he got up and tried to leave the house. The next day she would go to work exhausted and then come home and do it all again. That responsibility weighs on a person, and not in a good way. I didn't want to force someone into that type of obligation." Far below, a siren grew closer, and they watched an ambulance part traffic. "I'm most worried that I won't notice. That it'll creep up on me one day, but the psychosis will convince me it's real, and I'm terrified of that loss of control."

"Well, you've put my problems in perspective."

"This is the first time I've ever seriously wanted a relationship. It's the first time I've felt what my mom must feel for my dad. But I'm not the one who'll have to sacrifice."

"I don't think that's true. How many good relationships have you given up because of this? You need to tell Evie and let her make up her own mind. For one thing, it'll let you know how she really feels about you." Ian suddenly slapped Simone on the back. "Well, look at that. We both got the same relationship advice." He turned toward the street below and began singing the chorus of Spandau Ballet's Communication. "Communication let me down. And I'm left here." He turned to Simone. "No?"

"I don't think I've had enough alcohol for random singing."

Ian took her hand and led her back into the party. "We should fix that."

Simone's gaze once again found Evie, who was deep in conversation with a young blond woman Simone had never seen before. Ian was right. She needed to tell Evie and see what her thoughts were, because Simone was sure of one thing—she was falling, and it was only a matter of time before she would be too far gone to catch herself.

Chapter Twenty-four

Midnight was Evie's limit. Almost as soon as the hour changed and the night became tomorrow, she decided she couldn't wait any longer. She found Simone talking to someone from the costume department and sidled up behind her, whispering in her ear that they had more important things to discuss. She ran her hand along Simone's hip, enjoying the way she leaned back into her, accepting her touch.

When Simone turned, her eyes, with her lids low, conveyed her willingness to follow Evie anywhere.

They took Evie's car service back to Simone's place, the ride a prelude of things to come. Evie found it hard to keep her hands and lips off Simone, but somehow she managed and remained a respectful distance the entire ride.

The second they were in Simone's apartment with the door closed, Evie's reserve ended. They didn't even make it to the couch before Evie began removing Simone's coat, letting it drop to the floor where they stood. Next, she removed her headpiece, which she hung on the doorknob.

Simone's eyes were hooded and the most beautiful golden brown Evie had ever seen. As she pushed Simone against the door, her heart felt tight. She wanted to savour this moment. She wanted to memorize every freckle, the way Simone's lip curled at the end before she smiled fully, the way her hair hung over one eye, which she constantly flicked out of the way. The little gestures had Evie mesmerized.

Simone pushed Evie's jacket off her shoulders, and her gaze fell to the ample display of cleavage Evie had managed to achieve with her costume.

"I've been curious all night as to how you've been keeping this dress from falling." Simone reached for Evie, but Evie managed to evade her, laughing.

"A magician never reveals her secrets."

Simone wrapped her arm around Evie's waist and pulled her tight. Their bodies clashed, and Simone kissed her hard. Evie's lips parted, allowing Simone to deepen the kiss. The sensation swamped her senses, letting everything else disappear. She ran her hands the length of Simone's back, bringing with them the gauzy fabric of her costume. The entire night she'd watched Simone mingle, every movement sending the fabric swishing around her long, toned legs. It had been torture to watch. Now she got to touch, and she planned to take her time and explore.

Evie broke the kiss to pull Simone's costume over her head, revealing nothing more than a white lace bra and a matching thong. If Evie hadn't been wet before, she certainly was now. She stood back to admire the view, visually tracing Simone's body, from her long runner's legs to the small patch of fabric between her legs up her taut stomach and luscious breasts peeking out behind the lace of her bra.

Evie planted a kiss on each breast, then reached around and unclasped her bra. She kissed up Simone's neck back to her lips, where Simone captured her mouth.

Evie's heart, which had tightened at the thought of not being able to hold onto this moment, soared. Every emotion she had concerning Simone spilled out into that one kiss.

Simone pulled back, breathing in short bursts. "How does this contraption come off?"

"Maybe we should just leave it on?"

Simone shook her head. "As much fun as that might be, I've spent the entire night thinking about your body."

Evie gave a sideways smile and peeled the dress away from herself, revealing the secret to the dress's ability to stay on. She let it fall to the floor, revealing an intricate pattern of beige tape holding her breasts upright.

Simone laughed. "What have you done to your breasts?"

"The secret to this dress is massive amounts of boob tape. When I got dressed, I hadn't really thought about the end of the night. I mean, I hoped it would end with you, naked in bed. I just didn't consider that there might be some complications."

Simone ran her hand along the sides of Evie's breasts and underneath. It was like wearing a bra made of tape, and Evie knew it would be painful to remove. Simone circled her, presumably sizing up the problem. As she did, she glided her hands around Evie. Two pieces of tape above each butt cheek kept the dress from falling too low, and as a result, she hadn't worn underwear. Simone focused on those cheeks first, skimming her fingertips along the edge of Evie's ass, which sent tingles throughout her own body.

"If I'd known you weren't wearing underwear, I don't think we would've stayed at the party as long as we did." She ran her fingers along the inside of Evie's thigh, inching higher every second.

Evie's legs wobbled. She wasn't sure she could stand up for this. She also didn't want Simone to stop. So she stayed as still as possible, more aroused than she'd ever been.

"We'll have to combine a little pleasure with your pain," Simone said as she slid a finger up to feel the wetness between Evie's legs. At the same time, she ripped a piece of tape off her back. Evie moaned. No way would she be able to stand up much longer. Her legs already felt like Jello.

Simone grazed Evie's butt cheek with her fingernails. "Perhaps we should move this to the bed."

Evie nodded, unable to form a coherent sentence.

Simone pulled the covers back on her queen-sized bed and laid Evie in the middle. She climbed in and lay next to her, running her hands up and down the length of Evie's stomach, her muscles contracting. Simone planted a soft kiss below her left breast. She pulled at Eve's knee, spreading her legs apart, and began inching up her inner thigh, almost getting to the top and then starting all over again. As she reached the top of her legs, she dipped her fingers inside, quickly, and as she did, she tore a piece of tape off the underside of Evie's breast.

Simone licked the spot with her tongue and switched sides. As she briefly straddled Evie, she kissed her lips lightly.

Simone continued her slow climb, and each time she reached the top, she ripped a piece of tape off. Evie was panting hard before she was halfway done, aching in the best way possible. She bit her lip as Simone began circling her clit with the lightest touch imaginable. Evie's hips began to move in rhythm, and just when she was getting close, Simone jerked another piece off.

It revealed a nipple, which Simone immediately took into her mouth. Evie moaned, deep and throaty. She might not last until all the tape was gone. Her heart raced, and she felt like every inch of her could take off into space.

This time, Simone didn't switch sides. Her mouth stayed firm on Evie's nipple, and she began to apply pressure to Evie's clit. Her hips bucked as Simone ripped another piece of tape off. Evie put her hand on the back of Simone's head, her fingers entwining chestnut hair. Their rhythm well established now, Simone kept going, bringing Evie closer with every rip.

Evie gripped the bed sheet with her other hand. "Oh, God, Simone. Don't stop. I need…"

Evie came, hard, as the last piece of tape came off her breast.

"Well, hello, Sunshine." Shane checked his watch. The digital display rolled over from 11:59 to noon. "Or, should I say, good afternoon?"

Evie closed the door behind her. She still wore her Jessica Rabbit dress, although fully covered by a long, dark coat. Her hair, which had been perfectly styled the night before, was thrown into a messy bun, and her face looked fresh and clean. Gone was the sultry seductress. Now she looked like—minus the dress—she'd come in from a refreshing run around the park.

Without talking, Evie sauntered over to the coffee machine and poured herself a cup from the half-empty carafe. She took a sip and closed her eyes. "You make good coffee."

"Thank you. I spent four years in culinary school just for that."

"It was money and time well spent, my friend."

"Have a good night?"

Evie scrunched her face up. "Mostly good."

"What does that mean?"

"It means some of it was good." The parts that involved Simone were better than good and probably tipped the scale. "And some of it not so good."

"Which part do you want to talk about?"

Evie put her head on the counter and closed her eyes. When she thought of meeting the blonde named Leah at the party, her heart sank to her knees. "I met someone last night, the actress Cameron hired instead of the one Scott picked."

Shane crossed his legs and turned the stool he was sitting on toward Evie, his interest clear on his face. "Oh? I thought you'd already met someone. The someone you went to the party with."

"Not that kind of met someone." Evie lifted her head off the counter and took another sip of coffee. "This someone is a ticking time bomb."

"I didn't know humans could explode."

"This one can." Evie made her way around the counter and took the stool next to Shane. "Cameron hired this one for a bit part in our current episode, and reading between the lines of what she told me, she basically got the part because she had sex with him."

Shane's face rearranged itself into a surprised look.

"I mean, they say this stuff happens. And I know it does because I'm not new, except I thought we were getting past all this casting-couch bullshit. If it comes out, it could ruin the show, and now I don't know what to do. Should I tell Jess? There were rumours, or she overheard something and has been looking for who the possible person could be. I don't believe she thought it could be Cameron. Maybe one of the directors or producers. God. Should I tell her? Or just keep my mouth shut? If I don't say anything, that basically makes me complicit. I couldn't live with myself. What should I do?"

"You don't need my advice. You're having a perfectly wonderful conversation with yourself."

"No. I really do need you to tell me what to do."

"You've already made your decision. You need to let Jess know."

Evie paused to consider that remark, took a sip of coffee, then looked over at Shane, who was still in pyjamas.

"Hey. Why aren't you at work?"

Shane threw his hands at his cheeks and opened his mouth as if to silently scream. "I quit." He squealed a little. "I did it. I finally quit my job."

That remark physically threw Evie back a bit. Shane had been talking about quitting his job since he was hired there four years ago.

"Did you get another one?"

He shook his head, his hands still on his cheeks. Finally, he let his hands fall. "I'm going to try to make a go of my catering business. I have bookings for the next few weeks, and that always seems to lead to more bookings. I've been killing myself for months now trying to keep up with it all and do my own job."

Evie was silent. She was happy for Shane, because she knew how much it killed him to work the hours he did. And she didn't want to be the one to burst his dream bubble, but did it pay the bills?

Shane took her hand. "I know you want to ask without you even having to say anything. Of course I'll still be able to afford rent."

"Well, at least one of us will. If this all goes south, I'll probably be out of job soon too."

"Great. You can come work for me. I'll need good servers." He squeezed her hand and let go. "You know I'm just kidding, right? Your face is on half the billboards in the city. You have your choice of projects. You don't have anything to worry about. It's not like you're the one who's trading sex for parts. Tell Jess what you know, and you won't be complicit."

Chapter Twenty-five

For once, Evie wasn't early to the table read. She was becoming late, in fact. She had decided to take Shane's advice, which, as he pointed out, was really her own advice, to tell Jess what she knew. And she should definitely do this. However, in the abstract, the idea of someone on the show trading parts for sex didn't mean much. The reality of it scared the shit out of her.

Jess hadn't mentioned what she planned to do once she found the person. What if she went to the press and all this disappeared? Evie hadn't slept much last night thinking about it. She could bitch and moan about the perils of suddenly being thrust into the limelight all she wanted. But truthfully, she'd worked her ass off for years to get here. She didn't want someone else taking that away from her.

Everything was spiralling out of control, and she wasn't sure how to stop it. So here she was searching out Jess instead of showing up early to the table read.

When Evie finally made it, everyone was already there, and it put the spotlight on her late arrival. The only other person not there yet was Cameron, which was good, because she didn't know if she could look him in the face.

She took a seat next to Ian and flipped open her script to the first page. He pushed a coffee over to her, and smiled, then leaned over and whispered, "Did you get distracted by a certain intimacy coordinator?"

Evie smiled to herself and took a sip of the coffee. She hadn't seen Simone yet, and almost as if thinking about her summoned her, Simone walked into the room with her purse slung over her shoulder and a notepad under her arm.

"Sorry I'm late." She took a seat on the opposite wall. Her lip curled at the edge when she spotted Evie.

Evie's breasts began to ache at the sight of Simone. Her clit throbbed in response, and she crossed her legs and pulled her bottom lip in, biting hard to find her equilibrium. If this was the response she got from one look? She was in deeper shit than she'd thought.

Michael, who sat at the head of the table, pulled his script out and flopped it onto the table. "All right. Let's get started. We have some new storylines to go over today. You all know Jake, our newest cast member."

Jake waved from his seat at the table. He'd been introduced in the last episode as a single father who'd moved in next door. It was obvious they were setting him up to be the love interest for next year. It didn't mean that Ian would be going anywhere necessarily, just that Abby Bruce's life was about to get a lot more complicated.

Evie frowned as she reached the beginning of the second act. She'd read the script the night before, but for some reason it hadn't really sunk in how much Abby was willing to take on.

"Is something wrong, Ms. Harper?"

Evie looked up at Michael. "It's just, there's a hell of a lot of flirting for a woman who technically has a husband and a boyfriend." She shook her head because she knew that was the character. Abby Bruce was not incredibly likeable on most days. But as Entertainment Weekly had put it, Evie's portrayal brought vulnerability to the role and made you want to root for her, even if you didn't always like her. "I guess I'm just shaking my head at her lady-sized balls."

The room laughed.

"That's what makes for good television," said Michael. He flipped to the next page, moving the process along.

Evie actually enjoyed playing Abby because the two of them were so different. It gave her insight into the girls she went to high school with. Everyone always seemed so put together, so brazen, so feminine. And Evie had never felt any of those things. She identified as a woman, and she definitely fit the bill of feminine, but that was all surface. On the inside she was still a tomboy role-playing to fit in.

And none of those girls had figured it out. Everyone was just role-playing as well. It was hard, though, to change years of feeling inadequate. Not until she'd gotten to university and met Shane had she really started to feel like being herself was okay.

Acting for her was always a way to pretend she was normal, but she was good at it, and she didn't want to ruin this situation. She loved her job. Who wouldn't?

They continued through the script. Jake was turning out to be funny. She could see why they'd added him. Ian's character was very sombre and a little dark. He played into that tall, dark, and handsome fantasy. For Jake's character, Evan supplied some much-needed levity. Evie also liked the energy he brought to the table read. The cast had gotten into the habit of going all in when reading, even playing up the scene a bit, making it a lot more fun. Occasionally they'd have someone come in to read who brought the whole thing down by just delivering their lines as if they were in casting.

Near the end, Cameron came into the room and stood to the side. He seemed distracted, looking at his phone every few minutes.

Even now, Evie found it hard to believe that he was taking advantage of women the way he was. He played up the doting father and loving husband well and appeared to be happily married. Then again, maybe he was. Some people were able to turn that part of themselves off when they came to work. Maybe he and his wife had an arrangement. It really wasn't Evie's business. But using his power to take advantage of women disgusted her.

She'd had her fair share of encounters over the years and had been lucky enough to sidestep them and walk away from a role if she felt uncomfortable. But she also recognized her privilege. Many people weren't able to say no for whatever reason. And that's why it was so wrong.

Last night when they'd talked at the party, Leah, the actress who'd gotten the role by sleeping with Cameron, hadn't seemed like this was any different than other gigs she'd done. She probably even thought this was normal in some bizarre way. Or she didn't care. Maybe she felt like she was getting something out of it. But for every Leah, hundreds of others didn't think such behaviour was okay and went along with it because they didn't feel they had any other choice.

As much as she loved this show, she couldn't let Cameron get away with this. She had to speak up and say something.

As the table read came to an end, Cameron stepped forward. "Before you all leave, I wanted to announce that we have a slight change in who will be directing the last episode of the season. Originally Scott was, but he has a conflict with an upcoming project." He stepped forward and grinned as if this were one of the most exciting things he got to share with his people. "I'm happy to say that after much campaigning, Evie Harper is going to be the director of the last episode. She's done some amazing work over the hiatus that's getting a lot of recognition at the festivals, and we're happy to have her." He walked over to a stunned Evie and shook her hand. Leaning forward, he whispered, "Congrats. You deserve this."

After the table read, Evie didn't seek out Jess to tell her. Instead, she climbed the stairs to Simone's office, unsure whether to confide in her either. She needed to get her bearings. When she reached the top, she stopped and looked down through the middle of the winding steps all the way to the bottom. It was a long way to fall. Her career seemed to have hit this high, and one wrong move could send her down the stairway, where she'd inevitably land on her ass.

Whatever her plan, it had to be good. It had to be solid and well thought out. Clearly Cameron knew she knew about Leah. She wasn't sure how that conversation had occurred, but she could find no other explanation for why he was letting her direct the season finale.

Morally she knew what she had to do. She had to turn him down. She had to say no. Tell Jess what she knew and watch where the shit landed.

Evie knocked and entered.

Simone stood up from her desk, clearly excited. "Congratulations. This is what you've been working for." Evie smiled, but she didn't feel happy. "You're not thrilled? I thought you wanted this."

"I do." She thought about it for a moment. She wasn't happy because she didn't feel like she'd earned this. It was a bribe to keep her quiet. But she had another reason. "Part of me is worried that I want it for the wrong reason."

"You said you love directing."

Evie wanted to be seen as more than just a pretty face, especially when it didn't feel like that image reflected who she truly was.

"Why can't you have both?" asked Simone. "Why do you have to choose just one thing you love? The world isn't made up of people who are just one thing."

"I know I can do both. It's just I feel like people have put me in this bubble."

Simone took her hands. "It's you who has put yourself in a bubble. Who cares what other people think? You have to decide your own way and fuck everyone else. If you want to quit acting, you can. If you want to take a break and focus on directing, who says you can't. You have this idea of what people want from you, but what do you want from yourself?"

Evie took a step back and sat in one of the chairs in front of Simone's desk. She'd never thought of it that way before. She'd worked hard on her acting career because she believed she had to act while she still looked young and beautiful, but who said that was the kind of acting she loved? Abby Bruce's ugliness, the messiness, had drawn her to this character. If she stuck with pretty-woman parts, she'd spend the next five or ten years doing work she probably didn't like.

But she didn't have to do that.

This was like a revelation. She could choose not to act for a while and focus on something else she loved. She'd been so worried that the parts she wanted wouldn't be there when she wanted to come back. But that wasn't necessarily true. She'd weathered more than a decade of working crappy jobs in order to make it in this industry. Why did she suddenly think she couldn't handle tough?

"You're right," she told Simone. "I just need to get over my shit."

"That's good advice for everyone, really."

Evie slipped out of Simone's office shortly after. As she stood outside Simone's door, she realized she had another solution. Why did she have to turn Cameron down? It wasn't her fault he couldn't keep his dick in his pants. She could still accept the job and tell Jess what she knew. It was up to Jess to do what she wanted with that information.

Women were always taking this high road, which ended up hurting them in the end. Nothing bad ever really happened to the men in these stories. For all she knew, Cameron would go on to create another show, and in two years no one would give a shit that he had the morals of a baked potato.

The warmth had left the city. November barrelled in like an unwanted guest planning to overstay their welcome. Simone stared at her phone. Her opinionated and overbearing mother had officially stopped speaking to her. This fact hurt more than she'd thought it would. She kept expecting a sense of relief to wash over her, but it never came. Instead, she felt sad, angry, and guilty.

At least her mother was also not speaking to Gabriel. She'd just gotten off the phone with him, and things had gotten worse after Marissa had taken him back. They were united in their defiance. Simone had taken Gabriel's side and moved to a different province, so naturally she was enemy number one. Gabriel was in love with someone their mother didn't approve of, which turned out to be slightly less of a crime than living in another province.

She dropped her phone onto the couch and went into the bathroom to run a bath. As hot water filled the tub, she poured herself a glass of wine from an open bottle in the kitchen. Her only desire, now that winter had arrived, was to hibernate.

Evie had been away for the last two days on a location shoot, one that didn't need an intimacy coordinator. It surprised Simone how much she missed Evie, a new feeling for her. No one had stayed around long enough for Simone to ever miss anyone before. It felt nice, because it came with the bonus of anticipation for Evie's return.

Just as she stepped into the bath, her phone beeped, and Simone's heart skipped a beat, thinking it might be Evie. Instead, it was Shane.

He'd texted: What are you up to, RN?

Simone hated texting. She pressed the call icon instead of returning his text. When he answered, she said, "What do you need?"

He laughed. "You Frenchies are all the same. Straight to the point. You got me. Do you have time to help me out with some prep for a bar mitzvah I'm catering? I can pay you in wine and gossip."

Simone gazed down at the bath she'd run. It looked much more inviting than chopping vegetables for hours on end. Then again, chopping vegetables with Shane might take away some of her loneliness.

"Okay, but you also owe me a favour, and it better be good gossip."

"Deal."

❖

"Don't you have people to help you with stuff like this? Like employees?"

Shane put down his knife and sighed. "It looks bad, doesn't it? That I'm asking my roommate's girlfriend for help." He scrunched up his face. "Did I make the wrong decision? Should I have stayed working for a lunatic in a place that charges twenty dollars for something that is essentially skinny fries with salt?"

"Well, that sounds like he's ripping people off, so no. You definitely shouldn't have stayed there."

"A lot of places are like that. The high-end ones have horrible hours and usually shady assholes running the place. You stay for the cooks. Your friends. Because misery loves company."

Shane had transformed his kitchen into an assembly line, with stations for several different dish preps. Right now, Simone sliced red peppers. She wasn't sure what the final plan for them was, only that they had to be little centimetre cubes.

"To actually answer your question, I did have someone lined up for tonight, but he had to work an extra shift. So I was left high and dry. I don't have enough work to offer someone full-time yet, so all I can do is get part-time people. It means I'm not a priority. You were the only person I could think of—"

"Who wouldn't be doing anything on a Friday night?"

"Exactly." He smiled his big goofy grin, which she could tell had gotten him out of a lot of trouble over the years.

"Don't you ever feel like you're missing out on a social life? Evie tells me you don't even really date or go out anymore. You work. And then you quit your job so you could…" She pointed her knife at the spread before them. "Work some more."

"This is different though. I'm finally working for myself. It's all worth it when it's for yourself."

Simone raised an eyebrow. "Still looks like work to me. Are you getting paid more than you were before?"

"Not yet."

"You should take a break and just relax a little. When was the last time you actually went on a vacation?"

"A what? A vacation? What's that? It sounds like it might be fun. And expensive." He laughed and peeled the skin off a cod fillet. "In all seriousness, it's a lot of work, but this is my dream job. I've wanted to be my own boss when it came to cheffing for—for fucking ever. And here I am," he waved his knife—which looked like it cost more than several of Simone's more expensive handbags combined—around. "It's funny how Evie and I are getting our shots at the same time."

"Your shots?" Simone's English was flawless, but she noticed a few phrases, usually when she was around Shane, she didn't understand.

"Evie getting to direct. She's going to knock their socks off."

"Is she feeling better about it? She seemed conflicted earlier."

Shane set the knife aside and turned to Simone. "What an asshole, huh? I'm glad she went for it anyway. Fuck Cameron and his stupid fucking bribes."

"Bribes?"

"You know, with the whole Leah thing. About how she met the girl he gave a part to in the last episode at Ian's party, and now, all of a sudden, Cameron is letting her direct?"

Simone turned back to what she was doing and nodded. Evie hadn't said anything about any of this. Understandably. This was, she wasn't sure what it was, but it didn't sound good. Why hadn't Evie told her she'd found proof that Cameron had traded roles for sex? Because she'd gotten what she wanted from it. In Simone's eyes, that made her complicit. No, it made her worse than Cameron because she knew how wrong this was, and she was willing to just set aside her morals to go for what she wanted.

She was suddenly very angry. Evie had every opportunity to tell her about Leah, but she'd kept that information to herself. Well, she'd told Shane, which also hurt. And now she had her opportunity to direct as long as she kept her mouth shut, and instead of doing the right thing, she'd chosen herself.

A low vibration began moving across the floor at her feet. Simone's hand was shaking when she set down the knife. She didn't recognize the number.

"Hello?" She paused as she listened, growing alarm bells ringing in her head. "Is she okay? Where is this?" She turned to Shane as she hung up the phone, unsure of what to tell him. "I have to go."

"Of course. You've been amazing. Is everything okay?"

Simone nodded because she didn't know what else to say. In the span of five minutes her world order had crumbled. And at that particular moment, the least of her worries was that Evelyn Harper, the woman she was falling in love with, was not the person she thought she was.

CHAPTER TWENTY-SIX

Simone arrived first. The red flashing on one of the monitors and the tubes snaking out of her sister Mani's mouth struck Simone like she'd jumped into a pond of ice-cold water. She stood at the door forever watching the machines work to keep her sister alive.

Mani had chopped her hair short recently, or maybe not recently. They hadn't seen each other in over two years. Mani liked her hair long, always had. Braided or thrown up was easier to manage, she said. Sometime in the last year she'd gotten a pixie cut, and Simone couldn't tell if it suited her.

Dark-purple bruises covered the left side of her face, and a bandage wrapped around her ear. Both her right arm and leg were in a cast, everything white and sterile. Simone couldn't imagine what she must have looked like when they found her.

Mani had taken a job as a safety officer three hours north of Toronto, and while the details weren't yet clear as to what had happened, she had been in an accident, and they'd rushed her by helicopter to St. Mike's in Toronto.

Simone found something very familiar and unsettling about the accident that she couldn't wrap her head around. A nurse moved past her into the room.

"Are you family?" she asked. Her dark-purple scrubs were paired with lime-green Crocs, and her ID badge hanging around her neck said her name was Celia.

"I'm her sister."

Celia's warm smile filled the room. "She's lucky she had family close." She fussed around Mani, making sure none of her tubes or lines were crossed, noting the readings that were displayed on the monitor next to her bed. "Have a seat. The doctor should be in shortly."

"What's wrong with her? Do they know how this happened?"

Celia shook her head. "I don't think anyone's sure. She fell into something, maybe a vat, and wasn't found until morning because it was after hours." She stepped closer and placed a calming hand on Simone's shoulder. "She's getting the best medical care possible. And you're here now to give her the support she needs. The rest is up to fate."

This sentiment didn't comfort Simone. Fate had not been kind to their family over the years. Something told her that this scene had played out before. The fear that had gripped her earlier was wrapping its steely fingers around her heart and squeezing until it was hard to breathe.

Instinctively she reached for her phone, wanting to call Evie, but stopped when she remembered what Shane had told her. Could Evie really be happy to benefit from Cameron's situation? It didn't matter. She couldn't call Evie. She was alone in this situation.

Simone edged her chair closer and took ahold of Mani's rough, callused hand. Once it had been soft, unblemished by life. When they were kids and the weather was nice, they would head over to the river that ran behind the town. Where they lived the water was rough and fast, rushing over sharp rocks, but if they walked a few kilometres south, the river slowed and became flat and calm.

A tree that leaned over the river made a perfect spot to jump from. On Saturdays, they packed a lunch in their backpacks and walked through the forest until they came to the tree and spent the afternoon swimming and leaping into the river.

But that memory didn't seem real now. How could something so idyllic exist in this world with machines that breathed for you? How could this even be real?

One particular afternoon, when Simone was around ten and Mani was thirteen, they'd discovered a giant Styrofoam raft on the bank of the river, and Mani insisted they ride it down the river. Gabriel was too scared to get on, so it was just Simone and Mani.

What felt like two hours later, they hit a patch of particularly rough water and had to ditch. When they made it to land, they were scraped and bruised and soaking wet, several kilometres from home. Mani hadn't been deterred. She'd gotten them up a hill and through someone's backyard, where she knocked on the glass window and asked to use the phone.

They'd suffered the belt for that. Swift punishment from their dad. Yet Mani was ready to go back the next weekend. Nothing ever fazed her. She was ready for the next adventure. Perhaps that's why she moved around so much. She got bored easily and was always looking for that new adrenaline rush.

Simone always envied her sister for her bravery. Gabriel always wanted to be safe. He would join their adventures only until a certain point, and then he would bow out, too afraid to follow them farther. Simone, like the middle child she was, always played both sides. Certainly safer than Mani, especially when it came to her heart, she hadn't chosen the traditional route that Gabriel had.

Gabriel wanted only a good job that paid enough to raise a family, and Marissa seemed like the perfect person to fulfill that dream. Simone had never looked past her current job. She refused to consider the future, afraid it might hold something very different than what she wanted. So in that way, she was more like Gabriel—playing it safe her whole life. And after recent events, maybe that wasn't such a bad idea. If she'd followed her original instinct and not gotten involved with Evie, she wouldn't feel so shitty right now.

Simone put her head down on the bed and closed her eyes, still holding tight to Mani's hand. The rhythmic sound of a machine breathing lulled her to sleep.

❖

Simone woke to the sound of her mother's heavily accented English. When she lifted her head, the room was empty save for the machines and Mani, still alive thanks to their steady rhythm. Her mother's angry voice drifted down the hallway.

Simone yawned and stretched, groaning as the stiffness in her neck shot pain down her left arm. Sleeping hunched over a hospital bed hadn't been a great idea, but she hadn't wanted to leave Mani alone in a strange city. Mani wasn't a big-city girl. She'd always preferred out-of-the-way places where everyone knew each other–the opposite of how Simone felt. Simone loved the anonymity that big cities gave her. She felt more alone in a small town, where everyone knew your business, than in a crowd, where no one knew who she was. She could lose herself in a crowd, which felt more like home than her parents' house.

A nurse slipped in, a different one from the night before, this one much older. She had that no-nonsense, I'm-here-to-help-but-only-if-you-listen-to-me quality. She smiled at Simone as she checked Mani's bandages. "She's doing better today. We may be able to take her breathing tubes out, which will make it all look a lot less scary."

Simone nodded. The doctor had come in around eleven the night before, still dressed in scrubs from another surgery. Mani's right leg had shattered below the knee and was now held together with several pins along the tibia. It would take months, if not years, to get full use back. Her right arm had fared better. The fracture was clean, and they were able to set it without any problems. She'd also had internal bleeding, and they were watching for brain swelling, unsure if she'd hit her head in the fall. The bottom of her left ear had been neatly sliced off, from either the fall or something that had happened before.

They had a lot of questions only Mani could answer.

They still had no more word from where she worked about how the accident had happened, but they were reviewing security footage to see if they could find out who had attacked her.

Simone wasn't so sure it had been an attack. Last night, as she slept, she'd had a dream about a similar hospital room and remembered why this seemed so familiar. When she was thirteen, her dad had been in an accident. His accident. That's what they'd called it from the day it happened. But it hadn't been one. Her dad had tried to kill himself by jumping off the bridge across the river that ran behind their village. Where it crossed, the river was shallow, with large rocks jutting out. He'd managed to miss most of the big rocks and survived with two broken legs.

It had taken six months for him to begin walking again. He never returned to work, and from then on, their mom and his sister did everything for him.

Had Mani jumped into that vat herself? Would she have to move home and have their mom look after her the rest of her life? As much as she took issue with how her mom dealt with things sometimes, she didn't wish that on anyone. What kind of a life was that for someone? To care for your loved ones as if they were invalids. This brain disorder had ravaged their family, leaving everyone numb.

Simone felt numb only when she thought of her father. She wasn't even sure sometimes if she loved him, and that hurt more than thinking that this might happen to her someday, that she might hurt her loved ones the same way.

Her dad had an old chair in their living room so worn it showed the indentation from his ass even when he wasn't sitting in it. All he did, every day, was sit in that room and read magazines, books, anthologies. Every week her mom would come home from the library with a new stack for him to go through. Only reading would calm the voices. Words had become his obsession—hundreds of thousands of words all to focus his brain on something other than the voices telling him that aliens had infiltrated society and were picking people off one at a time.

Whenever someone died, he would look over at Simone with this knowing expression, like they were exchanging a secret. As if he were saying, see? They got another one.

❖

"How is she?" Gabriel entered the room and swooped Simone up in a huge hug. He held on tight as Marissa stood at the door, watching. Her blond hair pulled back into a messy ponytail, which had been slapped on top of her head. She had an overnight duffel in one hand, which she set at her feet, and a coat hanging over her arm. Both looked like they'd left in a hurry.

"They think she'll be okay. She hasn't woken up yet, but they're confident that she will." Simone pulled back to look at Gabriel. His bloodshot eyes and unshaven face made him look scraggly. "No guarantees though."

He bit his lip, as if about to say something but changed his mind. He looked down at Mani, who was still asleep, as she had been since the night before. Gabriel probably had all the same questions she did. Was this a real accident? Or had one of them finally started exhibiting symptoms?

"We don't know anything yet," said Simone. "This might not have anything to do with…" Gabriel's hard look stopped her.

"She hasn't been communicating with us for months. You said so yourself. She cut herself off, and that's what scares me the most, because she's probably been going through this alone."

They stopped talking and turned as Genevieve Lavoie stood at the doorway, watching them. Marissa moved aside to give her room to enter. She was an imposing figure, even at five two. Simone remembered getting caught taking a twenty out of her mom's purse when she was younger. She had that same air about her now, like she could make herself taller and more imposing just by remaining quiet. She sucked up all the air in the room with her anger. Only this time, Simone wasn't so sure she was angry. She couldn't tell what her mom was feeling.

She walked over to Mani's bedside and took her hand, then leaned over and whispered something in her ear. And that's when Simone realized what her mom was probably feeling. Resignation. She'd spent decades looking after their father. It was exhausting.

No one ever mentioned it, but she could tell her mom in some ways resented that she'd given up a lot so she could tend to her husband all these years. And now, here was her eldest daughter possibly facing a similar situation. And if, like her father, she refused to take medication, her life would be difficult. Genevieve sat down, still holding Mani's hand. As she sat, she sighed.

"She will get better," she said in French, a refrain she kept repeating. Simone took a seat opposite on the other side of the bed, and Gabriel and Marissa pulled up chairs facing the bed. They sat and waited for Mani to wake up.

Simone's phone buzzed. She slipped it out of her pocket to see a text from Evie. Without responding, she pushed it back in. She would deal with Evie later.

Simone stood at a row of vending machines, deciding if she could handle more chips or if she should go down to the food court. Gabriel and Marissa, on a tip from one of the nurses, had discovered the best food court was across the street at the Eaton Centre. They'd tried to get her to come with them several times, but Simone refused to leave Mani, as had her mother.

The two of them sat across from each other, not saying anything, waiting. It had been three days since Mani was admitted, and she still hadn't woken up. Simone's phone buzzed again. She didn't even bother looking. It would be Evie, wondering why she suddenly had stopped communicating.

Simone had invested all her energy in watching over Mani. She didn't have the mental capacity to deal with both her and Evie, which she feared she was now over. But none of that really mattered. Not when Mani was here.

"You should get that. It might be important." Genevieve stopped next to Simone, still conversing in French. She had refused to speak anything else since she'd arrived in Ontario, a province she loathed.

"It's not," Simone answered in English.

"Don't you have a job?"

"They don't need me this week." Simone had called Jess earlier and let her know what was happening. Jess was happy to give her the time off. She seemed tense and distracted, so Simone didn't talk long. "How's Dad doing?"

"We agreed it would be better if he didn't come. Your aunt's staying with him."

Everywhere she looked, the sterility of the hospital stared back. The atmosphere was meant to be calm, reassuring, and she should feel comforted that Mani was in a state-of-the-art facility instead of in a small one north of the city. Instead, the white invaded her senses, causing a headache that hadn't left since she'd arrived.

Simone slipped some toonies into the machine and chose a Diet Pepsi. Maybe the caffeine would help.

"You can't survive on soft drinks forever. Let me take you for some real food," her mother said. "It will be good for us to get out of the hospital."

Simone quirked an eyebrow. This was new: her mom offering to venture out into an Ontario city voluntarily. "Will you survive?" Simone was teasing.

"Bah. Grab our coats. It's cold."

Outside, the air was crisp, biting into Simone's skin. She pulled at her scarf, which was only a flimsy thing made of silk, and wrapped it tighter around her neck, tucking it into the front of her jacket. Her mother, of course, had come prepared. It was most likely ten degrees colder back home, so she had a heavy wool toque and cowl that matched her bulky winter coat. Completing the outfit were two dark red mitts, which she pulled on, clapping them together, a move Simone remembered from her childhood.

"Where shall we go?"

Simone shrugged. "I live in the west and work in the east end. I haven't explored this part of the city." They both stared at the busy traffic crawling along King Street.

The sky was a dark charcoal, and if you'd asked Simone what time it was, she wouldn't be able to say whether it was morning or evening. King was almost always busy, especially along this stretch. The end of the side street they ventured down emptied onto Dundas Square. With the open space and people milling about, it always looked like a party. They were in the heart of the city, and Simone once again marvelled at her mom's nonplussed attitude.

When they turned into the main square, and she saw the seductive and mischievous eyes of Evie staring back at her from a life-size billboard, she grew rigid and stopped in the middle of the street to stare until her mother nudged her.

"That's the show you work for, isn't it?"

Simone didn't answer. Instead, she chose a street at random and steered them right past the throngs of people milling about. As soon as she could, she guided them down a small side street, which brought them to a quaint area with small restaurants. As she turned the corner, her phone began to ring. She reached in and switched it to silence.

"Avoidance doesn't solve anything."

Simone's whole life could be summed up with that one word: avoidance. How long had she avoided life in general? "No, it doesn't, but if feels good at the time."

"That's what's wrong with your generation. You push everything until the future, hoping it will go away. It just comes back and, in my experience, worse than it was before." She nodded toward Simone's phone. "Who are you avoiding?"

Who wasn't she avoiding? That was a better question.

"Who is she?"

"Someone from work. It's not important." Everything felt so heavy, like she'd crawled under a blanket of snow, and it was starting to melt. She was finding it hard to focus on anything except being there waiting for Mani to wake up. That's the one thing she could do right now.

"Did I ever tell you about your Aunt Lilly?"

Simone shook her head. This was all new. She'd never even known she had an Aunt Lilly.

"Lilly was my older sister by two years. When she was seventeen she fell in love with a man from California. He was in Montreal for business, and we'd been in the city shopping for the afternoon. To say she fell in love doesn't explain it enough. She became infatuated with him. He asked her to marry him, and she agreed. What we both didn't realize at the time, or think about, because we were young girls, was that as soon as they were married, he took her off to California, and I never saw her again."

Simone stopped walking. "What happened?"

Her mother heaved her shoulders in a sigh. "She died giving birth a year after she was married. We never saw the child or heard from her husband again."

"Is that why you don't want Gabriel marrying Marissa?" Her mother started walking away, but Simone grabbed her arm. "You're afraid she'll take him to Vancouver, and you'll never see him again? Maman, you know that isn't going to happen. It's irrational."

"Life is irrational. I want Gabriel to be happy. How can he be happy with her?"

"Have you seen the two of them together? He was miserable when he couldn't spend Thanksgiving with her, when he thought he'd lost her. He isn't Lilly. First of all, because he's not going to die in childbirth, and second, because he's Gabriel. He loves you, and he isn't going to run away to Vancouver. His whole life is in Quebec, as is Marissa's. She has a job, friends, a life. They have no plans to leave all that. And you'd know that if you did something other than look after Dad. For once, put someone else first."

Her mother's eyes turned sad. "If I don't look after him…" She took a moment and continued walking. "If it's so unimportant. If she's so unimportant, how come she hasn't stopped trying to get ahold of you for three days? Unimportant people give up after a few tries."

Simone didn't press further. She knew the limits of her mother's patience.

Chapter Twenty-seven

Evie put the phone down on the counter in her trailer. She didn't even know why she was bothering anymore. Simone hadn't responded to a single message in two weeks. She also hadn't shown up to set or contacted Shane in that time.

Jess had mentioned there'd been a family emergency. In light of that information, Evie should've been willing to give Simone the time she needed. But something felt off. Something was wrong. If this only had to do with a family emergency, Simone would've contacted her to tell her she was out of town and that she'd be back. They would've been in communication. This was different. Simone had decided to shut Evie out of her life for whatever reason, and Evie deserved to know why. This hadn't been some fling, some one-night stand. She'd fallen in love with this woman, and now she was being excluded like none of that mattered. The not-knowing was killing her.

Here she was standing in a bra and tight jeans—her costume for this next scene—feeling vulnerable and uncomfortable about the upcoming scene, and their intimacy coordinator was nowhere to be found. She hadn't realized how much she'd relied on Simone's steady and comforting presence this season.

She jumped at the knock on her trailer door and reached for a dressing gown. "Come in."

Jess entered, a tablet tucked under one arm, some script sides under the other. "I hate to do this to you last minute, but they've made some changes to the script."

Evie groaned and accepted the sides. She flipped through the two pages and frowned. "What's going on here?"

Jess widened her eyes and then pulled out her phone and opened it to Instagram. "Looks like Jake had a change of heart. This was posted this morning, and he hasn't shown up to set."

Evie took the phone. It showed Jake lounging poolside in Puerto Vallarta with the caption, "On the set of my new project."

"Legal is going to crucify him."

Jess shook her head. "I just talked to Cameron. He was let out of his contract."

"What? Why?"

Jess leaned against the wall and tucked a stray curl behind her ear. "I think he knew something about Cameron's extracurricular activities. I talked to a couple of people, and it turns out Cameron was the one who hired Jake and pushed this storyline to the writers. I vaguely remember that but didn't give it much thought because this was back when I suspected Ian of being the one who was trading parts for sex." She folded her arms over her tablet and pursed her lips.

"So if Jake blackmailed his way into this part, which was essentially written for him, why is he in Mexico?"

Jess nodded. "Exactly. What does he know that we don't?"

Evie had shared her Leah encounter with Jess the next day. Jess had told her not to talk to anyone about it and that she would handle it. That was two weeks ago. Next week they started shooting the episode she was directing.

She was going through that weird experience she'd felt in Estonia, a combination of exhaustion and exhilaration. It didn't matter that she was tired. She was too excited to care. Next week she got to show everyone what she could do, and regardless of what happened to Cameron, she would still have this under her belt.

Evie suspected Jess had a plan in her back pocket that she wasn't sharing with anyone. After informing Jess about Leah, Evie had assumed her part in the whole ordeal was done. This new information told her maybe it wasn't. Something was about to happen, and both she and Jess were no longer in front of the information train. Somehow they'd ended up riding in the rear, and it was giving her heart palpitations. If only she could get ahold of Simone. She needed to talk to someone she trusted fully.

"Have you heard from Simone?" Evie asked.

"Just that her sister was in an accident and she's pretty much been living at St. Mike's."

"She's still in Toronto? I thought she went home to Quebec."

Jess shrugged, oblivious to the pain Evie had gone through for the past two weeks. "Maybe she went home. Originally she was in Toronto."

Which meant she was probably still in Toronto. Why would they transfer her sister from Toronto, a world-class health centre, to a small town in Quebec? Which meant Simone had been in the same city for two weeks and hadn't bothered to respond to any of the messages or texts Evie had left.

What happened? Evie had no idea. She'd gone away on a location shoot, and when she'd come back Simone was gone and had stopped talking to her. It had more to do than her sister being sick. Simone suddenly wanted nothing to do with Evie, and she was at a loss as to why. Her heart ached at the thought that Simone was going through this alone.

Evie took a seat on the couch in her trailer, remembering a few great moments she'd shared with Simone on the couch.

"What do we do now?" she asked. "I mean, do we try to talk to Jake, find out what he knows?"

"No. Whatever Jake knows will come out eventually, and there's really no way to be sure when that bomb is going to drop. Our best move is to be prepared for anything."

"It'll come out eventually that we knew something and didn't do anything."

Jess sat next to Evie on the couch. "Not true. The second you knew it was Cameron and could confirm it, you came to me. You voiced your concerns with production, and that's all you have to worry about. The rest is up to me." She patted Evie's knee, which wasn't very comforting, as it was awkward. "Keep going. We still have a show to produce, and now that you're at the head of it—"

"I'm directing this episode only because Cameron thought he could buy my silence."

"And he couldn't. You did the right thing."

Jess could say it, Shane could say it, but it didn't make it true. Evie still felt like she'd misstepped somewhere.

Jess stood. "They need you back in wardrobe. We still have a whole day of shooting ahead of us." Possibly the longest of Evie's life.

"What do you mean, she's been in Toronto this whole time?" Shane stood at the condiment counter of his favourite street-meat vendor slopping mounds of sauerkraut onto a foot-long sausage.

"Exactly what I said."

"And she hasn't contacted you?"

"Hasn't contacted me? Shane, she's fucking ignoring me." Evie had declined a hot dog and settled for a diet ginger ale instead.

"That's so weird because she must've been with me when she got the call about her sister. She ran off totally freaked."

"Wait. When did you see her?"

"When you were on location. I called her over to help out with one of my catering gigs." Shane had the good sense to look embarrassed about having to call in another favour from her would-be girlfriend. Scratch that. Former would-be girlfriend.

"What did you guys talk about?"

He shrugged and shoved half his foot-long into his mouth, mumbling. "I don't know. The usual. I mentioned how proud I was that you were directing the last episode." He chewed and swallowed. "And then I mentioned what a shithead Cameron was to think he could buy you."

"Why would you say that? I hadn't even gotten a chance to tell her about Leah." Evie turned toward the street, mortified. "She probably thinks I took the deal, that I'm directing that episode only because I kept my mouth shut."

"Why would she think the absolute worst of you? And if she did jump to that conclusion, then she's not worth your fucking time."

It wasn't that simple. Not in Evie's eyes. Yes, she was hurt, a little devastated even that Simone had chosen to freeze her out instead of asking what had happened. But she also knew that Simone might not be thinking straight. How would she react if Wes or Lucas were in the hospital? She had no idea, so she couldn't judge Simone based on what she thought she'd do. Right now, more than anything, Evie wanted to be with her to help her through this bad time.

Her phone beeped, telling her she had forty-five minutes to get to the studio. "I have to go. A production meeting."

"On a Sunday. You never work Sundays."

Evie shrugged. "We start filming tomorrow. We still have a bunch of stuff to go over."

"Okay. Don't be too late. I'm making bulgogi tonight."

"What's the occasion?"

"My best friend is directing her first big-time show, and we're celebrating how awesome she is."

Evie leaned close and kissed him on the cheek. "If you weren't male…"

"And you weren't a lesbian."

She waved and headed for the nearest subway stop.

"Cut," Evie called from behind the camera, wearing tight capris, her stiletto heels lying on their side next to her. It was just past nine on her first day filming the last episode. Nothing had gone right that morning, but at least they were finally filming.

When they'd arrived early that morning there'd been no power on the block, so all they had was the minimal, thanks to a generator that had been installed earlier that year because this seemed to happen a lot.

An accident on the DVP had shut down the southbound lanes, meaning several crew members hadn't made it in, including a few from wardrobe and makeup. They were now running three hours behind schedule.

So Evie had decided to shoot a scene today that was meant for tomorrow because it used the same set with a slightly different arrangement, which was why she was directing looking like a socialite who'd come in from shopping with friends all afternoon.

Ian had the flu but had shown up anyway because he knew how important this was to her. She felt lucky to have such good friends surrounding her. And if it wasn't for Jess, she didn't know how sane she'd be at that moment. Jess didn't get enough credit for how much bullshit she had to deal with on a given day.

As the lead in the show, she didn't see most of the behind-the-scenes drama because she didn't have to deal with it. Now, as the director, she was aware of every little hiccup. Everything that could go wrong that morning had, but she was determined not to let it get to her. She had to rise above it all and do the best job she possibly could.

In bare feet, she strode over to Ian and Will, standing in the Bruces' living room. "Will, every time you cross over to your second mark, a shadow comes across your face. Why don't we move your second mark to the couch, have you sit down? That way you can reach over for your phone from there. It'll save us from having to fuss with the lights."

Will nodded. "Okay. Are we keeping the line the same?"

"Yes. You say your line about finding something on Abby's phone. Then move to your second mark."

"Would it make sense? He's agitated. Would he take a seat?"

Evie paused and looked up at the lights. Will was right. That didn't make sense beat-wise. Everyone was looking at her, waiting for her choice. She knew from her time in Estonia that a large part of directing concerned the little details that no one saw in the final product. A million decisions went into any production. The silence dragged out, filling the studio as everyone watched, waiting to see if she could do this job. Perhaps they weren't. Perhaps this was all in her mind. And what felt like twenty minutes was probably not more than thirty seconds, but the illusion of time freezing stuck with her. The moment she made her decision, the back doors of the studio burst open.

She turned to Will to say, "How about this? We reverse your marks." And as she did—as if it were happening in slow motion—two officers in uniform strode into the cavernous room straight toward Cameron, who was standing in video village.

One of the producers said, "This is a closed set. You can't be in here."

An officer pulled out a piece of paper and explained it was an arrest warrant for Cameron. He was being charged with three counts of sexual assault. After that, everything seemed to speed up as the crew standing next to him backed away, and the officers cuffed him. They led him off the soundstage. It took almost a full minute as everyone processed what had just happened before they began talking again.

Evie immediately found Jess. "We need to take control of this situation."

Jess waved Tom, the executive producer, over. "You're right."

"You knew this was going to happen?"

"I knew there was a possibility. After Jake left the show, I began asking around, very quietly, and found out that the police were investigating Cameron. Three women had come forward with allegations against him, and they were deciding if they had enough evidence to press charges. I didn't say anything because, for all I knew, they might decide not to. I'm not certain, but I think

Jake knew one of the women and was betting on them not pressing charges either."

"But you have a contingency plan?"

Jess smirked. "Don't I always?"

Turned out they had a press release all ready to go, stating that Tom would take over as show runner, and they would complete filming and post production of the show. As for the future of Social Queen, that depended on the fallout. They would finish and release the second season, but Jess didn't know if they would continue with someone else at the helm.

The waiting room was empty save for one gentleman, who'd fallen asleep and snored softly. This had become Simone's routine. At lunch she would take her sandwich, which she'd bring from home, and find a solitary spot in the waiting room, away from her family, to have some quiet time.

It also happened to be the one vantage point where she could look out onto Dundas Square. She would eat her sandwich while staring at Evie's billboard. It made her feel less lonely, almost like she was eating lunch with her. She missed Evie terribly but didn't know how to contact her now that she'd ignored her for so long.

The texts and phone calls had stopped two weeks ago, around the time that Cameron had been arrested, which was splashed all over the news and social media. No one was saying whether the show would go on for another season. Jess had been in touch to talk to her about what that meant, since a few days before everything exploded she'd signed a contract for another season. The whole time she'd wanted to ask Jess about Evie but didn't feel like she had any right. Her heart felt heavy just thinking about the situation. She had to let her go.

Mani had woken up the day before yesterday, and they'd learned that she'd had symptoms for months, carefully hidden from friends and especially her family. Mani had inherited what

Simone had dreaded almost her whole life. The one bit of good news in the whole thing was that her mother had finally started speaking to Marissa and accepting her. It was a high price to pay. They could only hope now that Mani would be willing to take medication.

She'd given notice to Estela and told her that she would pay out the rest of the year but likely wouldn't be staying much longer. Her mother wanted her to go back to Quebec in a few days when they took Mani home. And the thought of sticking around Toronto for no reason had her feeling even lonelier.

"Well, fancy meeting you here."

Simone looked up to see Shane standing over her with a small take-out box. He plopped down beside her and handed her the box. "Thought you could use some good food, so I made you a little something."

Simone took the offering. For some reason she didn't feel like she deserved his kindness.

"I heard you'd been pretty much living here."

"From who?"

"Word travels."

Simone set the container on her lap, unsure what to say.

"She misses you. She won't say it, but I can tell."

"She has every right to be mad."

Shane laughed. "Furious. She has every right to be furious. I finally had to take her phone away from her to stop her from calling and texting. I told her if Simone was willing to see the worst in her, then she wasn't worth her time."

Simone's breath caught. He was right, of course, but it hurt to hear it. "You're not wrong."

He nudged her with his shoulder. "I hope I am. I hope it was all a giant lapse in judgment on your part because you were going through something terrible." He pointed down the hall. "I can't imagine what it must feel like to watch your sister in a coma for weeks. It's terrifying. And I'm not going to compare that to watching my friend's heart break. It's not the same."

"It probably feels the same. And you have every right to be furious too. You both do." Simone shook her head, wiping a tear away. "I'm not even sure why I jumped to the conclusion that she would let Cameron get away with something so horrible all for the sake of ambition. I don't think I was thinking straight. Not really. My mind was on other things. I apparently didn't give it much more than a cursory thought." Simone looked out the window. Evie's smile peered back. "Do you think I can fix this?"

Shane leaned back and put his arm around Simone's shoulder. "This will take a grand gesture. Something big and splashy and romantic as fuck."

Chapter Twenty-eight

The wind caught the side of Evie's tightly wrapped "scarf," which felt more like gauze than something meant to keep your neck warm. She peeked around the corner. Hundreds, if not thousands, of people filled Nathan Phillips Square, milling about on this abnormally cold December day.

She hated this. Tom, who now ran the show, had talked her into it, explaining they needed to be present in the media in positive ways, to distant themselves from the whole Cameron affair. Since she was the only Toronto native in the main cast, they'd asked her to host the festivities at the Cavalcade of Lights. Now here she was, freezing her ass off, and it hadn't even begun. She'd be here almost until midnight, and sure, she wouldn't be outside the whole time, but she was dreading the next seven hours.

Evie was all ready for Christmas. She loved nothing more than putting up a tree and hanging out with her brothers, making fun of her mom for making too much food—a throwback to when her brothers were younger and could eat an entire fridge full—the city becoming illuminated with Christmas lights.

However, even that thought was tinged with sadness since her mom and stepdad had put the house up for sale. This year they'd decided to have the family Christmas at Wes's house because he had the space.

She gave herself a little shake. It wasn't like her to focus on all the negative things. She had a lot going for her. The show had wrapped for the year, and even if the future of Social Queen was up in the air, she had plenty to look forward to. Her agent had been sending her scripts like crazy, some of which were incredible opportunities to work with directors she admired. There was even a script she was looking at directing, a feature-length about a boy who could taste sound, which was slightly based on the life of a man living in Cassis, France.

Evie was planning a trip with Shane to meet him this summer to start talks about directing the script based on his experience with synaesthesia.

She'd also had a chance to connect with Charlotte. After the entire ordeal with Cameron hit the media, she reached out to Charlotte to see if she was okay. It turned out Charlotte was having an affair with Cameron. Cameron had offered her the part of the neighbour, a part that became permanent only after she'd slept with him. At the time, she hadn't seen it as sleeping her way into a role. She'd genuinely—if not naively—thought that she and Cameron were having more than an affair. It came with all the old clichés about not loving his wife and needing someone who understood what he did.

Now looking back, she said she'd been manipulated into a situation she didn't feel comfortable with. When she told Cameron she wanted to end it, he gave her an ultimatum. Either she could leave the show or he would ruin her reputation and career. She was not one of the women who'd come forward but wasn't surprised.

Listening to Charlotte, the Cameron she described was no one Evie had met. The Cameron who ran the show was an easy-going family man who loved his wife and kids. It was obviously all a lie. Evie's only hope was that his career was over, but the way these things usually went, that might not be the case. Either way, he would never resume his control over Social Queen. Tom had promised her that.

"Two more minutes, Evie. Then you're on."

Evie nodded and adjusted the tiny mic snaking from behind her ear. Whatever happened with the show, she'd be okay. Everything had worked out for the best.

Well, almost everything. Despite her best efforts, she hadn't been able to put Simone out of her mind. At one point she'd almost gone down to the hospital. But that just wreaked of desperation, and Evelyn Harper was not desperate. She had a lot of things going for her. She didn't need to complicate her life with a relationship.

"Sure, Evie. You keep telling yourself that."

A tech from the other side of the stage waved angrily at her and motioned to his lips. It took her a second to realize she'd spoken out loud and her mic was seconds away from being hot. She gave him a thumbs-up.

The next few moments were a blur as she received her signal to start, walking onto the stage and being blown away by the applause and enthusiasm of the crowd. Her cheeks burned from the wind, and, smiling, she worried her face might freeze into a grin. She introduced the show and opening act and stepped off the stage.

In the front row had been a woman who looked a lot like Simone, and she worried her mind was starting to play tricks on her.

After she'd introduced the third act, she was convinced it was Simone, standing in front watching the entire show. For now, she wasn't sure what Simone's presence meant, but she was content to let that mystery lie and worry about it later. The rest of the show passed in a blur. They had ice-skaters, fire-breathers, performers, and she ended up having a much better time than she'd expected. They'd brought in outdoor heaters to warm up off stage, and it was easy to get caught up in the excitement of it all.

The holidays weren't far off, and even though they wouldn't be the same, she had to get used to things changing. Nothing could stay the same. For now, she still had Shane, and the show had its second season coming out next year. She still got to spend Christmas with her family. She had to be thankful for what she did have. Nobody could have it all, right?

❖

Evie flipped through a magazine mindlessly. She was now in that strange in-between place. They'd finished filming a week and a half ago, and a new project she'd signed on for a few days ago wouldn't start filming for another month.

Christmas was a week away, and she had no idea what to do with her time. She'd had lunch with Ian yesterday. He loved to spend a month decompressing and doing absolutely nothing. Evie needed activity to feel normal. Sitting around day after day was not her thing.

Shane had suggested a vacation, but he was unable to go because he'd finally taken his business to the next level—thank God—and was no longer using their kitchen for prep. He'd rented an industrial space and hired two people to help. The holidays were bringing in lots of business for him.

But it meant she'd have to go alone, and the last thing she wanted to do was sit on a beach by herself. How depressing was that?

As she flipped to the next page, Shane rushed into the room. "Is that what you're wearing?"

Evie looked down at her yoga pants and oversized U of T sweatshirt. "Yeah?… Why?"

He fluffed her hair a little and plumped her cheeks. "I guess it'll have to do. Put your shoes on. I'm taking you somewhere special."

"Shane, you don't have to do that. We've already celebrated." Her short film had made it into TIFF and Tribeca. Shane had taken her out to her favourite restaurant to congratulate her.

He waved her off. "This isn't that. This is something different. Bring your purse. Where's your purse?"

She frowned and pointed to the coat rack near the door. "Why are you acting so weird?"

He yanked at the hem of her sweater to pull her toward the door. "I'm not." He shoved a pair of worn Blundstones at her. "You can put these on in the elevator."

Evie pulled back. "I'm not going anywhere with you. Not until you tell me where we're going and why you're acting like you just killed someone and you want me out of the apartment so you can cut up and hide the body."

He pulled her into the hallway. "It's a surprise, and we'll be late if you keep yammering like that."

"Yammering? Did you also swallow my grandma? Who are you, and what have you done to my good friend Shane?"

He shoved her into the elevator and pressed the P1 button.

"We're driving?"

"Yes." He pulled out a bright-pink bandana and made a spinning motion with his hand. "Turn around so I can blindfold you."

She stepped back into the far corner of the elevator. "No. I am not going anywhere blindfolded. That's pure trouble."

"Please? It's part of the surprise. Otherwise, you might know where we're heading. I promise I'm not kidnapping you. Don't you trust me?"

Evie groaned and turned around. She did trust Shane, even if he was acting like a lunatic.

❖

By the time they pulled up forty-five minutes later, Evie was fuming. She'd had to keep her blindfold on the whole time. He'd helped her into a car that smelled new, but that's all she'd been able to tell about it. When he helped her out of it, she still couldn't tell you where they were. Forty-five minutes in a car could get you a lot of places.

Everything was deathly silent, and she smelled nature, not what High Park or Glendon Forest had to offer. This smelled like she'd stepped into actual nature, the kind with real forests and possibly real bears.

"Shane, where are we?"

"If I tell you now, I'll just ruin everything." He took her hand and guided her down a level path, and then, abruptly, he stopped her. "Okay. Here we are. I love you. Don't be mad at me. This is for your own good, mopey." Before she could ask him what he meant, he pulled the blindfold off her, and she found herself standing looking at one of the biggest observatories she'd ever seen. It stood in the middle of a field next to an old mansion that appeared to have been built sometime in the eighteen hundreds. She felt a little like she'd stepped back in time. The sun had long since set, this being December, when it disappeared long before most people got home from work.

She looked up to see hundreds of stars above her. It was everything she remembered from when she was younger.

"It's not a cottage in the woods, but I thought this might be better. You're not stuck for a week with one bathroom."

Evie turned at the sound of Simone's voice. She stood behind her, looking flawless in dark pants with knee-high boots and a fitted pea coat.

"Simone." She looked around, but Shane had disappeared.

"I'm sorry to have involved Shane in this event, but I wanted it to be a surprise. And…I wasn't sure if you'd want to talk to me, and I desperately wanted to explain to you why I was such a jerk."

Evie felt ambushed by both Shane and Simone, unsure what to say. Her pride wanted her to walk away, no matter how far out in the middle of nowhere she was. But her heart kept her planted. She wanted to hear Simone's explanation, if only to know for herself. She didn't need to make a choice either way.

Simone tilted her head toward the building in front of them. "Come. I want to show you something." She led Evie into a building that was completely dark save for tiny LEDs along the aisle guiding them toward the centre. They took seats in what appeared to be an auditorium, like they were here to see a show, and Evie was now thoroughly confused until the ceiling came to life with a giant explosion, and the speaker overhead boomed, "The Big Bang. Thirteen point eight billion years ago the universe began, at first a minuscule dense ball of fire that exploded."

"I wanted to give you the stars. You said you never get to see them in the city, so I brought you to them."

They watched as the ceiling sped through galaxies, stopping when it reached the Milky Way, showing what the dinosaurs would've seen when they looked up at our sky, what early humans would've seen, what the Romans and Egyptians would've seen.

After the show ended, Evie was surprised to look down and see that she was holding Simone's hand. She wasn't sure when that had happened, but it felt so natural, so comfortable. Above them the stars from a thousand years ago still shone, bathing the room in a soft glow.

"When I was a little girl, I remember my father taking me and my brother and sister out into this field. It was during a meteor shower. And it was beautiful the way they streaked across the sky. I remember thinking that the world was beautiful." Simone turned in her seat to face Evie. "A few days later my dad came into my room in the middle of the night and told me to get dressed, that we were going out. I was scared, because he was scared, but I did it. He said that aliens had come down with the meteors, and they were planning to capture us because we'd seen them. I didn't know it at the time, but that was the beginning of the end.

"My father has schizophrenia. He has both visual and auditory hallucinations. He also refuses to take medication for them. My mom, at a really young age, had to put her life on hold for him. She is essentially his keeper." The lights dimmed before changing to a different sky.

"My sister Mani had an accident, and until she woke up, we weren't sure if it was just an accident or if she was finally experiencing symptoms of schizophrenia. It's hereditary, so I've spent most of my life thinking that eventually I might turn into my dad, and the last thing I wanted was to put someone through what my mom went through. And then I met you. It was the first time ever when I wasn't thinking about horrible possibilities that could destroy my life."

Evie couldn't understand why Simone would think that would destroy her life, so she kept quiet. She'd never had to deal with this, so she didn't know. Her grandmother had had dementia, but she wasn't sure if you could compare the two. "You're worried you'll be a burden on someone eventually. Do you think your mom would've stayed with your dad all these years if she felt he was a burden?"

"You don't know my mom. She's one of the most stubborn people in the world, besides myself, of course. Leaving would've been like giving up."

"Maybe. Or maybe she loves your dad so much she stays because being without him would be more of a burden."

"I've never thought of it like that before."

"Maybe some people don't see it as a burden." Evie kissed Simone softly on the lips.

"When I heard about what happened to Mani, my mind went to all these horrible places. I shut down, and I shut you out, and that's unforgivable. Seeing Marissa there with Gabriel and the way she was able to comfort him, I realized I've spent my whole life worrying about maybes and that I pushed people away. I pushed you away."

"You're right. I'm not afraid of maybes."

Simone stood, pulling Evie up with her. "Come. Dance with me."

"There's no music."

Simone led Evie to an empty space in the middle of the planetarium, and as she did, the opening melody of Cyndi Lauper's Time After Time began playing.

Evie looked up at the stars above them. "How did you manage this?"

"Shane knew a guy."

Evie laughed loudly. "Shane always knows a guy."

Simone stepped close, gliding Evie around the small open space. Evie melted into Simone, and they fit together perfectly. "You don't know this," said Simone, "but this is the first song we ever danced to."

Evie pulled back to look at Simone. "We've never danced together."

"The first night I met you was at a club called Everything For Sale."

"That was you?" Evie asked, flabbergasted.

Simone nodded, pulling Evie closer. "I can't promise what the next few months will look like, or even next year, but I can tell you this. My life is so much better with you in it, and now that I've fallen in love with you, I can't imagine my life without you. And I promise never to shut you out again."

Evie grinned. "I've spent a lifetime working hard to achieve what I want, but falling in love with you was one of the easiest things I've ever done. I'd be an idiot if I didn't take this chance with you." Evie pulled Simone toward her, their lips locking in a searing kiss, that, if they were under the real stars, would've made them blush. And that's how they remained, locked together under the glow of the stars from millions of years ago while the strains of Time After Time played over them.

About the Author

CJ Birch is a Canadian-based video editor and digital artist. When not lost in a good book or working, she can be found writing or drinking serious coffee, or doing both at the same time.

An award-winning poet, CJ holds a certificate in journalism but prefers the world of make-believe. She is the reluctant co-owner of two cats, one of which is bulimic, the other with bladder issues, both evil walking fur shedders.

CJ is the author of the New Horizons series. *Between Takes* is her seventh book. You can visit CJ on social media @cjbirchwrites or www.cjbirchwrites.com.

Books Available from Bold Strokes Books

A Haven for the Wanderer by Jenny Frame. When Griffin Harris comes to Rosebrook village, the love she finds with Bronte de Lacey creates a safe haven and she finally finds her place in the world. But will she run again when their love is tested? (978-1-63679-291-0)

A Spark in the Air by Dena Blake. Internet executive Crystal Tucker is sure Wi-Fi could really help small-town residents, even if it means putting an internet café out of business, but her instant attraction to the owner's daughter, Janie Elliott, makes moving ahead with her plans complicated. (978-1-63679-293-4)

Between Takes by CJ Birch. Simone Lavoie is convinced her new job as an intimacy coordinator will give her a fresh perspective. Instead, problems on set and her growing attraction to actress Evelyn Harper only add to her worries. (978-1-63679-309-2)

Camp Lost and Found by Georgia Beers. Nobody knows better than Cassidy and Frankie that life doesn't always give you what you want. But sometimes, if you're lucky, life gives you exactly what you need. (978-1-63679-263-7)

Felix Navidad by 'Nathan Burgoine. After the wedding of a good friend, instead of Felix's Hawaii Christmas treat to himself, ice rain strands him in Ontario with fellow wedding-guest—and handsome ex of said friend—Kevin in a small cabin for the holiday Felix definitely didn't plan on. (978-1-63679-411-2)

Fire, Water, and Rock by Alaina Erdell. As Jess and Clare reveal more about themselves, and their hot summer fling tips over into true love, they must confront their pasts before they can contemplate a future together. (978-1-63679-274-3)

Lines of Love by Brey Willows. When even the Muse of Love doesn't believe in forever, we're all in trouble. (978-1-63555-458-8)

Manny Porter and The Yuletide Murder by D.C. Robeline. Manny only has the holiday season to discover who killed prominent research scientist Phillip Nikolaidis before the judicial system condemns an innocent man to lethal injection. (978-1-63679-313-9)

Only This Summer by Radclyffe. A fling with Lily promises to be exactly what Chase is looking for—short-term, hot as a forest fire, and one Chase can extinguish whenever she wants. After all, it's only one summer. (978-1-63679-390-0)

Picture-Perfect Christmas by Charlotte Greene. Two former rivals compete to capture the essence of their small mountain town at Christmas, all the while fighting old and new feelings. (978-1-63679-311-5)

Playing Love's Refrain by Lesley Davis. Drew Dawes had shied away from the world of music until Wren Banderas gave her a reason to play their love's refrain. (978-1-63679-286-6)

Profile by Jackie D. The scales of justice are weighted against FBI agents Cassidy Wolf and Alex Derby. Loyalty and love may be the only advantage they have. (978-1-63679-282-8)

Almost Perfect by Tagan Shepard. A shared love of queer TV brings Olivia and Riley together, but can they keep their real-life love as picture perfect as their on-screen counterparts? (978-1-63679-322-1)

Corpus Calvin by David Swatling. Cloverkist Inn may be haunted, but a ghost materializes from Jason Dekker's past and Calvin's canine instinct kicks in to protect a young boy from mortal danger. (978-1-62639-428-5)

Craving Cassie by Skye Rowan. Siobhan Carney and Cassie Townsend share an instant attraction, but are they brave enough to give up everything they have ever known to be together? (978-1-63679-062-6)

Drifting by Lyn Hemphill. When Tess jumps into the ocean after Jet, she thinks she's saving her life. Of course, she can't possibly know Jet is actually a mermaid desperate to fix her mistake before she causes her clan's demise. (978-1-63679-242-2)

Enigma by Suzie Clarke. Polly has taken an oath to protect and serve her country, but when the spy she's tasked with hunting becomes the love of her life, will she be the one to betray her country? (978-1-63555-999-6)

Finding Fault by Annie McDonald. Can environmental activist Dr. Evie O'Halloran and government investigator Merritt Shepherd set aside their conflicting ideas about saving the planet and risk their hearts enough to save their love? (978-1-63679-257-6)

Hot Keys by R.E. Ward. In 1920s New York City, Betty May Dewitt and her best friend, Jack Norval, are determined to make their Tin Pan Alley dreams come true and discover they will have to fight—not only for their hearts and dreams, but for their lives. (978-1-63679-259-0)

Securing Ava by Anne Shade. Private investigator Paige Richards takes a case to locate and bring back runaway heiress Ava Prescott. But ignoring her attraction may prove impossible when their hearts and lives are at stake. (978-1-63679-297-2)

The Amaranthine Law by Gun Brooke. Tristan Kelly is being hunted for who she is and her incomprehensible past, and despite her overwhelming feelings for Olivia Bryce, she has to reject her to keep her safe. (978-1-63679-235-4)

The Forever Factor by Melissa Brayden. When Bethany and Reid confront their past, they give new meaning to letting go, forgiveness, and a future worth fighting for. (978-1-63679-357-3)

The Frenemy Zone by Yolanda Wallace. Ollie Smith-Nakamura thinks relocating from San Francisco to her dad's rural hometown is the worst idea in the world, but after she meets her new classmate Ariel Hall, she might have a change of heart. (978-1-63679-249-1)

A Cutting Deceit by Cathy Dunnell. Undercover cop Athena takes a job at Valeria's hair salon to gather evidence to prove her husband's connections to organized crime. What starts as a tentative friendship quickly turns into a dangerous affair. (978-1-63679-208-8)

As Seen on TV! by CF Frizzell. Despite their objections, TV hosts Ronnie Sharp, a laid-back chef; and paranormal investigator Peyton Stanford, have to work together. The public is watching. But joining forces is risky, contemptuous, unnerving, provocative—and ridiculously perfect. (978-1-63679-272-9)

Blood Memory by Sandra Barret. Can vampire Jade Murphy protect her friend from a human stalker and keep her dates with the gorgeous Beth Jenssen without revealing her secrets? (978-1-63679-307-8)

Foolproof by Leigh Hays. For Martine Roberts and Elliot Tillman, friends with benefits isn't a foolproof way to hide from the truth at the heart of an affair. (978-1-63679-184-5)

Glass and Stone by Renee Roman. Jordan must accept that she can't control everything that happens in life, and that includes her wayward heart. (978-1-63679-162-3)

Hard Pressed by Aurora Rey. When rivals Mira Lavigne and Dylan Miller are tapped to co-chair Finger Lakes Cider Week, competition gives way to compromise. But will their sexual chemistry lead to love? (978-1-63679-210-1)

The Laws of Magic by M. Ullrich. Nothing is ever what it seems, especially not in the small town of Bender, Massachusetts, where a witch lives to save lives and avoid love. (978-1-63679-222-4)

The Lonely Hearts Rescue by Morgan Lee Miller, Nell Stark, Missouri Vaun. In this novella collection, a hurricane hits the Gulf Coast, and the animals at the Lonely Hearts Rescue Shelter need love, and so do the humans who adopt them. (978-1-63679-231-6)

The Mage and the Monster by Barbara Ann Wright. Two powerful mages, one committed to magic and one controlled by it, strive to free each other and be together while the countries they serve descend into war. (978-1-63679-190-6)

Truly Wanted by J.J. Hale. Sam must decide if she's willing to risk losing her found family to find her happily ever after. (978-1-63679-333-7)

A Good Chance by Ali Vali. Harry, Desi, and Desi's sister Rachel are so close to getting everything they've ever wanted, but Desi's ex-husband is coming back to get his revenge and rip apart their chance at happiness. (978-1-63679-023-7)

A Perfect Fifth by Jaycie Morrison. Streetwise pianist Zara Keller and Lady Jillian Stansfield couldn't be more different; yet their connection brings a new awareness of who they are and what they truly want in their lives—including each other. (978-1-63679-132-6)

Catching Feelings by Ana Hartnett Reichardt. Andrea Foster expected to catch a lot of pitches from the Alder Lion's star pitcher, Maya, but she didn't expect to catch feelings. (978-1-63679-227-9)

Defiant Hearts by Lee Lynch. In these stories, you'll find your lovers, friends, and lesbians you wish you knew—maybe even yourself. (978-1-63679-237-8)

Love and Duty by Catherine Young. All Princess Roseli wants is to marry her three lovers, but with war looming, she must instead marry Princess Lucia to establish a military alliance between their planets. (978-1-63679-256-9)

Murder at Union Station by David S. Pederson. Private Detective Mason Adler struggles to determine who killed a woman found in a trunk without getting himself killed in the process. (978-1-63679-269-9)

Serendipity by Kris Bryant. Serendipity brings jingle writer Annie Foster and celebrity pop star Bristol Baines together, and their undeniable attraction keeps them close, but will their different paths drive them apart? (978-1-63679-224-8)

The Haunted Heart by Jane Kolven. A ghost, a ring, and a quest to find a missing psychic—it's a spell for love. (978-1-63679-245-3)

The Rules of Forever by Nan Campbell. After reconnecting at their high school reunion, Cara and Lauren agree to embark on a textbook definition friends-with-benefits relationship, but trying to keep it uncomplicated is harder than it seems. (978-1-63679-248-4)

Vision of Virtue by Brey Willows. When virtue and desire come together, be prepared for sparks in this next installment of the Memory's Muses series. (978-1-63679-118-0)

Cherry on Top by Georgia Beers. A chance meeting leaves Cherry and Ellis longing for a different life, but when Ellis's search for truth crashes into Cherry's insta-filter world, do they have any hope at all of a happily ever after? (978-1-63679-158-6)

Love and Other Rare Birds by Angie Williams. Ornithologist Dr. Jamie Martin and park ranger Rowan Fleming are searching the Alaskan wilderness for a bird thought to be extinct and they're about to discover opposites really do attract. (978-1-63679-108-1)

Parallel Paradise by Mayapee Chowdhury. When their love affair is put to the test by the homophobia of their family, community, and culture, Bindi and Rimli will need to fight for a chance at love. (978-1-63679-204-0)

Perfectly Matched by Toni Logan. A beautiful Cupid named Hannah, a runaway arrow, and just seventy-two hours to fix a mishap that could be the best mistake she has ever made. (978-1-63679-120-3)

Royal Exposé by Jenny Frame. When they're grouped together for a class assignment, Poppy's enthusiasm for life and love may just save Casey's soul, but will she ever forgive Casey for using her to expose royal secrets? (978-1-63679-165-4)

Slow Burn by Missouri Vaun. A wounded wildland firefighter from California and a struggling artist find solace and love in a small southern town. (978-1-63679-098-5)

The Artist by Sheri Lewis Wohl. Detective Casey Wilson and reclusive artist Tula Crane are drawn together in a web of passion, intrigue, and art that might just hold the key to stopping a killer. (978-1-63679-150-0)

The Inconvenient Heiress by Jane Walsh. An unlikely heiress and a spinster evade the Marriage Mart only to discover true love together. (978-1-63679-173-9)